Fractured

DANI ATKINS

HEAD
ZEUS

For Ralph. For ever.
And of course for Luke, just because.
And mostly for Kimberley,
who helped make this happen.

My first life ended at 10.37 p.m. on a rainy December night, on a deserted street beside the old church.

My second life began some ten hours later, when I woke up to the blinding brilliance of the hospital lighting, with a large head wound and a life about which I had absolutely no recollection. I was surrounded by friends and family, and that should have made it better. But it didn't, as one of them had been dead for a considerable period of time.

I wanted to write down everything that had happened, to see if by committing it to paper I could make some sense of it all. Or perhaps I just needed to prove to everyone, even myself that I wasn't going crazy. For a long time I thought that this story should begin with what happened to me at the church, when my life literally came apart, but now I realise that to understand it all I have to go back much further than that. For it really all began five years earlier, on the night of the farewell dinner.

Chapter 1

September 2008

Long after the screaming had stopped, when the only sound to be heard was the soft crying of my friends as they waited for the ambulance to arrive, did I realise that I was still clutching the lucky penny tightly within my palm. My fingers refused to unfurl from around the tiny copper talisman, as though by sheer will alone I would somehow be able to wind back time and erase the tragedy around me.

Was it really only half an hour earlier that Jimmy had picked up the glinting coin from the restaurant's tarmacked car park?

'For luck,' he had grinned, tossing the coin up in the air and deftly catching it with one hand.

I smiled back and then saw the flicker of irritation

flash through his pale blue eyes as Matt had quipped, 'Jimmy mate, you should've said if you're a little short of cash, no need to go grovelling about on the floor for money!'

Matt had laughed then, and thrown his arm around my shoulder, pulling me close to his side. I thought the darkening expression on Jimmy's face was just a natural reaction to Matt's unnecessary comment, which highlighted the differences between their backgrounds. And maybe that was part of it. But it wasn't all of it. There was more . . . though of course I didn't understand that for a long time.

The three of us were standing in the fading sunlight of a warm September evening, waiting for the rest of our group to arrive. Jimmy had already been in the car park when Matt and I had driven in. Matt had made quite a show of circling the empty spaces, looking for just the right spot to park his new acquisition. I guess he was still in that strange honeymoon phase boys have when they're really in love with their cars. I just hoped he'd have the good sense not to gloat about it too much in front of the rest of the group.

The new car was shiny, sporty and expensive. That's as much as I know about cars. He'd been given it by his parents when the exam results had come out. That alone should tell you enough about Matt's family to understand why comments about money sometimes hit a raw nerve with the rest of us. For the most part, Matt was really good and didn't rub it in too much. But the odd glib remark occasionally slipped under the wire and lit a spark. I really hoped he wasn't going to say anything that would ruin what was probably going to be one of the last nights we would all be spending together for quite a while.

'You've been at work today, Jimmy?' I asked, knowing full well that he had but anxious to steer things back onto neutral ground. Jimmy turned and gave me the smile that I swear hadn't changed at all since he was four years old.

'Yep, this is my last week helping out my uncle, after that I'm happily handing back the wheelbarrow and the pitchfork. The gardening world and I are about to part company.'

'Still, look at the bright side, you've got a great tan this summer, you'd not have got that stacking shelves in the supermarket.'

And it was true, Jimmy's normally fair skin was coloured a soft golden brown, and his forearms were definitely more sinewed and defined from his months of outdoor work. Of course, Matt and I were both still sporting fairly decent suntans from our holiday in France at his parents' villa. That too had been another congratulatory gift – for both of us this time.

Actually, my dad had quite an issue over that one. Sure, he liked Matt well enough; he was a fairly familiar fixture around our house, and we *had* been going out for almost two years. But it had still been touch and go whether he'd allow me to go away for a fortnight with Matt's family. Part of it had been the money thing because, of course, Matt's parents had refused to accept any payment for the trip. The other part . . . the big part . . . had been the dad/daughter/boyfriend thing. I guess that's universal with dads, but it seemed even more so in our case, with no mum around to smooth things over. Eventually Matt and I had managed to persuade him; explaining how everything was going to be all above board, how it was strictly separate bedrooms and that we'd be with Matt's parents the whole time. Basically, we had just lied.

This chain of thought had made me wonder, and not for the first time, how Dad was going to cope when the time came for me to leave for university at the end of the month. I felt a frown forming and determinedly pushed the thought away. I'd spent most of the summer struggling with that one and I was *not* going to ruin the last evening my friends and I were going to have together by worrying over things I couldn't change.

Fortunately just then two cars, both considerably older than Matt's but no less appreciated by their owners, pulled into the restaurant's car park. The rear door of the small blue car nearest to where we stood flung open and Sarah ran over towards us in a clatter of improbably high heels. She tottered alarmingly over the uneven surface before enveloping me in a huge hug.

'Rachel, my lovely, how are you?' I hugged her back, feeling momentarily choked to realise that soon I'd only be seeing her during the uni holidays and not every day, as we had done for all of our senior school years. Apart from Jimmy, she was my oldest friend. And however close Jimmy and I were, and had always been, there were still some topics of conversation that were reserved only for your girlfriends.

'Sorry we're late,' Sarah apologised.

I gave her a wry smile. Sarah was *always* late. For a girl so naturally pretty, she still seemed to require an incredible amount of time getting ready to go out, with multiple hair and outfit changes before she could be persuaded to step away from the mirror. And she never seemed satisfied with the final effect, which was ridiculous, because with her heart-shaped face, her shiny brown curls and petite frame she always looked perfectly lovely.

'Have you been waiting long?' she asked, slipping her arm through mine and pulling me away from Matt to walk with her across the car park to the restaurant's entrance. This was most likely to ensure that she made it in one piece across the tarmac with those ridiculously high stilettos, although it could have been to avoid watching Trevor and Phil's knee-jerk reaction to Cathy as she climbed out of the car beside them.

'Just long enough for Matt to piss Jimmy off,' I replied in a voice low enough for only her to hear. She smiled knowingly.

'Oh, no time at all then!'

By now we had reached the patioed doorway at the rear of the restaurant and stood waiting while the various boys in our group of friends (Matt included) all tried to pretend that they were not noticing the extremely inviting cleavage being displayed by Cathy's low-cut top. Worn over skin-tight jeans and high-heeled sandals – which, to Sarah's chagrin, she appeared to have no difficulty walking in – Cathy looked every inch as though she was off to a photo shoot. Long blonde hair fell around her shoulders and everything about her seemed so perfectly put together that I instantly felt as though I'd got dressed in the dark with clothes that'd been thrown out from a charity shop.

Cathy had been a fairly new addition to our circle of friends. Prior to her arrival into our sixth form, our group had been a tight unit of Sarah and me and the four boys. I suppose the boy–girl ratio had been a bit unbalanced, but we'd all been mates for so long that it wasn't an issue. That said, Cathy's slow inclusion into our group had been welcomed quite vigorously by pretty much all of the boys, for obvious reasons. And, looks aside, Cathy was good fun to have around. Her family had moved to Great Bishopsford from a much larger town, and she had seemed much more worldly and clued-up than the rest of us. Added to that, she was extremely open and friendly with a wicked sense of humour and, when she wasn't flirting outrageously with every male within a five-mile radius, I actually really liked her.

Sarah, though, had her reservations, and on more than one occasion, when Cathy had ruffled her feathers or stepped on her toes, I had heard her mutter darkly, 'Last in. First out.'

When Jimmy sauntered across the car park to join us, Sarah stepped to one side and began to peruse the menu displayed inside a glassed-in case by the doorway. The others had all walked over to admire Matt's car, or Cathy's chest, I thought waspishly, as I watched her bend down low, supposedly to examine the alloy wheels. As if she cared about wheels!

'You look much nicer than her,' Jimmy whispered into my ear, knowing instantly what was on my mind.

'Am I that easy to read?' I asked, smiling back up at him. He gave me the grin I knew so well, the one that crinkled up the corners of his eyes and lit up his whole face.

'Like a book,' he confirmed, 'but a good one.'

'Like a battered old paperback, you mean, rather than a glossy magazine.'

He followed both my eyes and my analogy as we looked across to where Cathy was standing with Matt, listening raptly while he extolled something or other about the car.

'You don't have anything to worry about,' Jimmy reassured me, giving my shoulder a brief friendly squeeze. 'Matt would be crazy to look at her when he's got you.'

'Hmm,' was all I managed in reply and was surprised to feel that the warmth of his words had ignited a small blush. I quickly turned away to avoid him seeing.

Catching my reflection in the restaurant's window I didn't feel my old friend was being entirely honest. Or if he was, then he seriously should think about getting his eyes tested. What I saw in the glass was certainly never going to elicit the kind of reaction from men that Cathy did. Long dark hair, fashionably poker straight, big eyes, that hardly functioned at all without their contact lenses, and lips that were a little too wide. It was a pleasant enough face, but not stunning and I was honest enough to know I was never going to stop traffic. And that had truly never worried me before, but since being with Matt, who was, let's face it, undeniably gorgeous, I seemed more aware than ever of some of the shortcomings Mother Nature had dished up.

'And just remember, to me you'll always be the frecklyfaced girl with the gap in her front teeth, whose ears stuck out.'

'I was ten years old then,' I protested. 'Thank God for orthodontistry. Do you really have to remember every damn thing about my geeky childhood?'

'I can't help myself,' Jimmy replied oddly. And I would have pursued that strange comment if we hadn't just then been joined by the others.

'C'mon then,' urged Matt, grabbing my hand and holding it tightly. 'Let's go before they give our table to someone else.'

We walked en masse through the large double doors, arms linked or thrown casually around a neighbouring shoulder, never realising that in the next half hour our lives were going to be irrevocably changed for ever.

We were led straight away to our table, which was situated at the very front of the restaurant beside a large plate-glass window, where we had an excellent view of the high street and the church perched high up on the hill nearby. As we wove between the other tables to reach our seats, I could see Cathy drawing several appreciative glances from the male diners and I was pretty certain that Matt too hadn't passed among the women unnoticed.

I tried to stifle that small worried voice that had been whispering in my ear for several months.

Matt was a very attractive guy; he naturally drew the attention of other women, it was only to be expected, and while part of me relished the fact that it was *my* side he was standing by, *my* hand that he held in his as we slalomed between the closely packed tables, there was an unspoken worry that sooner or later I would have to address: what would happen when he was faced with inevitable temptation when we were apart? Would we be one of the couples who survived the university separation, or were we destined to become victims to the curse of the long-distance relationship?

I was pleased this line of thinking was interrupted by the softly accented Italian waiter, indicating we had arrived at our reserved table. Tight for space in the crowded restaurant, they had pushed two tables together to accommodate our party, which resulted in rather a narrow gap by a concrete pillar which had to be squeezed past in order to reach the seat beside the window.

Wishing Sarah had got there first, as she was much smaller than me, I nevertheless managed to manoeuvre through the gap without getting embarrassingly stuck. Matt slid into the chair beside me, as the others all found a place and sat down. Jimmy took the window seat directly opposite me, with Sarah claiming the chair on his right-hand side. I refused to look at the undignified scrabble of who was sitting by Cathy on the other side of Matt. I guessed pole position was opposite her anyway, with its excellent view down the front of her top.

Surreptitiously, under cover of the tablecloth, I tugged down on the hem of my own T-shirt, lowering the neck-line by an inch or two: then felt myself blushing like an idiot as I saw Jimmy's quivering lips as he noticed what I'd done.

'What's so funny, Jimmy?' Matt asked and suddenly, by some horrible coincidence, the whole table fell silent to hear his response. I knew my eyes were frantically telegraphing him not to say anything, and I needn't have worried. Jimmy calmly picked up the menu and gave a casual shrug.

'Nothing, just thinking of something my uncle said earlier, that's all.'

While everyone else followed Jimmy's lead and began to study their menus, I looked across and mouthed a silent 'thank you'. The smile he gave me back was so full of warm affection and friendship that for some strange reason my stomach gave an erratic flip. Confused, I broke eye contact and pretended to be deeply interested in the merits of the lasagne versus the cannelloni.

Matt's arm snaked around my waist, pulling me against him as we chose our meal and when I did look over to Jimmy a few minutes later, he was deep in conversation with Sarah, and although he caught my glance and gave me a small smile, my stomach remained exactly where it should have been.

It was impossible to ignore the nostalgia around the table, and the air of impending separation was almost as apparent as the tomato and garlic aromas wafting around us. While there were still a few weeks before I left for my place at Brighton, Trevor and Phil were both going to leave after the weekend, and Sarah only a few days later. Somehow I couldn't really imagine the condensed remains of our group: Cathy, Jimmy, Matt and me, all getting together in the remaining weeks.

This sudden reluctance to leave struck me unexpectedly with its intensity. It wasn't as though I didn't want to go away to university. Of course I did. I'd certainly worked hard enough to achieve the grades I needed to get on my journalism course. It was just that it finally seemed that tonight it was hitting home for the first time that this was really the end of a very important chapter in my life.

And just for the moment I couldn't really focus on the new beginnings, because all I could think of was leaving behind my boyfriend and my two closest friends. Ridiculously, I felt my eyes begin to water, and I hastily looked away, preferring the dazzling glare of the rays of the dwindling sun, than the reaction from around the table if they knew I'd been crying.

'You OK?' asked Jimmy softly, leaning forward so only I could hear his words.

Matt was placing the drinks order, so it was safe to quietly reply.

'Oh, you know, just feeling a little emotional, I guess. Changes coming, saying goodbye to everyone, stuff like that . . .' I trailed off, expecting some sort of ridicule, but instead was surprised when his hand reached across the table, encircled my fingers which were fiddling restlessly with the cutlery, and encased them in his grasp.

His grip felt oddly different; not the familiar clasp I had known since nursery school. Perhaps it was just the rough texture of the skin from his summer gardening, or was it more the way my hand felt so small, tightly encompassed in his own?

I felt, rather than saw, Matt's slow awareness of Jimmy's action, but rather than a hurried retreat, Jimmy gave my hand one last squeeze and took his time before withdrawing his own. In an instinctive response, Matt drew his body closer towards mine, reclaiming both my attention and his territory and it was only after a moment or two that I became aware that when taking back his hand, Jimmy had somehow transferred the lucky penny he had picked up outside the restaurant from his hand to mine.

I held the coin tightly in my palm, imbuing the small copper disc with more significance than it perhaps deserved. It was typical of Jimmy to offer to share even the possibility of good fortune with me. We had, after all, shared so much for so many years. He was more like my brother than my friend: in fact, when I thought about it, his whole family were closer to me than many of my own relatives.

Jimmy's mother and mine had been very good friends long before Jimmy and I were even born, and when my mum had died so suddenly when I was only a toddler, Jimmy's family had reached out and somehow drawn both Dad and me into their lives and their hearts. I realised with a shock that my dad wasn't the only family I'd be leaving behind when I went away; it was going to be almost as tough saying goodbye to Jimmy's parents and his younger brother too.

When the two bottles of wine Matt had ordered were delivered to the table, everyone took a glass to raise a toast.

'To going away . . .'

'To not dropping out . . . !'

'To our new lives . . .'

'. . . and old friends . . .'

The last was echoed by each person around the table, as glasses clinked together, catching a brilliant prism of evening sunlight.

As the others sat joking and bantering light-heartedly, I took a second to look around the table, trying to take a mental snapshot of the moment. I knew we were all destined to make new friends at our various colleges and universities, but just now it was hard to believe that the new bonds we would forge could ever be as strong as those that threaded between the seven of us around the table.

As my eye fell on each individual friend, a memory or emotion would erupt in response. So many, it was almost impossible to separate them, but each recollection was another brick in the wall of our friendship, which I had to believe would remain solid no matter where we all ended up.

When I looked at Sarah, I couldn't help but repress a smile. In a strange way I already felt jealous of the new friends she would be making on her art course. Crazy, loyal, funny and incredibly caring, Sarah's friendship was one of my most treasured possessions. Whoever they were, these new friends didn't know how lucky they were.

And then there was Jimmy. I'd spent so much of the summer stressing over how it would feel to be apart from Matt, that whenever the thought of also saying goodbye to Jimmy had intruded, I'd hastily stuffed it away to the back of my mind. I knew it sounded strange, but the thought of not seeing my old friend on a regular basis was just so huge, so hard to absorb, that I couldn't even allow myself the time to contemplate it.

I realised with some disappointment that I wasn't nearly as ready as I should be to let go of any of them.

As we waited for our meals to arrive, I glanced occasionally through the window beside me and up the road to the church. The sun was just beginning its leisurely descent and the sky was bathed in diluted shades of red and gold, turning the usually drab high street into a magical abstract of colours. I noticed there were few pedestrians, but the lines of parked cars flanking both sides of the road meant that the pubs and restaurants were all doing good business that evening. From somewhere in the distance the distinctive wail of a siren could just be heard.

'Rachel, are you listening?'

With a start I drew my attention away from the scene outside and realised that Jimmy had been speaking.

'Sorry, I was miles away . . . what were you saying?'

His eyes flickered for a second towards Matt, who was chatting to Cathy at that moment on his other side. Jimmy didn't look comfortable having to repeat whatever it was I had just missed.

'I was asking if you weren't too busy tomorrow afternoon, if you'd be able to come round to my house?'

The oddly hesitant request wasn't like him at all and I found myself momentarily confused, both by his tone and the formality of the invitation. Jimmy and I usually just pitched up at each other's front doors without asking; no invites necessary.

'Sure, I can do that. I was intending to come round to see your mum and dad again before I left, anyway.'

'Actually, they won't be home tomorrow.' Again, that oddly uncertain tone. 'No one will, just me. I . . . er . . . I just wanted to have a quiet word with you. Is that OK?'

Was it the red glow from the sun, or was he actually blushing?

He seemed anxious to elicit my response before Matt turned back, so I quickly reassured him. 'Yes, that's fine. I'll see you around two o'clock?'

He nodded then and sighed, as though some dreaded task had been accomplished, which only served to heighten my curiosity further. I guessed I would have to wait until the next day to find out what was on his mind.

The waiters had just arrived with the laden plates and begun to set them in front of us. Straightening up in his seat, Matt removed his right arm from where it had been resting around my waist, pausing to plant a firm kiss unexpectedly on my lips before pulling back.

'Pleeeease . . . people are trying to eat round here!' groaned Sarah, pretending repulsion.

I grinned back at Matt and held my face very still while he tucked a wayward strand of hair behind my ear.

It was just a chance inconsequential action, but later I would wonder what might have happened to us all if he hadn't been leaning so closely towards me and seen the car.

'What the hell . . . !' he cried.

I spun around to follow his gaze, mouth dropping in amazement as I saw a small red car, with all four wheels off the tarmac, catapult into view over the crest of the hill. Moments later a second car appeared, driving almost as fast and only slightly less recklessly; its flashing blue lights and discordant siren shattering the peace of the summer evening. In horror I saw a small van emerge from a side street and have to stand on its brakes to avoid losing the best part of its bonnet as the red car hurtled past with inches to spare. The car collided with grazing impact against the side of several parked vehicles, enshrouding the pursuing police car in a cloud of red hot sparks.

It was the shrieking scream of rubber from the van's brakes that alerted the attention of the rest of the group but Matt was way ahead of us all in assessing the oncoming danger. The red car was still comparatively high up on the hill, but at the speed it was travelling, that distance was being swallowed up with each passing second. When the police car began to narrow the gap between the vehicles, the red car veered crazily across the road, its driver clearly struggling to keep it from ploughing into the line of parked cars. Matt shot to his feet.

'He's lost it! He's out of control. That car's going to crash! Get away from the window! NOW!'

For the first time we all seemed to notice the vulnerability of our position, seated beside the large window at the front of the restaurant. Separated from the road by only the narrowest of low pavements and sited on the corner of a very tight bend at the foot of the hill, the inevitability of the danger suddenly seemed glaringly obvious.

I felt Matt's tight grip on my shoulder as he got to his feet, screaming out his warning. The panic became infectious as people around us also began to shout. I noticed distractedly the waiter dropped two of our plates of food on the floor before retreating hastily away from our table.

Well, that's made a horrible mess, I found myself thinking stupidly.

It wasn't as though I couldn't see what was happening; or that I hadn't fully understood my boyfriend's cry of warning. It was just that everything had suddenly and strangely slipped into slow-motion. There seemed to be no immediate rush; there was plenty of time to get away from the table. No need to have dropped two perfectly good dinners in the process.

Around me was a blur of movement. I saw Jimmy and Sarah get out of their seats and was aware of them running over to where Phil was standing, screaming out for the rest of us to move. Matt's hand remained embedded in the hollow of my shoulder as I felt him half drag me from my chair. With his other hand I saw him begin to propel Cathy, who was standing beside him, away from the table.

The chaotic scramble of flung-back chairs and knocked-over wine glasses could only have taken a second or two, but in that time I did something really dumb: I turned to look back through the window at the approaching car. Still coming way too fast, the vehicle, its engine roaring like a banshee, erratically straddled the centre line of the road, heading straight towards the bend – and the front of the restaurant – with no sign of slowing down.

And that stupid moment, when I stopped to check the car's approach, was when Matt lost his grip on my shoulder. When I turned my horrified face back from the window, I saw that he and Cathy were already some distance away. I stumbled forwards to follow them, but somehow when leaving, Matt's chair had been knocked over and was now wedged firmly against the pillar beside me. My exit was blocked.

Frantically I pushed at the fallen wooden obstacle, succeeding only in wedging it further between the edge of the table and the pillar.

'Rachel!' screamed Sarah at the top of her lungs. 'Get out of the way!'

Gasping in terror, I knew that from where they stood they must be able to see the car heading straight towards the window, beside which I was now trapped. I pushed and kicked at the chair with every ounce of strength, fear and adrenaline coursing through me, until the sounds of the restaurant diminished and all I could hear was the roar of the blood in my ears.

In desperation I looked up to Matt, and saw him begin

to move back towards me and then, unbelievably, Cathy grabbed his arm and held him back.

'No, Matt, no! There's no time! You'll be killed.'

I heard *that* all right, and crazily part of my brain, the part that wasn't busy trying not to let the rest of me get killed, even had time to absorb what I'd just seen Cathy do. If she thought I was going to let that pass, she was very much mistaken.

But then another noise screeched out from the street behind me, as finally, for the first time, the speeding car began to apply the brakes. Still thrusting uselessly at the fallen chair I glanced behind me for the last time. Yes, the car was braking, but it was much too late.

The sight of the speeding vehicle was growing ever larger in the window, so close now that I could make out the frightened face of the young driver, his eyes wide in terror as the inevitable approached.

I never saw him coming. He must have moved at incredible speed to get to me. One moment I was trapped in this tiny space between the fallen chair and the window, and the next two strong arms had appeared from across the table and fastened onto my own like a vice.

How he found the strength I never knew, but Jimmy literally hauled me out from where I was trapped and over the top of the table. I caught the look on his face as he dragged me across the clothed surface, mindless of the scattering bottles and glasses as I ploughed through them. His eyes were filled with indescribable fear and the tendons of his neck stood out like cables with the effort he was using to pull me towards him.

I grabbed onto him, trying to help, my feet scrabbling frantically over the cloth to propel me forward. Then from behind us I heard an ominously loud thump as the car left the road and mounted the pavement.

Jimmy threw me. That's the only way to describe what he did. One minute I was half across the table and the next I was lifted up, launched and thrown like a rag doll, slithering down to the floor some feet beyond the head of the table. But that act of impossible strength and bravery had taken up the last precious milliseconds between the car leaving the road and crashing into the restaurant.

Jimmy was still standing directly in the path of danger when the window exploded behind him.

The first thing I felt was the heat. Something heavy was over my legs, trapping them under a weight of pain that burned like fire. And there seemed to be water everywhere, thick, salty water running freely down from my forehead, over my cheeks, into my eyes and mouth. I tried to cry out, but no sound came. There was nothing left in my lungs but smoke-filled whispers of vapour. Someone was screaming behind me, someone else was crying. I tried to turn my head and realised I couldn't see properly with the sticky wetness blocking my vision. Tentatively I raised one hand to my head and attempted to rub my eyes. The hand came away covered in a slick red gauntlet of blood. All around me was a mountain of debris, so thick and dense I couldn't see beyond it to where the crying and screaming people were. The car was also blocking my view, half in, half out of what had once been the window, it was impossible to see what was left of the mangled vehicle, as the air was thick with a dense fog of smoke from the engine and disintegrated masonry from the front wall. I felt the shroud of glass over and under me and knew I must be lying among the remains of the window.

From behind me I heard the voices shouting frantically as masonry and rubble began to be moved and I realised that people were trying to reach us. Us. Not just me; *of course* not just me. Jimmy had been there when the car came through the window. Jimmy, who had left his position of safety and had come back to save me.

Ignoring the way the blood began to flow even faster when I turned my head, I managed to lift my neck an inch or two off the glass to look for him. The haze of dust and smoke was still too thick, but I thought I could just make out a shape some feet away to one side. There were huge broken masonry blocks and some long twisted piece of metal, which I guessed had been wrenched from the car, and they were all lying at a strangely skewed angle on top of a long white board. As my vision began to clear further, I realised that it wasn't a board at all; it was what was left of our table. And the reason why it wasn't lying flat against the floor, but was canted at that strange angle, was that something, or someone, was beneath it.

Mindless of anything else, I flung out my arm, raking it in a desperate arc towards the crushed table and what must be beneath it. At first I felt nothing, and then the very tips of my fingers brushed, just for a moment, against something soft.

'Jimmy!' I croaked hoarsely. 'Jimmy, is that you, can you hear me?' No reply. 'Jimmy.' I started to cry, the tears cutting small rivulets through the dirt and blood on my face. 'Jimmy, oh no, Jimmy. Say something . . .'

The dust and debris had begun to settle a little and I could just make out what it was I had been able to reach. Jimmy's forearm protruded at a strange angle from beneath what was left of the table. That was all I could see of him, just his forearm. The arm still looked strong and tanned, as it had a few moments before, when it had somehow found the strength to pull me away from danger. Only now it wasn't moving. Long before the ambulances reached us, I realised that it would never be moving again.

Chapter 2

December 2013

Five years later . . .

The wedding invitation was propped up on the mantel-piece, almost hidden by a small bundle of bills and fast-food delivery circulars. I suppose I was trying to bury it, or something. Perhaps I'd thought that by not seeing it, I could then claim to have accidentally forgotten about it and somehow missed the date. As if that was ever going to happen. Of course I'd replied with an acceptance card when the invitation had arrived a few months earlier, but that had been easy, when the thought of going back to Great Bishopsford had seemed like something abstract that was going to happen so far ahead in the future that I didn't need to really think about it. But now, when the date was only two days away; when I was standing in my tiny flat with an open overnight suitcase before me,

I didn't know why I'd ever felt that I would be strong enough to do this. To go back.

Abandoning my packing for a moment, I went to retrieve the small embossed card from the mantelpiece. *Mr and Mrs Sam Johnson request the pleasure of your company at the marriage of their daughter Sarah to David . . .'* I ran my finger lightly over the raised scrolled hand-writing of her name and knew then, as I had always known, that I *had* to go; that I couldn't make some pathetic excuse and not be at the wedding of my best friend just because it was taking place in my old home town. And was it really the town I was scared of, or the memories that I knew were waiting for me there? Memories I'd schooled myself to bury deep and never allow to surface.

Still clutching the thick cream-coloured invitation, I raised my head to look at my reflection in the mirror above the mantelpiece. In my eyes I saw the truth; returning to the town was only half the problem. The greatest fear was how I would cope with seeing everyone all together in one place again for the first time in years. Well, almost everyone. A haunted look fell over my face and that seemed appropriate, for I knew it wasn't a reunion with the living that was going to be so hard to deal with.

I packed my bag mindlessly, not really concerned about what I took. It was only for three days, and then I'd be back in my own flat, able to lose myself once again in the anonymity of a big city. To many, I'm sure, it might sound peculiar but I'd actually come to relish living somewhere where 'everybody *didn't* know your name'. The only items I took more care in packing were my outfit for the hen-night dinner and the deep burgundy velvet dress I had bought to wear for the wedding itself. Thank God Sarah had eventually given in and accepted my refusal to be her bridesmaid.

'But you *have* to,' she had pleaded, and for a second it could have been the old schooldays Sarah, imploring me to become involved in some crackpot scheme or caper she had cooked up. Only this time I had held fast in my refusal. I'd felt bad, of course. But then I'd known what she was going to ask me, even before the words had left her lips.

It wasn't often that she visited me in London, even though we kept in touch every few weeks by phone. Her job in the north kept her busy and of course her boyfriend Dave – *fiancé*, I mentally corrected – lived there too and quite rightly occupied most of her free time. I'd suspected what was coming when she had invited herself down for the weekend, and so saying no hadn't been as difficult as I'd imagined, when I'd had sufficient time to rehearse it.

'Oh Rachel, please think again,' she had implored and she'd sounded so crestfallen that I had actually felt myself wavering. 'There's no one else in the world I want as a bridesmaid except you, please say you'll do it.' And when I'd shaken my head, not quite trusting myself to speak in case she heard the chink of doubt in my resolve, she had inadvertently asked the one question that allowed me to abdicate from the role without her pursuing it further. 'But *why* won't you say yes?'

And it was then that I'd taken the coward's way out; answering her question by lifting away from my face the heavy swathe of hair I wore in a side parting and revealing the silver forked-lightning scar that ran from my forehead to my cheek. She'd pursed her lips and sighed, and in that moment I knew she had conceded defeat.

'Ah, so she's pulling the old disfigured face card again, is she?' I'd smiled in response. Everyone else I knew pussyfooted around the issue, but Sarah was the only one who had the courage never to dress up her words in anything less transparent than the truth.

'Well, if that's what it takes to keep me firmly seated in a back pew and not wearing some frothy pink creation up near the altar, then yes.'

She'd looked at me mulishly for a second, and I thought she was regrouping her argument for another try, but she then appeared to reconsider and backed down, only murmuring in her defeat, 'I wouldn't have *made* you wear pink, you know.'

I'd hugged her then, knowing I'd let her down in a big way and loving her because she had let me do it.

Before closing the case, I reached over to pick up the small brown bottle of pills on the bedside table, intending to add them to my toiletry bag. I frowned when I felt the weight of the container, holding the bottle up to try and count the contents by the weak light filtering through the window from the overcast December day. There were fewer there than I'd thought, barely enough to last for the next few days. That couldn't be right, could it? I checked the date on the front of the prescription label. It was only ten days old. I knew the headaches had been getting worse but I hadn't realised I'd gone through this many painkillers so quickly. A cold tremor meandered down my spine. This wasn't good. And while I could lie to my dad when he asked how I was, and even (stupidly) had tried lying to the doctors when the headaches had first started, I knew that sooner or later I'd have to face up to the truth. This was the warning sign they had told us to be on the alert for all those years ago. This was the reason why every phone call from my dad in the three years since we lived apart would follow the habitual pattern of 'How are you? No headaches, or anything?' And I'd been happy to report for the first two and a half years that I'd been fine; but for the last six months I'd been lying and saying I was still fine. Eventually I'd made an appointment to see the specialist I hadn't had to visit since my early days of recovery from the accident. He'd seemed concerned when I had told him about the headaches and their frequency, and I was concerned because I'd actually played down their severity quite considerably. The pills he'd prescribed were not the answer and he had urged me to make an appointment to go back to hospital for further tests. I'd taken the prescription but not his advice and had put off making the appointment I knew that I could no longer avoid.

And all of this I had kept from my dad. He had enough to worry about with his own health problems. He needed this time to try and get well, without concerning himself over me all over again. He'd done far too much of that already. However bleak the outcome of his consultation with his oncologists were, he always would end by saying, 'But at least *you* are all right now, thank God.' I didn't have the courage to take that away from him.

I'd sometimes wonder exactly how many mirrors we must have broken, or how many gypsy curses had been hurled our way to account for my family's unfortunate history. First Mum; then my accident; then Dad's illness and now these headaches. It made me wonder if there was some family out there who had been blessed with twenty-odd years of good health and luck, because we seemed to have been given their share of dark misfortune as well as our own. And it didn't matter that Dad said that no one was to blame for his illness, because I knew that he'd only begun smoking again after my accident. It had been his way of coping with the stress. And if he hadn't been doing that, then he probably wouldn't be ill now.

So many terrible things were linked to that one awful night. A blinding twist of pain, worse than even the severest of my headaches, stopped my thoughts suddenly in their tracks before they were allowed to venture down that forbidden avenue.

I intended to leave first thing in the morning and had looked up the times for the first train from London. I'd already booked two days off work, for although everyone wasn't meeting up until the Thursday evening for Sarah's hen-night dinner, I hadn't wanted to arrive late in the day. In reality I knew I would need the time to compose myself for the three-day visit and I had no way of knowing just how hard that was going to be until I was actually there.

I had refused Sarah's offer to stay at her parents' place. Much as I loved her family, they had always been more exuberant and excitable than my own, and I didn't think I'd be strong enough to face that particular brand of crazy in the run-up to their only daughter's wedding. They had seemed to understand and hadn't appeared offended when I'd declined their offer and had instead booked a room in one of the town's two hotels. Many of the guests would be doing the same, I imagined, although of course quite a large number probably still lived in the area.

As the train slipped out of the station and began the two-hour journey, I allowed myself to think of the people I would be meeting again that night. My friends from the past. It seemed strange that the bonds I had thought would bind us for ever had not proved as resilient as I had always believed. And it hadn't been the passing years that had slowly severed the threads apart. No, they had been sheared away by a young man's moment of insanity and an out-of-control stolen vehicle.

Sarah had been extremely careful and cautious when filling me in on news of our old group of friends. From visits to her parents and through the town grapevine she knew that after uni Trevor had returned to Great Bishopsford and was currently living with his girlfriend, who Sarah had yet to meet, and was working as a branch manager in a bank. I found it hard to imagine the rock-band guitar-playing Trev of my teenage years in such a sedate and respectable lifestyle.

Phil was apparently still living the life of a nomad. He'd taken a gap year after university which had grown into a second year of basically bumming around the world. This wandering lifestyle had somehow metamorphosed into a job as a freelance photographer, and although his family still lived in the area, Phil apparently spent little time there between assignments, often electing those which sent him abroad for months at a time. Sarah said that when their paths had crossed, she sensed in him a restlessness that seemed to explain his lifestyle and reluctance to settle in any one place.

And then there was Matt . . . and of course Cathy, for now their histories were inextricably linked. I could tell how hard it had been for Sarah to let me know about them. How carefully she had chosen her words, picking just the right phrase, uncertain of the pain she might be inflicting. It must be just over eighteen months since she had told me that Cathy and my ex-boyfriend were now an item. As the words had settled down the phone lines between us, I had waited for any shard of pain that this news would bring. There was none; merely surprise. And not surprise that those two unbelievably beautiful people were together, just surprise that it had taken Cathy this long to achieve her objective.

I pushed this thought away, as I had when Sarah had first broken the news to me about their relationship. If I allowed myself to think of Matt, then I would be opening the door to our own sad little story and break-up, and that would lead to the reasons . . . and that would lead me somewhere I never allowed my thoughts to go.

As the clusters of houses and built-up areas gradually gave way to fields and open spaces, I could feel a palpable tension beginning to rise inside me. I swallowed it back down with a mouthful of revolting, bitter coffee bought from the buffet car and tried to focus instead on the purpose of the visit. This was *Sarah's* weekend; *Sarah's* big day; I couldn't allow myself to ruin this time for her by having her worry about how I was going to cope with being home again.

That thought pulled me up sharply: *home again*. Was it really my home, was that how I still thought of it? I hadn't lived there for five years, so technically no, it was not. But then nowhere else actually felt that it deserved that title either. Dad's current address in North Devon, where we had moved during the long slow months of my recovery, was *his* home, not mine, despite the fact that I had lived there for almost two years. I suppose my small London flat was home, but it had always felt temporary and transient, chosen for its closeness to the convenient tube line rather than any emotional attachment to the building. Also, it was hard to form a deep emotional attachment to a rental property over a somewhat dilapidated laundrette in one of London's less salubrious locations. I should have moved on when I had earned my first salary increase, should certainly have considered it by the next one, but there was a comfort in the known and familiar, however lacking in style it might be. In my more light-hearted moments I would refer to my flat as shabby-chic, but without the chic. That about summed it up.

As the train's rhythm began to slow, I realised that the two-hour journey had passed much more speedily than I would have liked and when the androgynous voice of the tannoy announced 'The next stop is Great Bishopsford', I was alarmed to discover I was no more ready to face my return than I had been any time in the last five years. As the train shuddered to a halt I got to my feet and reached up to retrieve my small overnight bag from the overhead rack.

'Allow me,' a man's voice offered from behind me, and before I could decline, strong leather-clad arms reached up and lifted down the small case. As I looked up to thank the stranger I saw the quickly disguised look of sympathy on his face as he took in the jagged scar that became visible as I raised my head. I smiled briefly in thanks and lowered my head, allowing the thick curtain of hair to cover the worst of my marked face. It was a habit I had developed over time; it was easier to hide the scar than to have to deal with people's reaction to it. Those who weren't shocked into silence might be tempted to ask about its origins and I had made a decision many years ago never to speak of it, if at all possible. And perhaps that was what was scaring me so badly about being back home. Because how would the old group of friends get through this weekend *without* speaking of something so cataclysmic that it had altered each of our lives in some way?

I caught a taxi from the station, even though it was only a short walk to the hotel where I would be staying. But the walk would have taken me past our old school, and I wasn't prepared yet for the memories taking that route might elicit. Inside the leather-seated interior of the cab, I resolutely kept my gaze firmly fixed on my knees and the floor and tried to avoid the inevitable for a little while longer.

The hotel room was clean and impersonal. No memories here as I'd never set foot in the building before, so that was fine. It took all of three minutes to unpack my small bag. I glanced at the bedside radio alarm clock. It was nearly lunchtime and I toyed with the idea of going down to the hotel bar for a sandwich, but at the last moment lost my nerve and phoned down for room service. 'Baby steps,' I told myself encouragingly. 'Just take little baby steps and you'll be fine.' My reflection looked back at me doubtfully from the dressing-table mirror. If I couldn't even convince myself, how on earth was I going to get through the next seventy-two hours?

After I'd eaten, I called Sarah on my mobile to let her know I had arrived. I heard the relief in her voice and was dismayed that she had not been entirely certain I was really going to come. That strengthened my resolve to be strong, if only for her sake.

'Come over now, I don't want to wait till tonight to see you.' Her enthusiasm made me smile, but then Sarah always had. I just hoped Dave realised how lucky he was, getting to spend his entire future with such a special person.

'Maybe in a little while,' I promised. 'And you have me at your disposal all day tomorrow, so we'll get plenty of time to talk before you become an old married lady.' She groaned at my words and uttered a very unladylike phrase in response.

'Actually,' I continued, 'I think I'll take a little walk this afternoon. See if I can face up to some of those old memories after all.'

'Fancy some company?' I smiled at her offer. She must have a thousand and one things to do, yet I knew she'd abandon all of them in a heartbeat if I said yes.

'No, that's OK,' I replied, 'I think I might do this better on my own, and anyway I'm getting a bit of headache.' I brought my hand up to rub distractedly between my brows, as I realised this last was true. 'So the fresh air will do me good.'

'Well, don't walk so far that you'll be too exhausted for my hen dinner tonight.'

'As if I'd be allowed to miss that! Are you doing the L plates and tiara costume bit?'

'No,' came the swift response in mock indignation, 'I told you before, this is no tacky girly shindig. This is a mixed, grown-up and sophisticated dinner with all of my oldest friends, to celebrate my departure from spinsterhood. By the way, you *have* arranged a stripper for me, haven't you?'

'Absolutely,' I replied, and was still smiling when I hung up the phone.

The air outside was much colder than I had expected, and I was glad of my thick woollen coat and knitted scarf wound tightly about my neck. Without any conscious thought or instruction, my feet found their own rhythm and began to direct me down the twisting side roads which would lead me to my old home. I didn't intervene. This was the first stop I needed to make and this should be the easy one. No dark memories there, only happy ones from my childhood.

Someone had replaced the old picket fence with something much fancier made out of wrought iron, and the front door was now a garish green colour, but apart from that it all looked the same. There was a comfort in seeing that the house hadn't been altered too dramatically, although the garden was better kept, I noticed, but then Dad had never been much of a gardener. Also, fancy wooden blinds replaced the more homely curtains that we had preferred, but basically this was still my old home.

As I lingered on the pavement, I allowed a wave of memories to assault me, a kaleidoscope of images spanning the years. Yet still there were no dark shadows here. Up until five years ago this was the only home I had known and it still represented the feelings of safety and sanctuary which had eluded me in any subsequent accommodation. Standing on the pavement, feeling like I still belonged there, yet at the same time knowing strangely that I did not, I felt a dart of nostalgia pierce through me. I realised with a shock that this was the first time I had actually seen the house since the night of the accident.

The decision to move away, the packing up and sale had all been carried out during the long slow months of my hospital stay. Whether it was the right decision or not, who could say? My poor father had been desperate enough to do whatever he could to minimise my pain. Half demented with grief, I had clung to him desperately from my hospital bed and pleaded with him to let us move far away: so move we did.

Suddenly the memories coming at me were cyanide-bitter and I turned from the house and began walking briskly away. My eyes started to water furiously as a bitter icy wind blasted my face; at least I thought it was the wind doing that.

I walked face down against the gusting currents, my stride just short of a run. At the end of the street I stopped and hesitated. I was standing at a crossroads; in a physical as well as a spiritual sense. If it hadn't been so heartbreakingly sad it would almost have been funny. The headache, which the painkillers had dulled to a persistent throb, now threatened to go into overdrive. I *could* use it as an excuse not to make my next stop. But I thought I'd been hiding behind excuses for too long now.

My hand gripped tightly on the door knocker, as a fleeting glimmer of hope ran through me. Perhaps they too had moved? Sarah had never said but then we hadn't spoken of his family at all in the intervening years. Some wounds just go too deep.

If she was shocked by my appearance on her doorstep after a five-year absence, she hid it well. She also hid her reaction to my damaged face, which I knew she must have noticed with the wind whipping my hair about my head in long chestnut banners. I hoped I was as good at masking my own shock when I saw how much she had aged in the intervening years. Although she smiled and reached out to envelope me in a welcoming hug, the grief was so deeply etched into her face that I realised no new emotion was ever going to be powerful enough to erase it. Guilt sliced through me like a knife wound. It was *my fault* she looked like that. *My fault* she had lost her son.

It hadn't been an easy afternoon, and by the time I got back to the hotel, the tension and the emotions of the day had brought my headache to a never-before-experienced crescendo of agony. My first action on returning to my room was to blindly fumble in my toiletry bag for the bottle of pills. I ignored the dosage instructions on the label and immediately dry-swallowed two tablets instead of one. As I waited for the medication to kick in, I ran a deep hot bath in the small white-tiled bathroom.

The headache was still with me as I slid under the fragrantly perfumed water; slightly better when I emerged pink and beginning to shrivel almost half an hour later, and back to a manageable dull ache when I realised it was already time to get ready for the evening ahead.

I tried to keep my mind away from my visit with Jimmy's mother, knowing there was much I needed to consider about what she had said that day, and knowing too that this night was not the time to do so. I couldn't afford myself the luxury of thinking of that now. First, we all had to face the night ahead; a night of reunion and a time of celebration, all the while trying to ignore the fact that, for the first time, we would be meeting as six instead of seven.

'Baby steps,' I murmured again to myself as I settled before the dressing table and began to apply my make-up.

Sarah had chosen the location for the dinner well. We were booked at a fancy restaurant on the other side of town. A place far too expensive and sophisticated to have been visited by us in our student days. I got there deliberately early, a good thirty minutes before our allocated time, hoping it would give me some sort of mental advantage. Having given Sarah's name to the maître d', I declined the suggestion to wait at the bar and asked instead to be seated straight away.

I was ushered to a large circular table in the far corner of the restaurant. I chose a chair facing the doorway, wanting the advantage of being able to see who would arrive next. I could certainly have done without the large mirrored wall directly opposite our table though. I'd already spent far too much time stressing over my reflection in the hotel room. I didn't really need the indulgence of another half-hour of wondering whether my choice of midnight blue dress with the deep V neckline had been the right one. Having brought no alternative for the evening, there wasn't really much I could do about it either way. Nervously I kept checking my reflection, each time pulling my hair forward, making sure it swung deeply across my cheek.

Phil was the first to arrive, looking tanned and much more muscled and broad-shouldered than I had remembered. He crushed me to him in such a bear hug of an embrace, I felt sure some ribs were going to give way in the process.

'OK, need to breathe now.' He laughed and released me, sliding into the chair beside me.

'You're looking good, Rachel,' he began, and I had to almost sit on my hand to stop myself from automatically reaching up to check my hair was still hiding my face. If he noticed, he was too polite to say. 'It's been way too long. How have you been? Are you still living in Devon?'

We filled in the gaps in our histories, keeping it light, and his story was sufficiently varied to take us through until the next arrival: Trevor and his partner Kate. I didn't know that Sarah had invited partners, but as I introduced myself, after receiving a lift-you-off-your-feet hug from her boyfriend, I realised that Sarah had been wise to have included outsiders at our group's reunion. Somehow new faces would take the pressure off.

For the first time I counted up the place settings at the table, and wondered who the extra seat was for. I didn't have to wait long to find out, for Sarah burst into the restaurant with an infectious grin, a bundle of *Getting Married* helium balloons and her fiancé Dave in tow.

'Who brings their fiancé to their hen night?' joked Phil, standing up to shake Dave's hand warmly in greeting.

'What can I say? He just can't bear to be apart from me.'

I gave her my warmest smile and then nodded my head towards the balloons.

'Classy.'

'I thought so.'

'Well this is a really nice place,' pronounced Dave, pulling out a chair for Sarah before settling himself closely beside her. 'Very posh.'

'Uh-huh,' she confirmed, and then stage-whispered across to me, 'Better get on the phone and cancel that "*entertainment*", Rach.'

By this time, Trevor had been approached by the wine waiter and while a discussion ensued over what to order, Sarah took the opportunity to lean over and whisper in my ear.

'How are you doing, hon? *Really*.'

'Hanging in there,' I whispered back, and when I saw the concern cloud her brow, I knew I had to try harder. 'I'm fine, stop worrying about me.' She gave my hand a quick squeeze and leant back in her chair.

The first awkward moment occurred shortly after our chosen drinks were delivered to our table.

'So who are we missing then?' asked Trevor blithely and an uncomfortable silence ricocheted between us as the double-meaning of his innocent remark hit home.

'Matt and Cathy said they might be a little late,' Sarah quickly supplied and Dave, who really was in tune with his future wife, immediately forestalled any awkward moment by embarking on a long and improbable story about his recent experience with a parking attendant.

We were all still laughing when I noticed a few diners at other tables glancing up in appreciation towards the entrance to the restaurant. Without looking up, I knew they had arrived. Individually they had both always had the ability to turn heads, I knew that only too well from my own time spent by Matt's side. Together they were phenomenal. Magazine-photo perfect. Movie-star beautiful. The combination was almost breathtaking and as they made their way towards us I noted that they both looked, if anything, even more stunning than they had five years earlier. I'd never felt so plain in my entire life. And empty. Because I knew that in another life, with another turn of the dice, there would have been someone sitting at this table to reassure me that was simply not so.

Cathy had dressed to stun, that much was obvious. The figure-hugging black halter-neck dress did exactly what it was supposed to do; the neckline and thigh-high split simultaneously allowing tantalising glimpses of both cleavage and long tanned legs. Her hair was blonder than I remembered and fluffed to perfection about her face. But it was Matt who drew my eye; who had always drawn my eye, I admitted honestly. Like Phil, he too looked taller and broader than my remembered image. His dark suit and crisp white shirt looked expensive, and from their immaculate fit I guessed they hadn't been bought off the peg. His face was leaner, more chiselled than it had been, although his eyes, as they met mine and smiled in greeting, were still the same. I tried to smile convincingly back, thinking suddenly that this was just like earlier today when I had stood before my old house; that strange feeling that here was something that was mine, but yet clearly wasn't mine, all in the same moment.

There was the usual round of greetings and I was glad of the flurry of hugs, handshakes and hellos, for it meant that by the time Matt leant down to kiss me lightly on the cheek, I had pretty much suppressed my purely hormonal reaction at seeing him again. Cathy too leant over to kiss me hello, and I saw something unreadable flicker behind her eyes as she took in my scarred face. Not that the scar itself should be a shock to any one of them. They had all visited me in hospital many times in the immediate aftermath of the accident. Until I had driven them all away, that was.

The evening was a success and a failure both at the same time. On the surface we all appeared to be playing our roles just fine. There was the happy couple-to-be, surrounded by their old friends, gathered together from far and wide to wish them well. But it felt like we were all second-rate actors in a rather unoriginal play. We all said the right things, raised our glasses for toasts at the appropriate moments, but somehow the effort of *not* saying something about the last time we had all sat together around a dining table together was so immense that it suffocated any real pleasure out of the evening. I wondered how it felt to Kate and Dave and if they were aware of that too.

I had assumed, wrongly, that most of the old group had still met up during their university breaks, so it was surprising to learn that although they had seen each other in ones and twos, not once had there been an event where everyone had been together in one place. I hadn't known that the loss of Jimmy and my own disappearance had so effectively caused the glue between us to dissolve.

At least there were no awkward gaps in the conversation to contend with. There was enough ground to cover in bringing everyone up to date with their lives that silence wasn't the problem. We learnt that Matt had been working in his family's business since finishing uni and Cathy was something in PR – she did explain it, but to be honest I wasn't listening properly. I was far more fascinated with her body language than the words she was actually saying. From the moment she had sat down at the table, her every action seemed to screech out her possession of Matt. She was all but entwined around him as we waited to be served. In fact, given that most of her limbs seemed to be twisted in some way around his, I couldn't help wondering if she'd have an arm free to eat at all. And the weird thing was, I knew this show of display was all for me. But why? It had been years since Matt and I had broken up. Broken *apart*, in fact, would be a better way to describe it. And after several excruciatingly painful and abortive attempts, he had finally stopped trying get in touch in the hope that I was going to change my mind. I'd made it perfectly clear that I didn't want him in my life. And it was as true today as it had been back then, so what was with Cathy's astonishing behaviour?

As our last course was cleared discreetly away, the wine waiter appeared at my elbow to refill my glass. I quickly covered its surface with my hand.

'No, no more for me, thank you.'

'You're not driving, are you?' queried Trevor, who clearly had no intention of abstaining from any proffered alcoholic beverage.

'No, I came by taxi,' I replied. I'd been wondering when someone was going to notice that I'd had no more than a couple of sips of wine all night. 'I just think I'm going to need a clear head to cope with Sarah tomorrow. If not, she'll drive me totally crazy.'

Sarah pretended to look offended and everyone laughed. They all seemed to accept the lie. In truth, I was worried to drink any alcohol at all after the amount of painkillers I'd taken that day. And then, as if by thinking of it I'd woken a sleeping dragon, my headache flared up again in a sudden blazing torch of agony. I got to my feet, hoping nobody had noticed that I'd needed to rest my hands on the table to steady myself.

'If you'll excuse me a moment,' I said to no one in particular, and using every effort in my power I walked, in what I hoped was a straight line, towards the Ladies.

Once safely in the rather opulent cloakroom, I let out a long shaky sigh of relief and lowered myself gently onto a small velvet-covered bench. The pain was still searingly strong behind my eyes; so intense that my vision was begin to blur at the edges. It had only been this severe and intense a couple of times before, and I'd had much more warning on those occasions. Never before had the pain just erupted as it had done just now. I didn't doubt for a minute that the tension I'd been under all day had probably not helped the situation.

My fingers felt oddly shaky as I reached into my handbag for my pills. I almost cried in frustration as the childproof cap nearly defeated me, cracking my fingernail in my haste to prise open the container. Two pills again, once more without water. I closed my eyes against the brightly lit room and waited until I felt a little more in control.

I knew now that the time for putting off those hospital tests was long past. This wasn't just going to go away by itself. However frightening the results might be, something was seriously wrong and not knowing exactly what it was wasn't going to make it any better. There was, I supposed, some sort of black irony in realising I was still suffering from the effects of my injuries during the one and only time I'd returned to the place where I had sustained them.

Just let me get through this wedding weekend, I promised myself, and I'll make the appointment first thing on Monday.

By now I realised I had probably exceeded the amount of time I could reasonably be in the Ladies without having Sarah come looking for me. I didn't want her to think the reason I'd been missing so long had anything to do with tonight's territorial display put on by Cathy. And I *certainly* didn't want her to come in and figure out the real reason was because I was suddenly terrified there was something seriously wrong with me.

I got to my feet and was pleased to find that I didn't feel nearly as shaky as I had before and my vision was no longer blurred. I rinsed my hands under cool water and then carefully saturated and squeezed out one of the small folded flannel towels from the basket beside the basins and pressed the wadded cloth against my forehead. I was on the point of leaving to return to the others when the door of the cloakroom swung open and Cathy walked in.

'Everything OK?' she asked, and though she'd used the right words the tone was all wrong. Or perhaps it was just that her eyes held zero interest in my response. When had Cathy become so hard? Sure, there had always been an abrasive side to her, but we'd still been friends. What had I done to her to warrant this attitude? If anything, she should be grateful. It was clear she had always been interested in Matt; so I'd have thought she'd have been pleased that I'd voluntarily taken myself out of the picture on that score. And besides, that was all years ago. Teenage stuff. Surely we were beyond all that now?

'I'm fine. Just a little tired, it's been a hectic week at work,' I fabricated.

'Sorry, what did you say you do again?' Nice to know she'd been paying attention when I'd been talking about it earlier.

'I'm a secretary.'

'Oh, yes. Never did get to go into journalism then? That *was* what you were going to do, wasn't it?'

Bitch. How could she be so thoughtless? Surely she knew only too well why and how my plans for that particular life had been cut short and how I'd never been able to go to university as had been intended.

'No.' I hoped my voice sounded less venomous in reality than it did in my head. 'Obviously everything changed after . . .'

She nodded, and may have looked just the smallest bit shamefaced for the clumsy way she had forced the topic in a difficult direction. But just when I thought she might be showing just a modicum of compassion, that was completely obliterated when she made a great show of brushing back her blond mane of hair from her perfectly immaculate face and leaning closer to the mirror as though scrutinising for imperfections. There were none, I could have told her that. Whatever she saw, be it her own perfect reflection or my own scar-damaged one, the malice seemed to instantly dissipate. Clearly deciding that there was no competition to be feared here, she turned and gave me an artless smile.

'I hope you won't take offence, Rachel, but have you ever thought of seeing someone to see if something could be done about your face? You used to be such a pretty girl.'

Her use of the past tense was certainly not lost on me. For a wicked moment I considered playing dumb and innocently asking: 'My face? Why? Is there something wrong with it?' But I didn't. And anyway, as much as I was unhappy with the way I looked, I had no intention of visiting any plastic surgeon she was about to recommend to me. And I'd be crazy if I expected the shallow and unthinking person Cathy seemed to have become to understand that the problem wasn't that nothing *could* be done, but more that I didn't feel I *deserved* to have things improved. Certainly my father and Sarah, who had both raised this topic years before (with a great deal more tact and diplomacy) had been unable to comprehend what they saw as my martyred logic.

Fortunately the door of the cloakroom swung open at that moment to herald Sarah's arrival. There was an urgency about her entrance that was almost comical. She swept the pair of us with a knowing look and I knew she had instantly assessed what had been going on. I recognised a look on her face from many an altercation in our past, and shook my head almost imperceptibly. Reluctantly the fire in her gaze was doused. I realised then she had almost been looking forward to saying something to Cathy that definitely should remain unsaid.

'Have we moved my party in here then, girls?' she breezed, joining us at the mirror and linking her arm through mine, a move that even the densest person could not fail to realise was a display of solidarity. Cathy was insensitive, but not entirely dense.

'No, no. Rachel and I were just catching up. Let's go.' But then Cathy, being Cathy, couldn't resist one last poisoned dart. 'I'm sure Matt will be worrying about what's happened to me.'

If he *was* worried, he hid it well.

However, as I settled back into my seat, I picked up

on the threads of the one conversation that I had been dreading would be instigated all night. I felt my heart plummet in my chest like a wrecking ball.

Phil was clearly in the middle of saying something to Dave about Jimmy.

'. . . such a tragic and stupid waste . . . such a great bloke . . .'

Dave murmured a non-committal response, and I guessed that Sarah had already pre-warned him to try to divert the conversation from this topic if it surfaced.

'Nothing was ever the same after that night . . . not for any of us.'

The silence around the table that followed this remark was its own acknowledgement. I felt rather than saw almost every eye turn to me. I guess they were right in thinking that I had been affected the most, for the scars on my face were nothing compared to the ones that scored me deep inside.

'Come on now, let's not do this tonight,' implored Sarah.

'No, of course,' agreed Phil, and even though I'd kept my eyes averted to the tablecloth, I knew meaningful glances were being directed my way. It was all getting a little too intense and I was overcome by a sudden irre-sistible desire for the safe anonymity of my hotel bedroom.

'I hate to break up the party,' I began, and heard a small chorus of guilty noes from around the table, 'and it's not just because of . . . Jimmy.' My voice hesitated before being able to form his name. 'But I really do have a pretty bad headache, so if you don't mind, I think I'll call it night for now.'

Sarah immediately began to protest, but then the intuition our close friendship provided made her completely back down.

'Sure, sweetie. It's been a busy day for everyone.'

When I realised that she intended to wind the whole evening up, I felt instantly ashamed.

'No, Sarah. You all stay. You haven't even had coffee yet. I'll just grab a cab. Please don't break up the party because of me. *Please*.' I got to my feet. Sarah still looked as though she was wavering, but then Dave interceded.

'Let me go outside with you to hail a cab,' he offered. 'Trevor, why don't you order some coffees and brandies.'

I gave him a grateful smile. No wonder Sarah loved him. I decided he was worthy of her after all.

'No need for a cab,' a familiar dark voice interjected. 'I've got my car outside. I'll run Rachel back.'

I was so taken aback by Matt's unexpected offer for, apart from his initial greeting, this had been the first remark he had actually directed to me all evening. Before I even had a chance to react either way, he dropped a swift kiss on Cathy's forehead.

'Won't be long,' he assured her, then turning to look across at me, 'Shall we?'

I was about to protest; to insist that his offer really wasn't necessary and that getting a cab was by far and away the easiest solution, and then I caught sight of Cathy's face. Rage, disbelief and total indignation all battled for pole position. It was wicked, I knew, but that was what decided me. I owed her this for the cloakroom incident. I reached down, collected my bag and gave a general smile to the gathering of friends at the table.

'Sorry to leave so soon, but I'll see you all at the wedding on Saturday. Goodnight.'

As I walked away from the table, I felt Matt place a guiding hand at the small of my back to steer me past a waiter approaching the table with a tray of coffees. I heard the echoing chorus of 'Goodbyes' as we walked away. Strangely enough, Cathy's voice did not appear to be among them.

Once outside in the bracing December air, I took a step away from him, deliberately breaking the lingering contact of his hand against me.

'This way,' he instructed, raising his arm to blip a key towards a low dark sleek vehicle parked under a bright sodium arc light. He opened the passenger door and cupped my elbow briefly as I lowered myself onto a cream-coloured seat with leather as soft as butter. I waited until he had joined me in the car before commenting:

'Well, this is certainly far more luxurious than a taxi. A new toy?'

He gave a little shrug. 'It's a company car.'

'But you own the company.'

He shrugged again. 'And your point?' He shifted towards me, and although the engine had not been turned on, there was still plenty of light illuminating the car from the restaurant's security lighting. Looking into his face, being aware of the intimate proximity inside the car's confined interior, I forgot the point I was trying to make, if any. Hell, if he looked at me that way for a moment or two more, I was likely to forget my own name. I decided on a change of topic.

'Cathy didn't look too pleased that you'd offered me this lift.'

'Cathy'll get over it.' OK, that was clearly another conversational no-no. However he didn't drop that theme entirely.

'Cathy and I . . . you knew about that, didn't you . . . I mean before tonight?'

I gave a shrug that I hoped looked nonchalant.

'Sure, Sarah mentioned it . . . in passing . . . ages ago.'

His voice suddenly dropped in tone, sounding less self-assured than he had all evening. There was an echo of the boy I had known so well.

'And you were OK with that, were you?'

I may have hesitated for a second longer than I should have, before replying in a tone that was striving for breezy.

'Well, of course. Why wouldn't I be?'

He straightened suddenly in his seat, flicked on the ignition and headlamps and with a briefly instructed 'Fasten your seatbelt', reversed, at speed, out of the parking space. Clearly not the answer he had been hoping for, it would seem.

As we left the car park, he pointed the car in the direction of my hotel.

'I'm staying at the—'

'I know where you're staying,' he interrupted.

Oh, this was terrific. Now I had made him mad. At that moment I'd have given anything to have swapped this ride for the tattiest, smelliest cab that could be imagined. I sought for a topic that might be suitably innocuous to raise between us. But came up empty. There were too many landmines in our history to make chit-chat possible. In addition, the painkillers I'd taken for my headache had yet to kick in, so if we had to conduct the fifteen-minute journey in total silence, then so much the better.

I wasn't going to be that lucky.

When we stopped at the first set of traffic lights, which turned red as we approached, Matt caught me absently rubbing my fingers against the bridge of my nose to try to ease the pain.

'You really *do* have a headache? It wasn't just an excuse?' I heard the doubt behind the question. It made me snappier than I should have been.

'Yes, *I really do.*'

'There's a twenty-four-hour place up ahead, would you like to stop there and pick up something for it?' The unexpected kindness took me by surprise.

'No, it's fine. I've got some pills.' Not that they appeared to be working any more, I silently added.

Several more minutes passed and I thought we had probably escaped the awkwardness when he threw a live conversational grenade into the car.

'Cathy and I . . . it's not that serious, you know. More of a convenience thing . . . I just wanted you to know that.'

Too stunned for a moment to know how to respond, I eventually came up with: 'I very much doubt that Cathy views it that way. Not from the look on her face as we left the table together. And why would you possibly imagine I needed this information?'

He sighed, and I could see he was struggling to pick the right words.

'It's been hard tonight, seeing you again. All of us together again.'

With one notable exception, but I let that pass. He gave a laugh that fell short of having any real humour in it.

'It's just that all night I couldn't get rid of the feeling that I was sitting next to the wrong person.'

I didn't know how to respond. Should I feel flattered by the compliment, or offended that he was declaring such feelings when he was still clearly in a long-term relationship with someone else?

'Matt, I think you're just getting caught up in the nostalgia of the reunion, or something. You're confusing the past and present here in a pretty drastic way. We were just kids back then.' My voice lowered and trembled slightly. 'Something terrible happened and things changed. *We* changed.'

'We're not kids now,' he vowed, and without warning, his hand left the steering wheel and reached over to cover mine on my lap. I jerked it back as though I'd been burnt.

'No. Don't do that. You're with someone else, you're not free . . .' I carried on quickly when I saw he was about to offer something then, '. . . And even if you *were*, it wouldn't be any different. I still feel the same way as I did when we split up.'

This really grabbed his attention from the road, and he turned to stare at me in disbelief.

'Are you still blaming yourself about Jimmy? Dear God, tell me that isn't true. Not after all these years.'

'How long it's been is immaterial,' I began, wondering how many more people in my life I would have to keep justifying this to. 'If he hadn't been trying to rescue me, then he'd still be here now.'

'And you wouldn't be.'

I shrugged.

'So this is how you intend to repay that debt? By shutting yourself away like some dried-up old spinster all your life? Christ, Rachel, you're only twenty-three years old!'

I noticed the speed of our car had increased exponentially with his anger.

'And do you think this is what Jimmy would have wanted, for you to commit yourself to living a life all alone?'

'I'm not alone,' I refuted, sounding all at once a little too much like a sullen teenager.

'Well, have there been boyfriends?'

His attack stung, and I mindlessly sought to sting him right back.

'Hardly.' I swept back my hair to reveal the scar by the light of the street lamps. 'Not exactly a turn-on, now is it?'

He swore then, several times, my words seeming to have made him angrier than anything I had said before.

'Don't you do that to yourself. Don't bring it all down to that.'

The car jerked sharply into a narrow gravelled

forecourt and I noticed with surprise that we had already reached my hotel. He braked sharply in a little flurry of gravel chippings. His rage seemed to fade away with the thrum of the engine and he swivelled towards me, reaching across to lift my chin and tilt my face towards him.

'This scar . . .' his finger traced down its raised white-lightning path, almost reverently, 'it's nothing. It's not who you are.'

I pulled back from his touch, scared by the intimacy. I was tired, I told myself, and in pain, otherwise I would never have allowed him to have got that close. Desperately I sought to bring him back to reality.

'Your girlfriend doesn't think it's nothing. She thinks I should get it fixed.'

'Cathy can be . . . a little thoughtless. She only said that because she's afraid of you. And jealous.'

That really made me sit up in my seat.

'She's *what*? But why?'

His next words were so unexpected, I was literally rendered speechless.

'Because she knows I've never really got over you. That whatever she and I might have, it'll never be enough. There's no future in it for us.'

Things had gone much too far. I pushed him back so he was more squarely in his own seat.

'And there's none for us either, Matt,' I answered firmly. 'Please don't say this stuff to me, not again. I don't want to hurt you, and whatever she might think, I don't want to hurt Cathy either. If you're not happy with her . . .

then leave. Don't use me as the excuse. I'm not the solution to your problems.'

'It's not that—'

But I wouldn't let him finish.

'Look, Matt, I don't know where this has all come from, but whatever you think was going to happen between us, well, it isn't.' I tried to temper the rejection so the remains of the weekend would be at least bearable. 'Part of me will always . . .' I hesitated, anxious not to use the word 'love', 'have feelings for you. You were an important part of my past. But that's it. An awful thing happened, not just to Jimmy, but to all of us. And this, this feeling that I can't be with anyone . . . for now, at least . . . well, this is how I deal with it.'

'It's hiding. Not dealing!'

I stayed silent. That one had been used on me before. But his next words could not be so easily ignored.

'And do you really think this is what Jimmy would have wanted for you? To see you by yourself? For Christ's sake, Rachel, he was so in love with you he even sacrificed his own life to save yours!'

I gasped, struck by a pain that dwarfed my headache to the merest of irritations. He saw my reaction and looked stunned by it.

'What? You didn't know? You couldn't see it written all over his face whenever he looked at you?'

This was too much. To hear this again, for the *second* time in one day, was more than I could bear. I shook my head in denial, my eyes blurring with tears.

'You're wrong. So wrong. We were friends . . . just friends,' I whispered softly.

'For you, maybe. But not for him. Everyone else could see it. It was so obvious.'

I was so confused that my pained brain could hardly function.

'It's not true. I would have known. And he never said anything . . . not once, not in all those years . . .'

Something stirred at the back of my mind. An elusive memory, just out of reach.

'Why do you think he hated me so much?'

'He didn't *hate* you.' I jumped to my lost friend's defence, but even as I uttered the denial I had to acknowledge that there had always been a frisson of antagonism between the two of them.

Once more Matt reached out, securing my face between his strong hands. 'I had you, and he didn't. There must have been times when he found that unbearable.'

My heart twisted at the pain I had unknowingly caused. This didn't make anything better at all. It just made it a million times worse. I pulled back before he could kiss me, for I was certain that was what he had intended.

'I can't do this, Matt. Don't do this to me. It's just not fair.'

By this time my scrabbling hand had finally found the discreetly positioned door handle. I flung open the door, allowing cold December air and hopefully some sanity into the car. I was unbuckled and out of my seat before he could join me on the passenger side.

Perhaps he could see the distress he'd caused, or

perhaps the brighter illumination from the hotel allowed him to see I really did feel as sick as I'd been claiming, for he sounded conciliatory.

'I'm sorry if I've upset you, Rachel.'

I shook my head.

'Just go. Go back to the restaurant. Back to Cathy.'

He nodded, but he didn't look happy.

'Will you be all right?' His eyes searching my face were clearly concerned. 'You don't look very well.'

'I'll be OK. I just need to sleep off this headache. I'll be fine.'

I could sense his reluctance to leave me so I summoned up a manufactured smile from some unknown well of strength. 'Go.'

He smiled back. 'I'm not going to give up on you, you know,' he promised, getting back in his car. 'You drove me off once but I'm not going to give in so easily this time.'

'Go,' I repeated, the entreaty threaded through with a note of desperation. And at last he did, the car sweeping across the forecourt and disappearing into the darkness with a flash of brake lights as it entered the flow of traffic.

As I wearily mounted the three stone steps to the hotel's foyer, I couldn't help but think his parting comment had sounded more like a threat than a promise.

When I finally swiped the key card into its slot and entered my hotel room, I was surprised to see that it was only a little after ten o'clock. It had felt much later. I kicked off my shoes and sank gratefully onto the bed. Drawing a pyramid of pillows up behind me, I switched off all but the bedside lamp and lay back with my eyes closed. The headache was still at fever pitch, and I was afraid it had settled in for the night. I also knew it was far too soon to take more painkillers and at this rate the bottle would be emptied long before the wedding, so I knew I had to start rationing myself.

I tried for fifteen minutes to clear my mind but it refused to empty. The day kept spooling through my tortured head in slow motion. I saw again and again the look in Janet's eyes as she spoke of her dead son and how much she said I had always meant to him. I heard again my own denial, the same denial I had uselessly echoed to Matt when he had made the same claim. I couldn't believe they were both right. That *everyone* had been right.

Was it really possible to have been so blind, to have missed such a vital truth in our relationship? These were impossible questions to answer. And the tragedy of knowing I would never, could never, be sure was crumbling my resolve not to allow my thoughts to reach out for Jimmy. I needed him now, at this moment, more than ever; to hear his voice, to look into the smile that always lived in his eyes for me.

Without pausing to make a conscious decision, I swung my legs off the bed and groped around for my shoes. The lateness of the hour didn't worry me. I knew there was only one place I could go now to ask these questions, to say what I had to say.

★

The night had turned even colder when I once more walked past the bemused doorman who had bidden me goodnight on my way in only twenty minutes before. The cold wind numbed my face as I turned and began walking swiftly to my destination. If challenged, I could always claim that I'd taken the walk to find relief from my headache, but in reality I needed an altogether different kind of solace. And the location held no horrors for me. How could it? There was nothing to fear from a ghost when it was someone you loved.

The dark streets were almost deserted; it was too cold and late for an evening stroll. My feet crunched lightly on pavements already beginning to glaze with a light frosting of ice. When the wind bit into my face with icy fangs, I burrowed my chin deeper into my scarf and walked into its vicious jaws with steely determination.

My feet faltered for a second when I rounded the last street corner and the church came into view. It stood alone at the top of a hill, with no shops or houses nearby. Its closest neighbour was the town's railway station, and that stood almost two miles away. Even on a clear day, the red-bricked station building was completely obscured by the churchyard's high iron railings. Its isolation was perhaps meant to engender a feeling of peace and tranquillity, but on this dark December night neither of those emotions were foremost in my mind.

As I approached the large arched gate in the railings, I wondered what I would do if it were locked. Climb

over? I looked up and surveyed the height of the fence
. . . no, that wasn't going to happen. Come back in the
morning, I supposed. Yet the urgency to make this very
real and physical connection with Jimmy was so strong,
I didn't think I could wait until the following day.

The gate swung open on well-oiled hinges. Strange,
I'd felt sure it was going to creak and make the cliché
complete.

Once inside the churchyard my courage wavered
slightly. Was this an act of total madness, to be wandering
around a deserted graveyard at this time of night? Wasn't
this just the sort of behaviour I'd always ridiculed hero-
ines for in the movies?

A noise from an approaching car startled me, and
instinctively I ducked behind a large oak tree to avoid
being picked up in its headlights. I'd forgotten I could
be clearly seen by passing cars on the road. Plus, I wasn't
exactly dressed for covert manoeuvres in my long white
coat. I wasn't sure if I was actually committing a criminal
offence, or an act of trespass, but winding up at a police
station, trying to justify my actions, was not how I planned
to end the evening. My brush with disclosure decided me
against hesitating further, and as soon as the car was out
of sight I drew away from the tree and walked with
renewed purpose towards the rear of the church, where
the small graveyard was situated.

There weren't many graves in this part of the cemetery.
The larger, older section was around the other side, and
much of this grassy area was still awaiting the arrival of
its new occupants. I supposed the large crematorium in

the next town might account for the comparatively few new markers I could see in this more traditional place of rest. I instinctively knew that Janet would have wanted somewhere close by, where she could visit her lost son. I also knew that the easiest way to find him would be to look for the best maintained plot.

I didn't have to look at many before I found what I was searching for. Just long enough to read half a dozen moving and heart-wrenching epitaphs as I walked among the granite headstones. *Dearest husband*, *Beloved grandmother*, *Much loved father*. So much grief, so many tears, the frozen soil must be virtually saturated from those emotions.

Jimmy's grave stood slightly to one side, clearly newer than its neighbours. The headstone was sparkling white marble which seemed to glow under the winter moon's iridescence. I walked around and steadied myself for a moment before reading his inscription.

Jimmy Boyd.
Lost too soon at 18 years.
Cherished son and loyal friend.
Our love for you will live on for ever.

A sob broke from me, so raw with grief it sounded more animal than human in its anguish. I felt my knees begin to buckle and I sank onto the cold grass beside his grave. I had come here hoping to voice all of my feelings but none could reach the surface through the boiling swell of pain that swept me in its path. I had believed that over the years I had reached a place of acceptance, but I realised now that all I had done was pull a thin veneer of pretence over a gaping wound. I was incapable of words; only able to rock slowly back and forth on my knees, repeating his name over and over again.

This was too painful. I wasn't strong enough, either physically or emotionally, to cope with this grief tonight. It was madness to have come. Still hiccupping soft sorrowful sobs, I started to get to my feet and then swayed forward, only stopping myself from falling by flinging out my hand onto the ice-slick turf. My head felt suddenly strange, too heavy for my neck to hold. Then, giving a small helpless cry, my supporting arm gave way and I fell forward onto the cold, unyielding ground beside the grave.

The pain from my head now encompassed my entire neck and shoulders and I wondered if I had somehow struck myself on a rock when falling. But the cold grass beneath my cheek was clear of any obstruction. Very slowly, trying to minimise each movement of my head, I inched back my arms until both hands were flat on the soil on either side of me. I tried to lever myself up but although I exerted every ounce of my strength, my quivering forearms would not comply. After several abortive attempts, I realised I wasn't going to be able to get to my feet that way.

Suddenly the danger I was in was terrifyingly obvious. I was lying, sick and virtually immobile, in a deserted graveyard. No one knew I was here; no one was going to miss me – not until the morning at least. I could *die* here. The thought, so terrifying, managed to pierce through the vice-like pain in my head. I had no idea how long it took to die of exposure, or hypothermia. But I did know that giving up and lying down to die beside the boy who'd lost his own life while saving mine, was not going to happen.

Trying to ignore the agony in my head, I began to attempt to roll gradually onto my side. My progress was slow, each movement sending a paralysing spasm from my neck. I stopped several times to gather my breath, finding the strength to continue not in my desire to live, but more in the knowledge of what losing me, especially in these circumstances, would do to my father.

Eventually, when I had regained my breath a little, I gingerly raised my knees towards my chest. At least that area of my body wasn't in pain, but it did feel strangely numb, which I supposed must be as a result of lying on the frozen ground. With my legs in position, I realised I couldn't afford to tackle my next manoeuvre so delicately. I didn't have much strength left and it felt very much like this would have to be an all-or-nothing attempt. I braced my arm to support me, took a deep breath, held it and rolled with Herculean effort onto my knees.

Bright spots of light pinwheeled behind my eyes; I felt the sway of an incipient faint, and bit deeply into my lower lip to fight back against the weakness. When it had passed, I cautiously opened my eyes. I was still on all fours, and was so grateful not to have succumbed to unconsciousness that it took me a moment or two to realise there was something wrong with my eyes. Seriously wrong. An involuntary cry of pure terror escaped my frozen lips. My vision had virtually disappeared in my right eye, and my left had only tunnel-like vision, the periphery of my eyesight disappearing into a cloudy fog. This, I knew, wasn't anything to do with exposure, hypothermia or intense grief. The loss of sight was the last dire warning link in the chain of medical advice I had so unwisely chosen to ignore.

Telling myself that I couldn't afford to let myself panic, I groped out with my left hand, found the wide marble edge of Jimmy's headstone and pulled myself upright on legs that felt as stable as elastic. I realised I had stupidly left my mobile in the hotel room, so my only chance of aid was to try to get to the road. Hoping they would forgive me for the disrespect, I used the surrounding grave markers as handholds as I made my slow and unsteady way through the graveyard.

The sight in my left eye appeared to be decreasing at an alarming rate; the small circle of vision now felt as though I was looking through a narrow tube. I tried to ignore my greatest dread that this might be permanent. I just couldn't allow that thought to overwhelm my mind, or exhaustion to take my body. It was hard, particularly when what I wanted to do more than anything was lie down and close my eyes against this pain-wracked nightmare. Even walking was now proving difficult, and each shaky step I took had all the fluidity of a newly awakened zombie.

As I left the last gravestone support, I thought I could vaguely make out a distant sound. Was that just a train from the station or could there be a car approaching? It was probably not yet eleven o'clock, surely not that late for someone to be driving by? The road, although quiet, might still have the occasional passing car. But from where I stood, in the shadows of the church and its surrounding trees, I knew I would never be seen. The noise grew in intensity. It *was* a car.

'Help!' I cried out uselessly. 'Please stop, help!'

I lurched forward, trying to run and raise my arms to flag down the car. It was my last bad idea, in an evening full of them. Running isn't really an option when you can barely stand. Or see. I was already pitching head first towards the ground and oblivion by the time the car's headlights arced into the starlit sky.

Chapter 3

The first thing I became aware of was the continuing soreness from my head, which seemed to feel somehow strangely enlarged. I moved it slowly, just the merest fraction, and heard the soft scratch of crêpe bandage against cotton. I tried to raise an arm to investigate but stopped when I felt a painful tug from something embedded in my forearm. It would appear that I was attached to some sort of machine. A persistent beeping sound from a piece of equipment positioned directly behind me confirmed I was probably hooked up to some sort of monitoring device as well as being on a drip. Clearly I was in hospital, but why couldn't I see anything?

I blinked several times. My eyelids felt weirdly unresponsive, and it made no difference, everything was still in darkness. Why couldn't I see? What had happened to me? I felt a powerful wave of panic begin to engulf me. Why couldn't I remember? What was the matter with my head – and my eyes? I strained to recall. In small fragments I could see fleeting snapshots of the day before. I could remember visiting my old house, then a fast forwarded image of being at a restaurant. Then I'd gone back to the hotel. Had I taken a cab? I couldn't remember. Then I'd reached my room . . . and then . . . nothing. There was a gaping chasm where the rest of my memories of the evening should be.

I struggled to move, to sit up, even with all the wires and tubes attached. The noise of this ineffectual stirring did however alert someone in the room.

'Well, hello there. Welcome back to us, Rachel. It's good to see you awake. Let me just call your father.'

There was a sound of a door opening and footsteps rapidly receding down an echoing corridor. I realised I was alone before I could manage to command my numb lips to form a question.

Was she going to phone my dad? Had someone already informed him I was in hospital? Dread at how he would have reacted to that news rippled through me. He was too ill to cope with any more worry in his life right now. I wondered if they could bring the phone to my bedside. Perhaps if he could just hear my voice he'd be reassured that I was OK. But how could I calm and reassure him about my condition when I didn't even know what that was myself? I gave an angry moan of pure, impotent frustration.

'Hey, hey . . . none of that now. Everything's going to be all right.' Swift and sure footsteps approached the bed. How was this possible?

I started off the pillow, ignoring whatever agony might ensue. My head was already spinning in shock anyway.

'Dad? Dad, is that you?'

A warm and familiar roughened hand engulfed my own where it lay on the stiff hospital sheets.

'Of course it's me, my love.' His breath warmed my face as he bent to kiss my cheek, his beard scratching against me.

'Oh Dad . . .' I began, and then, although there were a thousand things I could say, *should* say, none of them managed to come out as I was helpless to stop myself from dissolving suddenly and very noisily into tears.

'There, there, there,' muttered my dad, frenziedly patting my hand in discomfort. I knew the look that would be on his face, even without the benefit of sight. He had always been fazed by my tears, either as a small child or in my turbulent teenage years. Knowing how difficult it was for him to deal with them, I made a real effort to stem the torrent.

'I'm so glad you're here, Daddy,' I sniffed, slipping back into the childish name without even realising I'd done so.

'I'm so glad to see you awake again, my love. You can't believe the fright I got when I first came in and saw you like that – all wired up and everything. It brought back so many horrible memories.' I heard the catch in his voice. Of course, he must have been unable to stop thinking back to the night of the accident.

I could only imagine the anguish he must have gone through back then, as he'd sat for days on end beside a hospital bed just like this one. It was many months before he had ever revealed to me the true terror he had lived through while I lay unconscious and unresponsive. And even though the doctors had reassured him that I just needed time; that the emergency services had got me breathing again before the threat of brain damage; that I *would* make a full recovery; he must still have been fraught with anxiety until the moment I had first opened my eyes.

That was the moment of relief from his heartache and the beginning of mine. For I hadn't allowed him to put off giving me the dreadful news; had refused to wait until I was '*stronger*'. And truly, who was ever going to be strong enough to hear the news that your best friend had died, while saving your life?

The accident of five years ago was obviously as much in his mind again as it had been in mine.

'Memories of the accident,' I said softly.

'Accident?' he sounded puzzled. 'No, love; memories of your poor mum.'

I was confused, he so rarely spoke of her. I suppose the thought of losing me had reawakened many painful recollections. I wasn't sure how to respond but was saved from the need to by the sound of the door opening and several people entering the room.

'Hello, doctor,' greeted my dad. It sounded as though he knew the man who had just entered my room, knew him quite well, in fact. For the first time I thought to ask the question:

'How long have I been in here?'

'A little over thirty-six hours, young lady,' replied the doctor, in a voice that I supposed was meant to be calming. I did *not* feel calm. As though in a game played against the clock, my mind frantically tried to fit together the jigsaw pieces of what had happened to me. Like an arc of electricity between two terminals, I suddenly remembered: the cemetery; the crippling headache; my sudden virtual blindness. I remembered it all.

I lifted the arm not encumbered with hospital paraphernalia to my bandaged head.

'Have you had to operate on me, for the headaches? The blindness?'

A deeply amused chortle came from the doctor. How could there be any humour in what I'd just asked?

'Bless you, Rachel, you're not blind.'

'But I can't see!' I wailed.

Again that laughter; this time even Dad joined in.

'That's because your eyes are covered with bandages. They sustained some minor scratches – you probably got those from the gravel chippings when you fell face down. You really did take a terrible old knock on your head.'

I turned my head in the direction of the nurse's voice. What the hell was she going on about? Clearly she either didn't see, or chose to ignore, the look on my face which clearly said she was an idiot, for she continued:

'That's what Dr Tulloch is here for now, to take off the bandages and check out your sutures.'

'But I *didn't* hit my head,' I insisted to anyone who would listen. I felt my dad once more take hold of my hand.

'Hush now, Rachel, don't get yourself upset. Things are bound to be a little fuzzy to begin with.'

'I think I'd remember if I hit my head,' I responded, more sharply than I intended. 'It was the headache, you see,' I tried to explain. 'It was absolutely excruciating.'

'You have a headache now?' enquired the doctor, with keen attention.

'Well no,' I replied, realising for the first time that although my head hurt, the pain was different from the splitting agony of the headaches I'd been experiencing. 'It just feels kind of sore . . .'

'I'm sure it does. It will settle down in a day or so. As the nurse said, it really was a nasty fall.'

I would have protested further but I was aware of hands reaching behind my head and beginning to release me from the swaddling bandages. With each rotation the pressure against my head lessened and my anxiety increased. When finally relieved from my mummy-like accessories, disappointment coursed through me.

'I still can't see anything. I'm still blind!'

The doctor's voice had a slightly more impatient edge. Clearly he now had me pigeon-holed as a major drama queen.

'Just let me remove the gauze first before you go off

and get a white stick, young lady. Nurse, if you please, the blinds.'

Deciding I didn't like the man, however much my father might disagree, I nevertheless turned my face towards his voice and allowed him to lift first one then the other circular coverings from my eyelids. I blinked for the first time, enjoying the unfettered freedom of the movement. The room had been darkened by the lowering of the blinds but enough daylight fell through the half-shut venetians for me to make out the vague shapes of four people around my bed: the doctor, a white-coated young man standing beside him, the nurse and, on the other side of the bed, my dad.

'I can see shapes,' I declared, my voice a strange mixture of joy and disbelief. 'It's cloudy but—'

'Give it a moment. Nurse, a little more light now, I believe.'

She obliged by a further twist on the corded blinds. Suddenly things began to clear and I saw the white-haired senior doctor, the young bespectacled intern, the middle-aged nurse. I began to smile broadly, a reaction they all mirrored.

I turned to my dad, my grin wide, and then froze, the look on my face unreadable.

'Rachel, what's wrong? Doctor! Doctor what's the matter?'

The consultant was beside me in an instant, flashing a small torch in my eyes, checking my reactions, but I fought against him to look again at my dad.

'Rachel, can you tell me what's wrong?' urged the

doctor. 'Are you in pain, is your vision disturbed in any way?'

Disturbed? Well yes, I should say. But not in any way that he meant.

'No, I can see all right. Everything's clear now.'

'Then what's wrong?'

'It's my dad.'

'Me?' My father sounded totally confused. Well, join the club. I forced myself to look at him slowly and with greater concentration then. But what I saw made no sense. The doctor's voice had adopted a tone I guessed he usually reserved for those with mental illnesses.

'What about your father?'

I couldn't find my voice.

'Rachel honey, you're scaring me. Can't you just tell us what's the matter?'

'Is there something wrong with your father, Rachel?'

I turned to the doctor to reply to his question and then back at my only parent. My newly empowered eyesight took in his plump cheeks, his bright eyes – albeit clouded now in concern – the small paunch he was always planning on joining a gym to lose. There was no sign of the haggard, prematurely aged, cancer-raddled man I had last seen three weeks ago.

'No! That's what's the matter. There's nothing wrong with him at all!'

Chapter 4

December 2013

Also five years later . . .

The man must have been watching me for a considerable period of time before I first became aware of him. Of course he could have been right beside me on the crowded underground platform and I'd never have known it, packed as we were like cattle during the usual Friday evening exodus from London. Moving along the twisting tiled passages while changing underground lines, I wasn't really aware of anything except the annoyance of having to drag my small suitcase behind me through the rush hour. I stopped apologising after I'd run over about the fifth set of feet. It had been a huge mistake to leave it so late to begin my journey: it would have made far more sense to have driven down with Matt that morning as he had suggested, but I had an immovable deadline for an article I'd been working on that just couldn't be ignored.

'Shall I wait for you, and we'll drive down together when you're done?'

I'd considered that for a moment but then dismissed the idea.

'No, there's no sense in both of us being late. You go on ahead, I'll finish at work and then catch the fast train down.'

It had seemed like such a good idea at the time, and now . . . well, not so good at all. Between my attempts at weaving through the crowds with the suitcase in tow (which was how the five sets of toes got mangled), I kept glancing frantically at my watch, knowing time was fast running out if I was going to make the mainline train out of London for Great Bishopsford. At this rate I would be lucky to get to the restaurant before the desserts were being served. Guilt at letting Sarah down added impetus to my stride and I cannoned between two suited businessmen earning a very ungentlemanly comment from one of them.

'Sorry,' I mumbled, not even glancing back to see if my apology had been heard.

I looked again at my watch; I had less than twelve minutes until the train left. I was going to have to make a run for it. As I lowered my arm a sudden flash of brilliance arced back at me, momentarily dazzling in the reflection of an overhead light. Damn! That showed how harassed I was, because I couldn't remember the last time I'd forgotten to hide my ring before catching the tube home. In one swift movement I swivelled the large diamond on my ring finger so that it now nestled against my palm, showing only a plain platinum band on my exposed hand. Matt would have been furious if he'd known I'd forgotten. He really didn't like me wearing it for travelling, but what was the point of having such a fabulous engagement ring if it had to be kept locked up in a safe all the time?

God knows how but I made the train with barely seconds to spare. My heart was still thumping furiously in my chest from my sprint down the platform as I stowed my case in the overhead rack and sat down on legs trembling from the unaccustomed exertion. I promised myself that this year my New Year's resolution would be to actually *go* to the gym I spent so much money on each month and hadn't visited for three months or more. Like so many areas of my life, all my good intentions had swiftly been buried in an avalanche of work.

I was lucky that Matt was every bit as busy as I was and perfectly understood the demands of my job, otherwise we'd never have survived together until now. Long hours at the office, plans that had to be cancelled at the last minute, late nights and working weekends, these were all things we were equally familiar with. When I thought about it, when I had a free second to think about *anything* that wasn't work-related, I wondered how anyone ever managed to find the balance between a successful career and a relationship. And if at the back of my mind there was a nagging voice telling me that things shouldn't be the way they were right now, then I just ignored it, telling myself this was only a temporary glitch and that everything would be sure to settle down some time next year when Matt and I eventually found somewhere to live together. That's supposing we ever found enough time to clear our schedules to go flat hunting.

Perhaps if I still didn't feel very much the 'new girl' at the magazine, I'd be able to relax more. But each time I considered doing less, I could hear the echo of doubts that had been voiced at my interview as my prospective employers read my CV, detailing my very provincial two years' experience on a local newspaper. But I had, against all the odds, been offered the job above people who I knew were, at least on paper, far better qualified and experienced than I was. That was eight months ago, and I was still trying to prove both to them, and more importantly to myself, that they had made the right decision. And if that meant being the first to arrive each day and the last one to leave at night . . . well, that's just what I had to do. For now.

It was only when I realised that I was seeing more of the office night-time cleaners than I was my own fiancé, did I consider that perhaps I needed to relax my work regime a little more. And it wasn't only Matt I had been neglecting. I hadn't been back to Great Bishopsford to see my father for nearly six months, and it was really not to my credit that I'd continually postponed visiting him, knowing I'd be going back in December anyway for Sarah's wedding.

The train rattled through a station, the waiting commuters a multicoloured blur as we flashed past. It was only when we bulleted back into the darkness that I caught the reflection of the man sitting diagonally opposite me on the other side of the gangway. The perfect blackness mirrored from my window showed a thick-set, balding man sitting upright in his seat, uninvolved with the travellers' usual pastimes of newspapers, iPod or the like. No, this man seemed to have only one distraction on his mind. Me. Although I made no move, he must have seen that I'd noticed him staring at me. Unabashed, he didn't look instantly away, as convention demanded. Instead he seemed to intensify his scrutiny and then slowly, revealing ugly and distorted teeth, he began to leer. An ice cube of unexplainable alarm trickled down my spine.

I pulled a magazine from my bag and in an instinctively defensive pose angled my body away from the rest of the carriage and towards the window. I flicked through ten or twenty pages before acknowledging I had no idea whatsoever what had been on them. I swear I could physically feel the intensity of his gaze upon me, and surreptitious glances into the reflection from the window confirmed this was still the case. The hair on the back of my neck prickled uncomfortably. It was unfortunate that during one such furtive inspection, he caught me watching him watching me, and gave again that slow ugly smile, followed by an almost imperceptible licking of his lips.

That did it. A different sort of woman might have raised her glance and challenged him, either verbally or with a meaningful stare. I wasn't one of those women. Feeling foolish, but working purely on instinct, I plucked my coat from the seat beside me and moved to a vacant place on the opposite side of the carriage some distance away. As I hurried down the narrow passage between the rows of seats, I thought I heard a low, dirty, self-satisfied laugh from somewhere behind me.

I chose a seat opposite a middle-aged women engrossed in a book. I now had my back to the stranger and his reflection was no longer visible. But instead of being comforted, I almost instantly regretted the move, feeling more vulnerable than ever now that I couldn't see his whereabouts. This was ridiculous. What on earth was I getting so worked up about? This wouldn't be the first time I had had to fend off some undesirable male attention. And while I was certainly not in the same category as my old schoolfriend Cathy, any passably attractive young women could normally handle unsolicited male advances with scarcely a second thought. Yet I couldn't help feel that this stranger's intentions towards me didn't fall into that familiar category at all.

It was one of the most uncomfortable train journeys I could ever remember, but there was at least a reassuring safety in the number of people in the carriage. When the guard came through to check the tickets, I considered for a millisecond mentioning the man. But then, just as quickly, I dismissed the idea. However menacingly the man had stared at me, I really had no grounds at all to alert the guard. I could almost imagine the inevitable reaction to such a complaint: '. . . And he was looking at you "in a funny way", miss, is that correct?' Yet even as I swallowed back my complaint there must still have been some betraying anxiety in my eyes that alerted the guard; for on returning my ticket, he stopped and scrutinised me carefully before enquiring: 'Are you all right? You look a little . . .' His voice trailed off. I silently filled in the blanks: paranoid/manic/sheer out-and-out crazy. The woman seated opposite lowered her book and openly awaited my response. A little diversion from the monotony of the usual commute home. I was happy to disappoint her.

'No, I'm just fine, thank you. Just concerned I'm going to be late for a special dinner tonight, that's all.'

'Well, we're running right on schedule, so you can't blame British Rail this time,' he joked. I joined in his laughter, which sounded, even to my own ears, over-jovial and forced.

As the guard moved on to the quartet of seats directly behind me, I risked looking over my shoulder and was just in time to catch a glimpse of a bulky figure clad in a scruffy tan-coloured jacket exiting the carriage, striding with some haste to the adjacent one. My sigh of relief was so loud that the woman sitting opposite once more lowered her book and looked at me with questioning eyes. I smiled briefly and returned my attention to the magazine.

The rhythm of the train was soporific and before long I lowered my magazine, settled my head more comfortably against the headrest and closed my eyes. It felt strange to be going back home; even stranger to be meeting up with friends I had not seen in years. It was impossible not to feel guilty when I realised the vows we had all made to keep in touch had been empty promises, full of more good intentions than actual resolve.

It had been easy to stay in touch during our student days, returning as we did to our families at the end of each term. Not so easy now though, when we were scattered the length and breadth of the country with only one or two people still remaining in the Great Bishopsford area. For most of us, our old home town had been too small to hold us when careers and relationships began to tug us away.

Pursuing my own career in journalism had made my move to London an inevitable one. The same applied to Matt, who had needed to be based in the capital for his business since taking over from his parents after their retirement to Spain. I still saw Sarah whenever I could, of course; some friendships would always manage to endure any distance of separation or neglect. But there were people I had thought I would always have in my life; important people, who had somehow just faded away.

I had been looking forward to the evening ahead and was disappointed that my work commitments had meant the reunion would already be several hours old by the time I arrived. More than anything I was curious to see if the threads of our friendship were still there, or if the unravelling of the old group was sadly irreversible.

The man, whose unwanted attention had so disturbed the beginning of my journey, never returned to the carriage. And while this should have quietened my fears,

I couldn't stop myself from checking the commuters who disembarked the train at the various stations, my eyes scouring the darkness, hoping to catch sight of a shabby tan jacket. I didn't see him. Knowing he was most likely still on the train did very little to calm me. At one of the major stations the train had emptied dramatically and it had been impossible to check for him among the throng of commuters on the platform. There was only a handful of stations left until we reached Great Bishopsford and even fewer on the line beyond that. What were the chances of him alighting at the same stop as me? Greater now than they had been, I supposed. The ice cube down my spine was back.

From the station I intended to catch a cab across town and go directly to the restaurant. It was a shame there wasn't time to go to the hotel and change first but I was going to be ridiculously late as it was. I regretted now not asking Matt to meet me at the station but it had seemed selfish to drag him away halfway through the evening. Grabbing a cab had seemed the best option. I only hoped there would be one ready and waiting at the rank.

With only ten minutes until my stop, I delved into my large handbag and extracted a compact and comb. As I was, by then, one of only three people left in the carriage, it didn't seem too inappropriate to reapply some make-up on the train. And while the overhead fluorescent light wasn't exactly flattering, it did at least allow me to tidy up some of the ravages of the day. I applied powder, touched up my eyeshadow and streaked a smooth layer of gloss across my lips. Unfortunately the size of the compact made it impossible to view the overall effect. I tried angling the mirror both up and down in an attempt to get a better look, which wasn't very effective, and I was on the point of snapping shut the compact when in the corner of the mirror I caught a fleeting glimpse of tan reflecting in the tiny glass.

I spun around in my seat as though electrocuted, imagining the strange man from earlier to be standing directly behind me. There was no one there. The carriage held only myself and two other occupants, both of whom appeared to be asleep. Cautiously I stepped away from my seat, terrified the bald man was somehow lying in wait behind one of the banquettes. As I hesitantly moved down the gangway, I kept my eyes firmly aware of the location of the nearest emergency cord. Screw the £250 fine for misuse, if anyone had so much as said 'boo' to me at that moment, I was ready to bring the train to a halt in an instant.

Of course there was no one there. And by the time I was halfway down the carriage I had already begun to feel more than a little ridiculous. I had already managed to convince myself that what I thought I had seen in the mirror was most likely a flash of orange reflection from a passing street lamp. It was just my over-active imagination that had made a quantum leap to the wrong conclusion. No one was lying in wait and unless I intended to search every last carriage on the train – which I most *certainly* did not – I just had to let go of the crazed-stalker notion.

With relief I heard the tannoy announce the next stop was to be Great Bishopsford, which left me only a minute or two to retrieve my case from my first seat and my other belongings from my second one. I was waiting with impatience by the automatic doors and was one of the first people to alight from the train when it eventually slowed to a standstill at the station. I was pleased to see three other people disembarking from a carriage further up the platform, and trotted as quickly as my suitcase would allow to keep pace with them.

Climbing the long flight of stairs dragging my case behind me caused me to lose ground, so I'd lost sight of the other commuters when I heard, or thought I heard, someone on the platform below me, someone out of sight of the pool of light from the staircase. Someone who had got off the train after I had.

I ran up the remainder of the flight of stairs, my suit-case literally bouncing over the concrete treads. When I reached the small ticket office I looked around for either the other commuters or a guard. There was no one to be seen but I could hear a car pulling away from the station entrance so I could only assume they had all been met by someone. But surely the guard should still be here? It was only just ten o'clock; did they really leave the station unmanned this early?

'Hello?' I called out shakily, my words a quivering echo in the empty foyer. 'Is there anyone on duty?'

The responding silence was its own answer. Suddenly aware of my vulnerability at the top of the stairs, I quickly stepped far away from the stairwell. Whoever had got off the train after me would certainly be in the ticket area in a matter of moments. I strained my ears to hear their footfall on the stairs but could make out no sound.

There were two options here: either I had imagined hearing someone on the platform below me, or whoever had got off the train was now lying in wait on the darkened stairs rather than revealing themselves in the foyer. I preferred my first option – better to be paranoid than a potential crime statistic. I decided there was no virtue in staying to prove I was not going crazy and all but ran across the ticket office and out into the winter night.

The taxi rank was sited to one side of the station, and I was grateful for the bright security lighting that illuminated my way as I followed the building around. I was in luck, there was just one cab parked in the bays, its engine idling, the yellow beacon on its roof glowing brightly in the frosty chill of the air. I raised my arm to claim the driver's attention at the precise moment the engine increased its revs and the cab pulled away from the kerb.

'Wait!' I cried out helplessly. 'Please stop!'

Abandoning my case in the middle of the pavement I began to run after the departing taxi, my arms windmilling crazily overhead in an attempt to be seen. From the darkened interior of the departing vehicle it was impossible to see if there was already a passenger within or whether the driver had simply decided to call it a night and go home. I ran on for a few more metres, knowing it was useless but unable to stop myself until the tail lights were mere red specks in the distance.

Tears of sheer frustration pricked at my eyes as I slowly walked back to retrieve my case. There were no other cabs in sight, and for all I knew there would be no more until the next day. I had no other choice but to call Matt and ask him to meet me. But even as I pulled my mobile from my bag and started to key in his number, I was already realising that it would take him the best part of half an hour to reach me. And it wasn't the prospect of waiting all alone for my fiancé to arrive that caused my fingers to tremble as I punched in the familiar number on the keypad; no, it was the more terrifying realisation that I may not be alone at all.

As I waited for the number to connect, I turned to face the station entrance, wanting to have a clear view of anyone leaving the building. When the familiar ringing tone failed to sound against my ear, I jerked my mobile away. Two words. Innocent enough in almost any other time or place but totally horrifying to see right now. *No signal.*

'No, don't you do this to me,' I implored the mobile, as if reasoning with it alone could alter the reception. I pressed redial, drumming my fingers with impatience against the phone when it seemed to take an interminable amount of time to tell me exactly the same thing.

Forgetting about looking foolish, I raised my arm and held the small silver phone high above my head, slowly sweeping an arc across the air, trying to pick up a signal. As I pivoted around in my futile attempts to gain reception, I thought I saw a fleeting dark shadow break the shaft of light falling from the station entrance. I froze. Like a rabbit in the headlights my eyes were riveted to the light. It wasn't until they began to water from the strain that I realised I was staring so hard I'd forgotten to blink. Although I saw nothing else from the station doorway, I knew I had not been mistaken; something or someone was inside that building and, for reasons that seemed unlikely to be innocent, they were still lurking out of sight within the shadows.

Knowing it was useless, but compelled to try anyway, I once more pressed the redial button. Frustration at its repeated failure to perform its most basic function almost made me throw the phone on the pavement in disgust. Fortunately good sense prevailed. The irony was there was a bank of payphones inside the station. I'd been standing right beside them after climbing the stairs. But I could no more force myself to walk back into that building than I could pluck a signal from the airwaves by sheer force of will. I had to face facts. I was alone in a remote area on a dark December evening, with no means of communication and no way of knowing if the man who had so terrified me earlier that evening had followed me off the train.

I tried to calm my racing thoughts, which were beginning to get away from me like stampeding ponies. Focus on the problem in hand; the problem that was fact and not a terrified flight of fantasy. I had to communicate with someone, be it Matt, a cab company, or the police, and I had no means of doing so. Well, stripped down like that, the answer was obvious. Find another phone. There were still payphones on British streets, weren't there? Mobiles hadn't entirely taken over our civilisation yet, had they? And while I couldn't remember the last time I had actually used a telephone kiosk, I knew that I ought to be able to find one somewhere. I swept my glance around the car park and taxi rank area. Well, no, there wouldn't be any here when there was a perfectly adequate bank of phones sitting a few hundred metres away inside the station. And they'd be ideal – if it weren't for the homicidal maniac lying in wait right beside them. A small laugh, more hysterical than amused, bubbled up as my over-active imagination elevated the possibly-not-even-there stalker to deadly criminal status.

And then I remembered. There was a payphone on the pavement just outside the old church. Or at least there always used to be. And the church wasn't that far away, a mile or two at most, I reckoned. And worst case scenario, if the phone booth *had* been removed, I would at least be halfway towards the main town, where I'd be sure to find another one, or even hail a cab. Having a plan was like antacid on the burn of my panic.

With exaggerated slowness I began to step back towards the road that would lead me to the church. Although I wasn't sure how far sound could carry in the night, I wanted to be as quiet as possible as I made my retreat from the station. So I didn't risk dragging my case along on its casters but picked it up the handles instead. Carrying it might slow me down a little but the rumbling sound of the wheels would lead anyone straight to me like a tracking device. And even though it was cumbersome to carry so many things at once, I still kept my mobile phone open in my hand, trying it every twenty seconds or so, ever-hopeful that it would respond.

*

I can't remember when I knew for certain that he was behind me.

I thought I'd been so quiet. Until I was some distance from the station I had lowered each foot into careful place on the pavement, effectively muffling the sound of my tread. Only when I felt positive that I was out of earshot did I break into a really brisk walk. I risked looking backwards on numerous occasions, never once seeing anyone. There were several roads that led away from the station. If he hadn't seen me leave, it would be impossible to know which one I had taken. I had just begun to feel the vice grip of panic loosen its fingers from around my heart when I heard the noise. A light tinkling sound, followed by a rolling noise. As though someone had accidentally kicked a bottle into the road.

Standing statue-still, I strained my ears and my eyes. There were no street lamps on this stretch of road; they would not appear until I'd reached the church itself. And the leafy street, lined with thickly trunked trees, could provide a hundred hiding places for someone to conceal themselves, when the only light around was from an icy moon and a frosting of stars.

This was not the time for caution. I ran. And as I did I heard the sound of heavier footsteps begin to do the same. It was impossible to be certain but I was grateful to hear that the sound was not as close as I had first thought. Needing to know how much of a lead I had, I threw a backward glance over my shoulder and although

I could still hear the heavy pounding on the pavement, I still couldn't see anyone. I picked up my legs and drove myself harder.

I wasn't particularly fit; I'd proved that already from my dash to catch the train, but it's amazing the effect that pure adrenaline can achieve. I hadn't moved this quickly since my school days, yet still I could hear the echoing pounding of my pursuer. I wasn't breaking ahead, just maintaining the distance. I knew I couldn't keep going at this pace, not for much longer. My shoes, designed for fashion rather than a survival sprint, had several times skidded on the rime of ice lying on the pavement's surface. On one particularly icy patch I totally lost my purchase and felt my feet slide from beneath me. My arms cartwheeled in an attempt to regain my balance, and my case dropped with a thud to the pavement. Somehow I didn't fall, but I left the case where it lay. Less than twenty seconds later I heard a crashing sound, and a loud cry. At least now I knew how far behind me he was. It was too much to hope he'd broken his ankle in the tumble, but even the idea of him being injured gave me the spurt of extra drive to keep going.

I wasn't far from the crest of the hill. In the moonlight I could just make out the spire from the church. I was really close. I think I had half convinced myself that there would be no phone box when I got there. Everything about this evening had seemed to be set against me; so the exhilaration of seeing the kiosk a hundred metres or so up ahead at first felt like a beautiful mirage. My heart was thundering in my chest and my side felt as though it was being ripped open by a stitch, but I didn't slow down. I hadn't heard any more from behind me but I still needed time to get to the box and dial the call: 999. How long does it take to get through? Could I summon help before he reached me? Would I have enough air left in my lungs to speak at all? The only answer to any of these questions was to run harder, which I did, my thumb still convulsively pushing the redial button on my mobile, as it had done since I left the station.

I was almost there. My fingers were literally outstretched towards the handle of the phone kiosk when a handful of my coat was yanked viciously from behind me, and I went down. No arms came out to break my fall this time, and I hit the icy pavement hard, my head cracking painfully upon the ground. I fell with such force that I took him down with me, and I heard the thump of his stocky body crashing down behind me. I don't think I was even aware of the warm sticky flow of blood from my head as I scrambled to my knees. No bones appeared to be broken, I could still move, and though I'd probably lost layers of skin off both my hands and knees I wasn't even aware of the pain.

But before I could raise myself any further than being on all fours, a cruel vice grip caught my ankle and I was down again. I kicked back instinctively and knew from his cry that my heel had struck him somewhere where it hurt. His grip fell away and I immediately attempted to crawl away, using my elbows and arms to drag me along commando-style. I had gone about a metre when he was on me again. His knee hard in the middle of my back. I could hear him muttering and swearing as he used his full body weight to hold me motionless. I felt the fight drain from me. I had tried and failed. My vision was almost obliterated by the fast-flowing stream of blood from my head, and I could feel myself begin to slide into unconsciousness. I wanted to fight it but there were no reserves left to draw upon. The man roughly grabbed the sleeve of my coat, the white fabric already stained with my blood, and yanked my arm up at an unnatural angle. He said one word, just one – 'Bitch!' – as his thick fingers found my hand and yanked off my engagement ring. The weight on my back was suddenly gone. And so, I realised, was the man.

That was what it had all been for? The damned diamond ring? Had all this happened just because I'd worn the ring while travelling? And I wouldn't even be able to identify my attacker, because I'd never seen his face. It might never have been the man from the train at all.

The darkness around me seemed to be growing thicker and I felt as though I was teetering upon the edge of a dark hole. A faint thrumming noise sounded by my ear, and I thought at first it was the rush of blood until the truth pierced through my consciousness. It was a ringing tone. Somehow my hand had never lost its grip on my phone, and finally my compulsive attempts had at last achieved success.

'Rachel, are you there?' The voice sounded tinny and small and very far away indeed.

'Help me . . .' I cried out, and then the blackness sucked me under.

Chapter 5

They sedated me. I suppose they had to, although it seemed crazy waiting nearly two days for me to wake up, only to put me straight back under again. And the more I struggled and begged my dad not to let them do it, the more panic and concern I could see mirrored in his eyes. As the consultant barked sharply worded instructions to the nurse to prepare the sedative, I was still pleading with my dad to explain how he had got well again so quickly, and when he wouldn't reply, shaking his head helplessly in confusion, I only became more distressed. It was quite a relief when the drug they inserted into my IV flooded into my system and my lids fell closed.

My eyes flickered open sometime later, and although the room was darkened, it seemed to be full of people.

I could hear hushed whispers from voices that were tanta-lisingly familiar. My eyelids felt leaden, too heavy to open more than the merest slit. I couldn't really make out who was in the room, just four or more tall shapes, all darkly clothed I thought, or perhaps they were all just in the shadows. Sleep reclaimed me.

I briefly woke for a second period some time later on that night. The group of people, whoever they had been, were now gone. I had absolutely no idea what time it was but the room was in total darkness except for the small pool of light directed down towards a chair pulled up to my bedside, in which my father sat sleeping. There was an open book lying across his lap, and an empty food tray on the unit beside me. I correctly guessed he had not left my side all day. From his slightly open mouth a soft snore emitted with each indrawn breath. He looked tired and dishevelled . . . and yet still, unbelievably and impossibly, he looked completely well. I needed to speak to him; I felt desperate to find out what was going on, as nothing made any sense, but the struggle to stay awake was too much. Sleep overtook me once more before I could call out his name.

The clatter of a food trolley woke me the next morning. I blinked in protest at the surprisingly bright morning light falling into my hospital room.

'Good, you're awake in time for breakfast,' my dad announced in an overly cheery tone. I was slow in turning my head towards him, hopeful that the strange episode of the previous day had just been imagined. He must have seen the look in my eyes as I once more took in his obvious good health, for his smile faltered a little. I felt a stab of absolute mortification. Had I actually been hoping to see my only parent still in the throes of his battle with a terrible disease? What sort of a person did that make me?

I tried to smile back.

'G'morning,' I mumbled. My mouth felt as though someone had stuffed it with cotton wool in the night.

'How are you this morning? Are you ready for something to eat?'

I shook my head, the thought of food making my stomach roll in horror.

'Tea,' I croaked, my throat as parched as my tongue. I tried again with more effort. 'Just some tea, please, Dad.'

His eyes never left me as I raised the utilitarian white cup to my lips and didn't lower it until it was emptied. He seemed pleased to see me performing such a mundane function without incident or outburst. Was that a measure of my sanity? Didn't crazy people drink tea?

'Shall I see if the nurses can get you another one?' I nodded, and was grateful when he left to pursue a second cup as it gave me a minute or two to collect my thoughts. He was gone nowhere near long enough for me to even begin to have sorted out my bewilderment. I drained the second cup and felt, physically at least, a little revived.

'So how is your head this morning, sweetheart?'

'Better, I think. Dad, what's going on here?'

He looked uncomfortable, before bouncing the question back to me:

'Going on here? What do you mean?'

'Stop it, Dad. I mean it. What's happened to you, and why haven't you told me about it? Have they got you on some miracle drug or something? Are you in remission?'

The look on his face was tortured; he was clearly searching, and failing, to find the right answer to give me.

'Rachel, love, I think you are still a little confused—'

I interrupted him, struggling to sit up more fully in bed, causing me to wince from what felt like a thousand bruises which I had no idea how I got. I tried to speak really slowly, articulating each word in a reasonable tone; the last thing I wanted was someone calling for me to be sedated again.

'Dad, I am not confused; well I am, but not in the way you mean. Three weeks ago you looked . . . well, you looked absolutely terrible. The chemo had made you so sick and weak, and the weight you'd lost . . . well, just everything. And now . . . now it makes no sense, you look completely better.'

His dearly loved face looked so troubled as he studied me, his eyes beginning to well with tears.

'Rachel, I *am* completely well.'

'How can you have been cured so quickly?' This was all just too much to absorb. My father began to reach for the bell push above my bed.

'Perhaps we should ask if the doctor could come and see you again now.'

'No!' I shouted, my voice thick with the frustration I

knew was on my face. Shaking his head sadly my father lowered his arm from the emergency button and let his roughened fingers reach for and encompass my hand, patting it soothingly.

'I haven't "been cured", Rachel, because I've never been ill in the first place. I *don't* have cancer and I can't imagine why you thought I did.'

The nurses had come in then, one to remove the breakfast tray and another to help me to the bathroom. In truth I was glad to be taken away. For some reason my father was hiding what had happened to him from me. My sluggish mind, still addled from the sedative, couldn't think of a single reason why he was keeping such a thing secret.

I was grateful for the nurse's assistance in the sparse white-tiled bathroom. Thankfully, my IV had been removed sometime during the night, and although unencumbered by having to wheel a tripod around, I still couldn't have managed either the short walk down the corridor or the removal of my hospital gown without assistance. With the ties undone, the nurse turned on the shower and, after establishing that I felt confident enough on my feet to be left alone to wash, she slipped out of the room.

Under the surprisingly forceful jets of water I tried to clear my mind of its endless questioning, but it refused to be still. And even the innocuous act of washing myself threw up further unanswered puzzles. An unperfumed white bar sat waiting in the soap dish, but it wasn't until

I began to revolve it slowly between my palms that I noticed the grazes upon them.

I washed off the coating of suds and turned them thoughtfully this way and that under the spray from the shower. Both hands were equally grazed, as though I had fallen heavily and tried to save myself. But for the life of me I couldn't remember when or how I had done this. I did remember falling to the ground beside Jimmy's grave in the churchyard, but I had landed upon grass, not concrete. The only possibility I could come up with was that I must have grazed them against a headstone when I had finally collapsed. The progression of that thought left me wondering who it was who had found me in the cemetery and brought me to hospital. In the light of the larger more puzzling questions, I was happy to let that one go.

I wished there had been a mirror in the small utilitarian washroom, so I could see if my head or face bore any signs of injury, for as I soaped and rinsed the rest of my body, I found several other places that were both grazed and bruised. Again they all looked too raw and angry to have been sustained in anything less than a very hefty fall. I was beyond puzzled. I appeared to be covered in injuries where there should be none, while my father had an illness that had simply disappeared. I wondered if Alice had felt this confused when she had fallen down the well into Wonderland.

Still trying to resolve the irresolvable, one idea suddenly occurred to me as I dried myself briskly on the rough hospital towel. Perhaps the reason my father wouldn't admit to his illness was because his treatment hadn't been legal. I almost threw the idea out as preposterous. He was so honest, I couldn't even remember him getting so much as a parking fine in his entire life. But the more I thought about it, the more sense it made – in a totally nonsensical way. Maybe he was paying privately for some unlicensed medication or treatment forbidden in the UK. And if that *was* the case, well then he'd probably *have* to lie in order to protect whatever secret trial or doctor had helped him.

As I waited for the nurse to return with a clean gown, I felt happier to have found a workable solution to the mystery. Very probably, when away from the confines of the hospital, he would confess it all, when it was safe to betray his secret without others hearing. And as for secrets, well I had been hiding a pretty big one of my own from him too: the recurring headaches. I just hoped I would be able to find the time to speak to the doctor in private about the symptoms that had precipitated my collapse by the church.

As she took my arm to help me back to my room, the nurse supplied another surprising piece of information.

'I'd better warn you that you have a police officer waiting in your room to talk to you now that you're awake.'

I stopped mid-step and turned to the young nurse in consternation.

'A policeman? Why? Whatever for?'

She gave me a curious look, as though amazed I could ask such a thing.

'Well, they obviously need to get all the details about what happened by the church the other night.'

I looked back at her dumbly. *What happened by the church?* Were the police really so light on crime in this area that they had sent someone to question me about trespassing in the churchyard late at night? Was that really even a crime at all? It wasn't as though I'd been vandalising the graves. Surely I wasn't going to be charged with some petty misdemeanour? How much weirder was this day going to get?

In my wildest of dreams, I could never have guessed.

The policeman was seated half out of sight behind the door of my room. Dad had clearly been talking about me, judging by the guilty way in which he shut up like a clam as soon as I appeared at the threshold. In my peripheral vision I took in a dark uniform as the policeman rose to his feet.

'Rachel, hon, the police need some information from you, but don't look worried . . . look who they sent.' He sounded as triumphant as a magician pulling a rabbit from a hat, and I turned for the first time to look at the officer.

The room swayed; I knew my face must have drained of all colour. I reached out blindly for the doorframe, knowing it wasn't going to be any use. As I crumpled to the floor, in a swoon worthy of any Victorian gentle-woman, I had time to say just one word:

'Jimmy!'

The good thing about fainting in a hospital is that they know what to do with you right away. It was only a moment or two before I once again became aware of where I was. Seated on the chair that my father had occupied the night before, with my head stuck securely between my knees, I could feel the comforting hand of the nurse holding a cold compress against the back of my neck. I struggled to sit up.

'Don't go rushing to get up yet, Rachel. Take a moment or two.' Then, presumably directing the next comment to my dad, 'She may have been under the hot shower a wee bit too long, she'll be fine in a moment.' I very much doubted that. I strained against her hand, and sat up.

I didn't scream, or shout out, or even faint again, I just stared, totally transfixed, at the face that had been missing from my life for five dreadful years. He smiled but something in my scrutiny caused it to waver and the greeting was rearranged into a look of deep concern.

'Rachel?' His voice was hesitant.

I asked the only question that came into my mind.

'Am I in heaven?' The nurse clearly found this quite amusing.

'Well, I don't think I've ever heard anybody call an NHS hospital that before!'

I ignored her.

'Is this heaven? Are we all dead?' That shut the nurse up. I saw the look my dad flashed to Jimmy. *See?* it said, as plainly as if he had spoken the words out loud. *I told you she was acting strangely.*

The nurse had regained enough composure to switch back into her briskly professional role.

'Come along, back to bed now, Rachel. I think you need to have a little lie down.' She was definitely annoying me now. Disregarding her once more, I directed my question only at Jimmy.

'Did I die in the churchyard beside the grave?'

I guess his policeman's training was the reason he answered such a bizarre question so calmly.

'No, Rachel, you did not die in the churchyard. And beside whose grave?'

My next answer, not surprisingly, took the polish off his professional demeanour.

'Yours, of course.'

I don't know who pushed the emergency button this time. It could have been any one of the three of them. Hell, it could even have been me. I think we all needed some medical intervention at that point.

A young doctor I hadn't seen before came speedily into the room. There was a rapid flurry of conversation. I caught the words 'delusional' and 'sedative' and 'tests'. They all meant nothing. I could only stare at Jimmy as they laid me back on the bed, swabbed briefly at my arm and slid the hypodermic into my vein.

It was a much milder sedative than the day before. I guess they couldn't risk pumping someone with a head injury with too much sedation. Although my limbs were relaxed as though I were floating on a buoyant bed of feathers, my brain was still working. My eyes had closed, but I was still awake. It was a pleasantly drunk feeling, without the room-spinning element.

'Did she *really* mean that? Did she actually think I was dead?'

My father's voice sounded broken.

'I don't know, son, who knows. She thought *I* was dying of cancer.'

There was a long silence.

'She must have hit her head harder than anyone realised. She's not going to be answering any questions today. Nothing she tells you right now will help you catch the bastard who mugged her.'

'I realise that.'

'You probably don't need to be hanging around here. That doctor was ordering up a whole load more tests. I can call you when she's more . . . with it.'

'I'm not going anywhere.'

I was wheeled from department to department. I had an MRI, two further X-rays and several other tests with electrodes affixed to my head. By then I was awake and alert enough to be asking questions. But no one was talking to me, except in soft placating tones designed not to evoke another one of my 'episodes'. When I was finally transported back to my room, it was empty. The staff nurse who helped me back into bed advised me that my dad and all the rest of my guests had moved down to the canteen for a cup of tea. When I asked who the 'all' referred to, she did not know.

So I sat bolt upright in bed, staring at the door, waiting to see how many more deceased visitors I would be receiving that day.

They came in in single file: my dad, then Jimmy, followed by Matt, Cathy and Phil. I stared at them in turn as they arrived. I was still looking a little surprised to see the last three when Matt broke away from the others, rushed to my bedside and kissed me tenderly on the lips. I flinched from the brush of his soft mouth upon mine, instantly looking over his shoulder to see how Cathy would react. Amazingly her face gave away none of the rage she must surely be feeling.

'Matt,' I hissed, my eyes flashing a warning towards his girlfriend. I could suddenly remember the vow he had made when dropping me back at the hotel: that he was not going to let me get away again. Did he really think this was the appropriate place to start that campaign?

Besides, I couldn't concentrate on anyone other than the person standing at the foot of my bed. At some point during the day I guessed he must have gone off duty, for he was now out of uniform, wearing jeans and a dark shirt. But the most amazing thing of all was that no one else in the room seemed in the least bit amazed that he was there. It was like that old saying about ignoring the elephant in the room. This was so enormous, so ludicrously and mind-blowingly 'wrong' – how come everyone wasn't reacting like me?

And then the answer came to me. How could it have taken so long for me to get it? Especially when I'd seen *The Sixth Sense* so many times I knew parts of it off by heart.

'Can anyone else see Jimmy in the room?'

I can't begin to describe the pity on their faces as they all exchanged extremely meaningful looks. My dad answered for them all.

'Of course we can, love.'

'No, Dad, don't humour me. Just be honest. I can see Jimmy's ghost right there at the foot of my bed. Now can anyone else see him or not?'

Dad's pain was obvious as he tried to formulate an answer but before he could reply the incredibly solid-looking 'ghost' of Jimmy came up to sit on the bed beside me, gently picking up my hand. I felt the mattress depress when he sat down, felt too the warmth of his fingers against my grazed skin; the ghost theory was losing ground fast.

'Rachel, just listen to me for a moment without speaking, would you?' I opened my mouth to protest but he gently pressed his forefinger across my lips. 'No interruptions, right?'

God, if he *was* a ghost he was a bloody bossy one. And that finger against my mouth had felt so strong . . . so real.

'You've taken a nasty blow to your head.' He carried on as though I was going to contradict him. 'You'd travelled back here for Sarah's wedding.'

At last, something I could agree with. 'Yes, I *know* that.' There was a communal sigh of relief that I had grasped at least that one truth.

'Now something happened, we think you were probably mugged, after leaving the station. And we think that somehow, when you were attacked, you must have hurt your head. And all these . . . strange . . . thoughts and ideas you are having right now are because of your injury.'

He might as well have saved his breath.

'Then this must all be a dream,' I announced, seizing upon the only other solution that made sense. Someone, I don't know who, gave a loud sigh of despair. I ignored them. 'This is all just a very real and very vivid dream, but it's all in my subconscious. Any minute now I'm going to wake up.'

There was a long silence, which no one seemed to have the words to fill. It was though my absolute determination to stick to my own beliefs had sucked all protests clean out of the room.

Silently, Matt came up to the other side of the bed and rested his hand lightly against the back of my neck. Something flickered in Jimmy's eyes as he immediately let go of my hand and got up from the bed. This dream was *really* peculiar; it was like going back to when we were teenagers all over again. The awkward moment was interrupted by a softly ringing bell from the nurses' station.

'I think that's the end of visiting,' my father announced with relief. 'Perhaps you should all go now, I think Rachel could do with her rest.'

Actually, I was feeling much calmer now I'd finally worked out that none of this was really happening at all.

'Look, why don't you go home and rest too, Tony,' offered Matt, unexpectedly. 'You look really exhausted. I'll stay with Rachel.'

Dad looked reluctant, but Dream Matt was insistent. 'Go on, you go and get a few hours' sleep.'

But my dad still appeared unwilling to go.

'I don't know, I think I should stay. I'd feel wrong

going home and leaving her.' Adding in final justification, 'She's my daughter; she needs me here.'

Matt's response was firm.

'I understand that but you're not much use to her if you're dead on your feet. Go home. I'll take good care of her, Tony. I know she's your only daughter but you're not the only one who wants to look after her; after all she *is also* my only fiancée!'

I jolted with surprise and instinctively looked over at Cathy who was picking up her coat and handbag and getting ready to go. Matt's words didn't seem to have affected her at all.

'Although right now she's a fiancée without a ring,' observed Jimmy in an unfathomable tone.

I stupidly looked down at my left hand as if to seek confirmation. There was obviously no jewellery upon it, although as I looked more closely I could see the faint white mark where a ring had obviously sat. Also strangely, the knuckle appeared reddened and swollen, something I'd not noticed before amongst the others cuts and bruises. It looked as though whatever had been on my finger might have been pulled off quite roughly.

I looked up, my face registering a sort of dazed surprise, and interrupted a very dark exchange of looks between Matt and Jimmy as they stood facing each other on either side of my bed. The thin veil of friendship between them looked stretched to the point of rupturing.

'Ring or no ring, she's still my fiancée, mate.'

Oohh . . . this dream was getting more interesting every minute.

Chapter 6

Sometime over the next twenty-four hours it all stopped being quite so funny.

When does a dream become a nightmare? I'd always thought it was when the familiar suddenly becomes strange and threatening; or when you get lost somewhere you thought you knew well; or even when you feel over-whelmed by a feeling of impotence – when you know you're speaking clearly but no one appears to be listening. And it's true, a nightmare is all of those things. But *my* true nightmare began with the realisation that I wasn't waking up: that somehow, impossibly and unbelievably, this was all *really happening*.

This realisation didn't come all at once but slowly pricked away at my conscious with a questioning voice that refused to be quiet. The first indicators to concern me were the continuing and detailed vividness of the dream. There were no strange shifts in time or place; this dream had continuity and even monotony. What dream could I ever recall having before that had incorporated the truly mundane details of day-to-day life? In this one I ate the unappetising hospital meals, I slept (who does that in a dream?), I even visited the bathroom. None of this had any place in a 'real' dream.

Of course, when Matt and I had been left alone in my room, after my other visitors had left, I was still happily ensconced in blissful ignorance. I was content to sit back and let events around me unfold like a play. This was just a dream, after all; nothing I did or said had any real consequence.

So I made no protest when Matt drew a chair up close to the bed and entwined his long tanned fingers around mine. I winced slightly as he caught the grazes on my palms, never stopping to think how odd it was to actually experience the sensation of pain in a dream. I let his lips cover mine as he bent to kiss me tenderly, whispering soft and low between kisses how frantically worried he had been about me. And when he eventually pulled back, I could feel my heart fluttering madly against my ribs like a frenzied canary. Well, that wasn't really a surprise; it had been a long, long time since I'd been kissed like that – either in a dream or wide awake.

What I hadn't expected after such a display of tenderness was for him draw back and for his tone to turn so quickly to one of censure.

'Rachel, I have to ask, what the hell were you thinking of, setting off alone from the station and walking down that deserted road? Didn't you realise the stupid risks you were taking?'

I blinked up at him slowly, caught off guard by the sudden switch in his mood.

'Why didn't you phone me to pick you up, or get a cab, or just wait with the other passengers?'

He was looking at me intently. Clearly expecting some coherent reply. I had none.

'I'm sorry . . .' I offered lamely. 'I don't remember anything except . . .' Except everything that *really* happened: the dinner, the ride back to my hotel, and then the disastrous visit to the cemetery.

'Except?' he prompted hopefully.

'Except waking up here.' Even in my dream I was smart enough not to keep on insisting that *my* reality appeared to be completely different from everyone else's.

'And it's not just about losing the ring, don't think that – though thank God we had it well insured.'

The ring? Was that what was concerning him, losing the engagement ring? Jeez, Dream Matt was certainly all about the money.

'You could have been seriously hurt, it could have been so much worse than just cuts and grazes and a bump on the head. When I think of what that guy could have done to you . . .'

He seemed to be waiting for me to say something, so I nodded slowly as though absorbing the dilemma that my dream persona had apparently brought upon myself.

'When we got that call, when you cried out for help . . . well, I've never felt so useless in my entire life. Thank God Jimmy was there – and it's not often you'll hear me saying that!'

I gave a watery smile in response. Then curiosity to learn more took over.

'Why, what did he do?'

'Took charge. I guess it's his policeman's training to act like that in an emergency. We were all about to go charging off God-knows-where to find you but he was the one who kept calm and cool and called his police station. He figured you were probably at the railway station or somewhere nearby and got several cars out looking for you before we had even got out of the car park! A squad car found you by the church only ten or fifteen minutes after your call and you were off in the ambulance before we were even halfway there. I guess it pays to have a copper on hand in a crisis.'

So Jimmy had saved me once again. I guess I could see why, in a dream, I had once more cast Jimmy in the role of hero. It was, after all, how he'd lost his life.

'Not that his behaviour afterwards was very professional though.'

My ears pricked up at that comment.

'Why, what happened then?'

'Well he really lost it while we were at the hospital waiting for you to be assessed: when we didn't know how seriously you'd been hurt. He started yelling at me about how could I be so irresponsible; how I never should have left you to travel alone at night. I particularly liked the bit about how I didn't deserve to have you, if I couldn't look after you properly.' He rubbed his hand ruefully over his handsome chin. 'And then he took a swing at me!'

I sat up sharply. 'He did?'

Mistaking my total astonishment for loving concern, he patted my arm in reassurance.

'Don't worry, he didn't do any damage; Phil had a hold of his arm before he even made contact. Damn unprofessional of him though, even if he was off duty. I *could* make an official complaint . . .' He saw the look in my eyes and continued quickly, 'I won't, of course. I realise it was all just heat-of-the-moment stuff. Don't worry, I'm not going to get old PC Plod in trouble. And I guess it *is* understandable, feeling as he did about you all those years ago.'

There it was again. Even in my dream I couldn't seem to get away from someone trying to convince me that Jimmy had been deeply in love with me.

'I think he must have forgotten how strong-willed you can be. And independent. After all, you haven't been in touch with him for quite a while now, have you?'

I wanted to say: *Well no, not without the aid of a Ouija board.* But settled instead for a less controversial, 'No, not really . . . we must have kind of lost touch.'

I was really quite glad when the nurse came in at that point, wheeling a laden trolley of pharmaceuticals. She tactfully reminded Matt that visiting hours were long over and he took the hint, kissing me lightly on the forehead and leaving with the promise to return the next day.

As I lay on the starchy hospital sheets, waiting for the pills I'd swallowed to take effect, I pondered on the curiously complex scenario my subconscious had summoned up. All the facts and characters were present but the details and events were twisted into such a bizarre parallel reality. It was my life but not as I knew it, for here it was all so much better: Jimmy was still alive, my Dad wasn't sick – and neither was I, apparently – and Matt and I were engaged to be married. It was almost a shame to wake up.

And I didn't. Well, that's to say I slept and when I opened my eyes it was a new day, but still the dream continued. That's when the voice first started up, telling me something was really wrong here. They had scheduled me for God knows how many more tests that morning, and my pleasurable euphoria of living in a dream began to gradually dissipate when my real life failed to return. I even resorted to the old trick of pinching myself hard, a real old Chinese-burn style pinch, whilst waiting outside the room for a second MRI scan. Nothing happened, except that I gave myself a very nasty-looking red and white mark on my forearm. Even then, I only stopped contorting the soft flesh when I caught the pitying glance from the nurse who had wheeled me down for this latest test. Clearly news of the delusional new patient was widespread and all comments directed at me were in the softly spoken sing-song tones usually reserved for dealing with those under five or the imbecilic.

Somewhere between the blood tests, the scans, and the X-rays I started to get really scared. I felt like a prisoner in Neverland; it might be nice place to come for a visit, but I really, really wanted to go 'home' now, however bad things might be there. One of the worst moments came when I caught sight of my reflection for the first time in the small square mirror positioned above the basin in my room. A nurse had come running at my cry, and I could tell she was at a loss to know what to do, when she saw me running my fingers frantically over the smooth unblemished skin of my cheek. And who could blame her; what was the poor woman supposed to say when I rounded on her, crying, 'My scar. Where's it gone? What have you people done with my scar?'

I just about held myself together until the afternoon, when I was due to meet again with the consultant. The nurse who came to collect me with a wheelchair looked disappointed to see my untouched lunch. Fear and confusion had robbed me of my appetite, well, that and the appalling culinary offerings of the hospital kitchens.

When they wheeled me into the doctor's consultation room, I was pleased to see my (newly-restored-to-good-health) father waiting for me.

'Good afternoon, Rachel. Are you feeling a little better today?' The doctor's voice was kind and solicitous. Clearly he was expecting an answer in the affirmative.

I shook my head slowly, unable to speak as hot tears began to course down my cheeks. My father reached across from his chair and took my hand. Tactfully choosing to ignore my distress the doctor continued.

'Well, I have good news, young lady. We have done just about every test imaginable, and I'm happy to report there is no serious or permanent damage resulting from your little escapade.' He turned in his chair to indicate an illuminated X-ray of a skull, presumably mine, on a lit panel behind him. 'Everything looks completely normal. No injuries to the brain or cranium whatsoever.'

'Thank God,' breathed my father in fervent relief.

'But it's all wrong!' I cried out, ashamed at how pathetic my voice sounded.

'Oh no, Rachel, I can assure you the tests are all conclusive. We repeated several of them, just to be sure. They most definitely are not wrong.'

'Not the tests,' I contradicted, striving not to lose control again and be sedated before I could make them understand. 'If you say the tests are right, then I suppose I have to believe you. Why would you lie to me about that? But everything else is wrong!'

'Hush, hush, Rachel.' I could tell from his tone that I was scaring my dad again. Hell, I was scaring me again, but I had to get through to them this time.

I drew a deep shuddering breath and tried to continue in a less hysterical tone.

'I know this sounds crazy to you but please just hear me out. I don't know what is happening here, but none of this is real – at least not to me. In my life – in my *real* life, my father is sick, very very sick and I think I am too.'

The tone the doctor used was mild and placating.

'So you believe you have cancer as well, is that it?'

He was making me really angry now. I truly did not like this man.

'No, not cancer. I have something wrong with my brain.' Strangely enough no one butted in to refute that one. 'It's all due to the accident . . .'

'When you were mugged?' asked Dad.

'No, the car accident at the restaurant; the one where Jimmy died and I got badly hurt.'

The doctor looked across in confusion at my father, who was shaking his head as though trying to see a solution through a fog.

'Are you aware of the accident Rachel is talking about?'

'Well yes,' replied my father hesitantly, and I almost cried out in relief that he wasn't going to tell me that I'd imagined that too. 'A car *did* crash through the window of a restaurant where Rachel and her friends were sitting. It must have been, oh I don't know, about five years ago or thereabouts, just before they all went off to university.'

'And people were seriously hurt? Was Rachel injured?'

'I think the driver of the car was badly hurt, but Rachel and her friends managed to get away from the window just in time. Rachel was one of the people to come off worse; she fell whilst running from the window and was knocked unconscious for a minute or two, and of course there was also Jimmy, he had quite a nasty cut on his head.'

'But no one died?' prompted the doctor.

'No one died,' confirmed my dad.

'But Rachel *did* hit her head?'

'She did. She had mild concussion.'

'And five years later she is mugged and sustains a second injury to her head . . .'

The doctor made a church steeple with his fingertips as he paused to assimilate all he had been told. 'I do believe it is all beginning to make sense now.'

It was? Not to me, it wasn't.

Dr Tulloch leaned across the table, a benign smile upon his face. Unconsciously my father and I leaned towards him to hear his conclusion.

'Rachel, I believe I now understand what is causing your problems. It seems clear to me that you are suffering from a rather severe case of amnesia.'

If he was expecting his diagnosis to be met with whoops of joy, he was sadly mistaken.

Amnesia? I don't think so. In fact I knew it wasn't that. For a start isn't amnesia when you forget things? Well if so, that clearly *wasn't* what I was suffering from. My trouble was remembering things that apparently weren't real – not forgetting them! Yet when I challenged him on that one, he had a medical explanation.

'There are many many different types of amnesia. It is far more complex than just the "bang-on-the-head-who-am-I?" stuff you see in the movies.'

'I see,' said my dad, and I swivelled sharply in my chair to look at him. Was he really buying into this? Did this answer really make sense to him?

'And how long will this amnesia last, doctor?'

'I don't have amnesia.'

'Well that depends, it can really vary quite considerably: a day or two, a few weeks. In some cases a full recovery from amnesia can take many months.'

'I don't have amnesia.'

'And with Rachel's type of amnesia, where she believes she is remembering something which hasn't actually happened . . . well, that is rather . . . unusual, shall we say, so it is hard to say how long it will last. I would like to make arrangements for her to see a specialist in this field.'

My father then asked the question I had been most afraid to hear voiced aloud.

'Could her amnesia be permanent?'

There was a long silence. I hadn't realised I was holding my breath to hear Dr Tulloch's response until I began to feel dizzy from lack of oxygen.

'There is that possibility, although it is far too early to say for sure,' he replied in gentle tones. 'The specialist will be better able to give you a clearer idea on that.'

He got to his feet then and shook my father's hand, our consultation clearly at a close. As my father pushed the wheelchair from the room, I took one last look back at the white-haired doctor, who was already shuffling my pile of papers and case notes into a neat pile. His eyes met mine.

'I don't have amnesia.'

On the doctor's advice I was to be discharged from hospital the following morning. The specialist appointment would take some time to set up and it was felt I would recover more speedily in my own home. I felt that was highly unlikely, as the last time I saw my own home in Great Bishopsford there were clearly other people living in it. However, I *was* anxious to get out of hospital, if only to prove to everyone that I wasn't suffering from some weirdly interesting medical condition and that I was, in fact, telling the truth. And obviously I wasn't going to be able to prove anything from a hospital bed.

'Who knows,' said Dad hopefully, 'once you're back home you might find everything just clicks back into place.'

He looked so optimistic, I didn't have the heart to point out yet again the facts I knew to be true.

'Maybe,' I offered. 'Although even in your world I don't live with you any more, do I? So don't go expecting it all to come rushing back, eh?'

He looked anguished, as though I'd deliberately tried to hurt him with my words.

'There is no "your world" and "my world", Rachel. That's just your injuries talking. You'll see that once we get you back home.'

I tried to smile, and was pleased to see I must be a better actress than I had thought.

'I'm sure you're right, Dad.'

Matt had clearly been primed about the meeting with Dr Tulloch and its outcome, for when he came in to see me during visiting hours, half obliterated by the most enormous bouquet of flowers I had ever seen, he immediately bent to kiss me and spoke in a strangely irritating conciliatory tone.

'Rachel, my love, poor you. Amnesia. No wonder you've been acting so strangely since you came round. Do you remember anything at all? Do you know who I am?'

For one devilish moment I thought of playing along with it but I backed down in the last instant. That was just too cruel.

'Yes, Matt, of course I know who you are, we've known each other since we were teenagers. It's just . . . well, I've kind of "forgotten" things that happened recently.'

He passed the flowers to a nurse who had come in to take my blood pressure.

'Can you put these in water, nurse?'

She didn't look too happy to be distracted from her duties by a visitor, but she took the mammoth bunch of flowers and I mouthed a small apology to her over Matt's shoulder. That was one thing I hadn't forgotten: Matt was used to getting his own way and could come across as somewhat arrogant, if you didn't know him better.

'So when you say you can't remember things that happened recently, just how recently do you mean? The last few days?'

I shook my head.

'The last week?'

I shook my head again.

'Longer than that?'

Shaking my head wasn't going to do it this time.

'I've kind of "lost" the last five years.'

He sat down heavily in the chair. 'Shit!'

I stayed quiet, letting him absorb the impact of my words.

'So you don't remember anything about us? Nothing beyond when we left school? You don't even remember us getting engaged?'

I bit my lip, knowing he was in shock, but unable to share his emotion. I had, after all, broken up with Matt five years ago. And the Matt I had left behind had been an eighteen-year-old boy, not the bewildered man who sat staring at me now in helpless confusion.

He was quiet for some moments, and even though I hadn't known this new Matt for very long at all, I could tell his mind was already working at finding a solution. Presumably that was why he was such a success in business: if there was a problem, you fixed it. It was as simple as that.

'Well I think it's a good idea that you're going back to your dad's for a while. You obviously are going to need someone to look after you for the time being.'

'I'm not ill, Matt.'

'No, no, I realise that, Rachel. It's just that I wouldn't like to think of you back in London on your own, and you remember I have that important meeting in Hamburg I have to leave for tomorrow.'

'Actually I didn't know that. Amnesia, remember?' Oh, that was almost too cruel of me, but I couldn't resist.

He looked confused. When had Matt lost his sense of humour?

'Oh, oh, of course you didn't know. Well, it's been

planned for months . . . If there was any way of rescheduling it, then you know I would, but at this late stage . . .'

I reached out and patted his arm. 'Relax, Matt, don't worry. I'll be fine.'

He left not long after that but not before taking me in his arms and kissing me in a way that had felt oddly familiar and completely new all at the same time. I had tried to hold back, but he silenced my protests with his warm mouth and I had ended up returning the kiss with barely concealed eagerness. I might not actually be his fiancée but that didn't mean I couldn't at least enjoy something pleasant out of all this madness before I finally made sense of it.

Both of us were a little breathless when we finally broke apart.

'Well, at least we haven't forgotten how to do that now, have we?' There was a confidence now in his eyes and his voice. 'And if you have forgotten everything else, well I'm just going to have to make you fall in love with me all over again.'

He left, promising to call me at my father's from Germany and assuring me he would only be away for a little over a week. That was perfect. That should easily give me enough time to try to sort out this whole stupid mess. I didn't care that everyone else was perfectly happy to accept the amnesia theory. I *knew* that it wasn't true. Somewhere out there was my real old life and the sooner I was able to get out of this hospital ward and prove that to everyone, the better.

Chapter 7

The following morning a nurse brought me the clothes they said I had been wearing when I had been brought in. I didn't recognise them, but when I slipped them on they appeared to fit me perfectly. And while I didn't like the feel of wearing someone else's clothing, it was either that or walk out of there clad only in a hospital gown.

What really surprised me was when the nurse placed a large expensive-looking leather bag on the bed.

'Whose is that?'

There was sympathy in her voice as she replied.

'That's yours.'

I don't know why she was sounding sorry for me. I appeared to be the owner of a Gucci handbag! As I fumbled to open the unfamiliar clasp, I wondered if it had been a present from Matt; it looked like his style of gift. I held the open bag upside down and tipped the contents out onto the faded hospital blanket. There wasn't much to give me a clue: keys, a purse, a comb, a make-up bag. I flicked open the purse: the back pocket held more money than I ever carried around and the card slots were filled with an array of credit and store cards, all in my name. My own purse held a solitary debit card.

But it was the mobile phone that interested me most of all. Small and sleek, its shiny mirrored surface glinted brightly under the overhead light, sparkling like treasure. Which it very well could be. I snatched it up and found my fingers were trembling as I struggled to flick it open. It took several infuriating moments while I paused to try and figure out how to display the menu. When I did manage to access the right screen, I was initially disappointed to see that the phone book display held no immediate answers.

I had been so sure that there would be some clue to be found in this tiny device. I scrolled through the list of names: a few were familiar but most were not. I was about to snap shut the phone when the final entry on the list caught my eye. Dr Whittaker. Those two words, illuminated by the pale green backlight of the screen, shone out at me like a lighthouse through a fog. Dr Whittaker was the consultant I had been under after the accident. He was the one who had prescribed the medication I was currently taking for my headaches and it was him I'd been intending to see back in London to investigate why they had suddenly become so much worse.

With trembling fingers I pressed the call button and

the wait seemed interminable before the familiar ringing purr came back in response. The connection had just been picked up when the door to my room swung open and in breezed a staff nurse carrying the flowers Matt had given me the night before.

'I'm sorry, dear, you can't use your mobile in here.'

Rudely I ignored her, swivelling my body away from her and putting a finger in my free ear, the better to hear what was being said at the other end of the line.

'Really, I'm going to have to ask you to hang up. I'm afraid you'll have to wait until you get outside.'

I gave her a look and something in my eyes must have told her to drop it.

'You have reached the offices of Dr James Whittaker,' a tinny voice announced in my ear. 'I'm afraid there is no one here to take your call. Our hours are . . .' I flung the phone down on the mattress in frustration.

The nurse eyed me warily as I frantically sought for pen and paper among the stranger's handbag debris on the bed.

'Look, I really need you to do me a favour,' I urged, ripping a back page from a diary and scribbling hurriedly upon it. 'This is the name and number of a doctor in London who has been treating me for . . . well, it doesn't matter. It's just he'll know who I am. Can you get Dr Tulloch to call him and he'll be able to confirm everything about my headaches and . . . and, well, all the other symptoms.' I thrust the paper towards her and she hesitated for a second before taking it and placing it in the pocket of her uniform.

'You will remember, won't you? It's very very important.'

Her look of annoyance at catching me using a mobile had been replaced by one of saddened compassion. I think I preferred her angry face.

'Ask him to ring me at my father's when he's got through to Dr Whittaker. Any time – day or night. It doesn't matter. Everything will all make sense then.'

She was still looking incredibly sorry for me as she placed Matt's flowers slowly down on the bed, as though on a graveside, and left the room.

When my father came to collect me a little while later, I decided not to tell him about finding the doctor's number on the mobile phone. It would all make sense soon enough, once the hospital were able to confirm that everything I had told them was true. There was no need to endure another unsolicited explanation of how 'this was all part of the amnesia'.

Of course, I hadn't yet figured out how confirming my medical history could answer any of the other glaring anomalies that surrounded me. Little things: like people being back from the dead, cured of illnesses, and let's not forget the unexpected addition of a fiancé. Mentally I threw these problems to one side as though they were wafts of confetti. I wouldn't allow my racing thoughts to get sidetracked. Dr Whittaker first: the rest would all fall into place after that.

Our old house looked the same. That's to say the same as it had five years ago, which was conversely not the same as it had been when I'd stood before it a few days earlier. The iron railings and wooden shutters had disappeared, as if they never were. The front door and window frames had regained their unkempt look and could now all do with a fresh coat of paint. Likewise the state of the garden had suffered an obvious decline. It all looked wonderful.

The first surprise came only seconds after opening the front door. I stepped across the threshold, closely following my father, and then took a sharp step backwards as a bolt of something long and black streaked across the hall and into the lounge.

'What the hell was that?'

'It was only Kizzy. We must have startled her.'

She hadn't been the only one.

'And Kizzy would be?'

'Our cat. Well, *my* cat now, I guess, since you left home.'

I took a second to absorb this surprising information. My childhood had been remarkably bereft of pets, aside from the odd goldfish or two, and it was peculiar to learn that my father now owned one.

'You bought her for me when you left for university. So I wouldn't be so lonely, you said.'

Well, that had been quite nice of me.

I followed him slowly down the corridor taking in this new revelation. *I had gone to university.* And as I walked into the shabbily familiar lounge there, proudly displayed on the wall, was the evidence of that. My own face stared back at me from the large gilt-framed photograph. Swathed in gown and wearing a mortar board, there was no mistaking the look of pride in those eyes as I held in my hands a fancily engraved scroll. Absurdly I felt my eyes begin to prickle with tears. I had graduated. I had gone to university, gained a diploma and achieved my dreams. For the first time I actually questioned why I was so driven to tear down a world that might actually be far better than the one in which I really lived.

'Cup of tea?' questioned my dad, already halfway towards the kitchen to put on the kettle. He came from a generation where no problem was so huge that it couldn't be solved by simply pouring hot water onto a bag of tea leaves. I called out my response, but instead of sitting down to rest in one of the well-worn but comfortable-looking armchairs, I found myself wandering restlessly around the room, searching for . . . I'm not sure what I was searching for: was it definitive proof that this whole world around me was false, or was it to find evidence to prove that, unbelievably, it might actually all be real?

My graduation photo wasn't the only picture on display in the room, for the mantelpiece held several other frames. I walked over to examine them more closely. The first two I recognised: my parents on their wedding day, the dated fashions and hairstyles obliterated into insignificance by the brilliance of their smiles. I had always loved that picture. The next was the only photograph we still had of the three of us. It had been taken on a day trip to the seaside, and I stood between them on the pier, I can't remember where exactly, one hand held tightly in the palm of each parent. The photograph suddenly began to blur and waver, and I felt overwhelmed, as I hadn't in years, by a shaft of despair and loss for the mother I couldn't even remember having.

There were still two photographs yet to examine. The first brought out a bubble of laughter, which was just the antidote I needed right then. It had been taken on a school sports day when I was about seven years old. In the picture Jimmy and I held between us a small silver cup for having won the three-legged egg and spoon race. It was the only race I think I ever won during my entire schooldays. Of course, I could have turned out to be a decathlete at university, who was to say? Our eyes shone out in the picture, a happy combination of pride, friendship and pure unadulterated happiness. We were both grinning from ear to ear, seemingly unaware that the huge gaps we sported in our front teeth did little to improve the picture.

The last photograph I hadn't seen before, and I lifted it from the shelf and took it to the window to study it better. It was clearly taken quite recently, as I didn't look any different than I had when I had seen my reflection that morning. The hair was the same, and so too was the unblemished face. The venue looked like a fancy hotel or restaurant; there were gifts piled in clusters upon the table in front of us and in the centre of the photograph were its main subjects: Matt and myself. His arm was tightly wound around my waist, his left hand encompassing mine, holding it aloft to allow the camera to capture the dazzling brilliance of the impressively large ring upon my finger. The radiance of the diamond seemed almost too bright to be contained by the small glass frame.

I turned swiftly, almost guiltily, as the rattle of tea

cups heralded my father's return. Hastily I replaced the photograph where it had come from.

'Ring any bells?'

I shook my head sadly. 'I remember those ones' – I indicated the much older snapshots with a wave of my hand – 'but I've never seen this one before in my life.'

My father lowered himself into an armchair, looking sad.

'Nice ring though,' I observed, trying to elicit some sort of smile from the man I was causing so much concern. 'I bet he never got that one out of a cracker.' There it was, the smile I'd been waiting for.

We sipped our tea in silence, the hot drink taking away the need for conversation. I hated to disturb the tranquillity of the moment but I had to prepare him for something important.

'Dad, I'm expecting Dr Tulloch to call us later on. Let me know when he does, will you?'

Dad looked up, surprised.

'What would he be calling about? Hasn't he signed us over to that amnesia chap?'

I sighed, trying not to show how 'amnesia' was now my newest least favourite word.

'Yes, well I left a message and asked him to find out something for me, and when he does I'm sure he'll be calling us here. Don't worry. It will all make sense then.'

My father looked a little bemused but agreed to let me know when the call came.

He was in the process of trying to persuade me that I might want to go and have a lie down while he prepared us some lunch, when we were both suddenly startled by an angry hissing and spitting sound as the black cat I had seen earlier landed on the settee beside me, took one look at me, and sped off across the room, the hackles on her back raised in a high ridge of fur.

'What the heck . . .' began my father, as the cat, halfway out the door, stopped in a scuffle of claws against the carpet, turned to look at me and gave a low angry growl.

'Kizzy!' shouted my dad in remonstration. 'What's got into you?'

I drew back a little in my seat, not certain if the angry feline was going to pounce. She continued to stare balefully at me across the room, claws out, eyes as staring as large green emeralds. With one last angry spit she turned and fled the room in a streak of fur and fury. My father and I stared at each other in amazement. I broke the silence first.

'Does she usually do that?'

'No. Never. I've never seen her act like that before in her life. That cat really adores you.'

'That's lucky then. I'd hate to see what she'd do if she didn't like me.'

He laughed hollowly, but as he gathered up our dirty cups and prepared to leave the room, I could see he was still puzzled by the cat's inexplicable reaction to me.

Sometime later that afternoon he knocked on the door of my old bedroom with yet another cup of tea. I'd had gone there initially to find something warmer to put on than the silk suit I'd left the hospital in, but had become completely sidetracked by going through the contents of my old wardrobe and chest of drawers. Beside me on the floor lay piles of old magazines, clothes and mementoes.

My father picked a precarious path through the debris and laid down the steaming mug on the bedside table.

'I guess I wasn't too hot on throwing stuff out when I left home.'

'You could say that. Still, it might come in handy now. Jog your memory a little.'

I swept a hand across the random collection on the floor. 'Most of this stuff is from ages ago. I knew it all already.'

And though I knew it pained him, I had to let him know how I was really feeling. 'I haven't changed what I believe, Dad. I know you're desperately hoping I'm suddenly going to have a huge revelation, and start remembering stuff, but I really don't believe that's going to happen. You see, I haven't *forgotten* anything. There are no blanks in my memory. None at all. I can detail the last five years for you moment by moment. It's just a *different* five years.'

The mixture of pity and love in his eyes forced me to stop there. I wasn't helping either my own case or his to understand it any better.

'Let's just see what the specialist has to say, Rachel. How about that?'

I nodded slowly. I had to let him hold on to that for a little while longer. He still believed in the omnipotence of a medical 'specialist' almost as strongly as he did in the curative powers of tea.

Before leaving me to pack away the residue of my youth, he stopped at the doorway.

'By the way, I reckon I've figured out what must have spooked the cat earlier on.'

I looked up from a huge pile of magazines destined for the recycling bin.

'Yes, I've been thinking about it all day, as it was just so strange. Then I realised it must have been your smell.'

'Well that's nice, Dad.'

'No, I don't mean like that, but you probably smell of the hospital; you know, antiseptic, medical kind of smell. That was what must have made her act so crazy. She'll be fine with you now, you'll see.'

I wanted to believe him, I really did, but to me it looked far more like the cat had simply been defending her territory from someone she had never seen before in her life.

By the morning there had still been no phone call from the hospital. In fact the only call at all had been one from Matt telephoning from his hotel room in Germany. I tried to hide the disappointment in my tone when I realised it wasn't Dr Tulloch on the line but instead my newly acquired fiancé. Fortunately Matt didn't seem inclined to chat, and the whole conversation was over and done with in under ten minutes.

'How's Matt?' enquired my father when I had hung up, and something in his tone snagged my attention and made me look up.

'He's fine. Pretty busy with work, I guess.' Working on pure instinct I leapt in feet first with the next question.

'You don't like Matt much, do you?'

He fumbled with the newspaper he was flicking through, and I think he took a fraction too long before replying.

'Of course I do. What nonsense. Why ever would you think that?'

'I don't know, something in your tone, in your eyes . . .' I trailed off.

He met my enquiry full on.

'Even if I did . . . have doubts, I would never say anything when he is clearly the one you want to be with. And you've been together for a very long time now.'

'Not in my world we haven't. We broke up shortly after the . . . Well, shortly after leaving school.'

My words seem to ignite a strange look of curiosity.

'Interesting, that: that your amnesia has manufactured a world where Matt isn't your fiancé at all. I wonder what that could all be about?'

And clearly thinking he was onto something with this line of thought, he continued, 'And tell me, are you and Jimmy an item in this "other" life of yours?'

I gave a sigh. Did no one listen to what I was saying?

'No, hardly, Dad. Not with him being dead and all.'

There was a strange and pregnant silence between us. Our eyes met and held for a long moment before we both decided it was wisest to drop the subject.

★

I wandered into the kitchen the following morning, hair still dripping from my shower, wearing an old dressing gown that was several sizes too small. Dad was busily piling a small yellow mountain of rubbery scrambled eggs on a plate. Suddenly the hospital food was starting to look pretty good.

'Dad, you shouldn't have. Toast is all I can usually manage.'

'Nonsense,' he replied firmly, and I could see here the makings of a campaign. 'We're not going to build you back up to strength with just a dry old bit of crust for breakfast.'

I was on the point of explaining that possibly my problems might require more than just a cooked breakfast to fix, when I was spared by the ringing of the doorbell.

'Get that, will you, while I dish up?'

I went to the front door, still squeezing out droplets of water from my sodden hair. Behind the frosted panel was a tall dark shape. My heart gave a small leap in my chest as I opened the latch to greet the visitor. There's nothing like a visit from a dead friend to truly take away your appetite.

Jimmy followed me down the hall to the kitchen, bringing with him a huge cardboard box.

'Good morning, lad. You're just in time for breakfast, care to join us?'

Jimmy eyed the yellow concoction with the same enthusiasm as I had.

'Sorry, Tony, I've already eaten. I only popped in for a moment to say hello.'

I knew he was lying about the breakfast even before his eyes met mine. We had always been able to read each other like a book. Or maybe we hadn't. Absurdly I felt a warm pink blush flush my cheeks and was all at once aware of how inadequately covered I was, in the tiny dressing gown, to be receiving visitors.

'So what's in the box?' It was just as well my father had asked; I was so preoccupied with the strangeness of sitting in my old kitchen with my long-dead friend that it probably wouldn't have occurred to me to ask even if he'd have walked into the room with an elephant in tow.

'It's not from me,' Jimmy explained. 'A delivery van was just dropping it off and I offered to carry it in. It's for Rachel.'

I looked up from where I had been desperately trying to stretch unstretchable towelling edges more closely together.

'For me? What is it?'

My dad looked over my shoulder. 'Oh that must be the box with some more of your clothes. Matt said he'd have it sent down for you. He knew you wouldn't have much to wear.'

'He's right there,' I agreed. 'That was really thoughtful of him to go and sort that out for me.'

There was a small humphing sound from Jimmy's direction. 'Most likely he got his secretary to do it.'

The snipe had come as a reflex and just as swiftly I thrust back in Matt's defence. 'He's very busy, you know. He had to fly to Hamburg last night.'

A speculative look crossed Jimmy's familiar features but he knew better than to offer another criticism. My dad, who seemed completely oblivious to the verbal sparring going on, added, 'By the way, Rachel, I completely forgot to tell you, Matt also wanted you to know that he contacted the magazine on Monday and told them what had happened.'

Baffled, I shifted in my kitchen chair to look at my father.

'Magazine? What magazine?'

'The one where you work.'

I felt the familiar flipping sensation in my stomach as yet another bombshell got dropped.

'I don't work at a magazine.'

Here we go again. The look the two men exchanged was so blatant they might as well have shouted out the words. *Poor Rachel, still suffering with that old amnesia.*

Suddenly I was angry and got up so hurriedly the wooden chair almost toppled over behind me.

'No, don't you both look at me like that! Like "Oh-oh, Rachel's gone crazy. It's kid gloves time again." Don't you think I'd know something as basic as where I work?'

'You haven't been there long, you probably remember working on the paper better. You were there much longer.'

'I worked on a newspaper? I'm a journalist?' There was wonder in my voice at achieving my own goals before I shook my head angrily to dispel the fantasy. 'I *don't* work there. I think I would have remembered if I did, don't you?'

'Seems like you've forgotten a whole lot more than just that,' mumbled my father, and it was the first time I heard in his voice that he was beginning to lose patience.

Jimmy, as calm and collected as ever, reached over and took my hand. 'Sit down, Rachel, please.' And when I didn't comply, he gently tugged on my arm, forcing me back down to the table. Angling his chair towards me and speaking without any agitation, he asked slowly and clearly, 'Where *do* you work, Rachel?'

His eye contact with me was unbreakable and I wondered if this was a technique they taught policemen when interrogating suspects.

'Andersons Engineering in Euston. I work as a secretary for the sales department. I've been there over three and a half years. The telephone number is 020 7581 4387.'

If he was startled at the glibness and speed of my response, he hid it better than my father.

'What the—'

Jimmy silenced my dad with a warning glance and immediately turned his full attention back to me. This was definitely policeman stuff.

'And who can we contact there to confirm . . . or rather to tell them that you won't be in for a little while?'

'Mrs Jessica Scott in Human Resources. Her extension number is 203.' I saw the flicker in his eyes at the immediacy of my response, but his voice was smooth and firm when he asked my dad:

'Tony, do you mind if I use your phone and give them a call?'

By reply my father released the cordless phone from its mount and passed it to Jimmy. Before dialling the number he turned to me.

'Would you prefer to speak to them yourself?'

I shook my head, they would probably both think I was lying. No, let him speak to Human Resources, that way everyone would see, once and for all, that I was telling the truth.

I repeated the number and he quickly keyed it in. It seemed an eternity before the switchboard picked up and he then asked for the required extension. Infuriatingly he had risen to his feet to make the call, so I could no longer hear even the vaguest of responses from the other end of the line. I had to content myself with piecing together the conversation from Jimmy's side of things.

'Could I speak with Mrs Jessica Scott?... Good morning, Mrs Scott. My name is Jimmy Boyd and I'm a friend of Rachel Wiltshire. I was just phoning to let you know that unfortunately she's been involved in a small accident and won't be in for at least the rest of this week, possibly longer.'

There was the longest pause.

'In the Sales Department . . . Yes. . . . Yes . . . All right, yes. I see. . . . Thank you very much. Goodbye.'

He pressed the red button to disconnect the call and turned slowly back to face us both. I fidgeted in my chair like an impatient five-year-old.

'Well? Well? What did she say?'

He hesitated, his face unreadable. I didn't think I was going to like what was coming next. I was right.

'Rachel, she said she'd never heard of you. You don't work there.'

OK, so it probably wasn't very mature of me to burst into tears but I just couldn't help it. Every time some small glimmer of hope was dangled in front of me, it was suddenly seized from my grasp. I leapt up from the table in a cyclone of tears and dismay, this time succeeding in knocking over my chair, and thundered up the stairs to my room where I threw myself face down upon the bed.

And just like the angry teenager I appeared to have morphed back into, I ignored their entreaties to open the locked door, shouting at them both to 'Go away' until I was too hoarse to shout any more.

It was beginning to get dark by the time I eventually emerged from my room. I must have cried myself to sleep, for I'd woken up several hours later, the dampness of the pillow sticking to my cheek. My father was in the lounge, pretending to watch the early evening news on the TV.

I slid onto the settee beside him, ignored the cat who gave a muted hiss and swiftly vacated his lap, and laid my head against his shoulder.

'Sorry, Dad.' He squeezed my hand in response. 'It's just so difficult. Nothing makes sense. It's all just topsy-turvy. Maybe you are all right. Maybe I *am* going crazy.'

He turned to me then, an unexpected anger in his

eyes. 'Don't you go saying anything of the sort. No one has ever said you're crazy! You've had a nasty blow on the head and a terrible shock. It's no wonder you're just a little . . . muddled . . . That's all, yes muddled. It's all going to come right soon, love, you'll see.'

And this time I was too tired to argue.

He must have really been worried about me though, because several times during the night, in the twilight between sleep and wakefulness, I caught the distinctive bouquet of his aftershave and I knew he had crept silently into my room to check up on me. He never said a word, and I never let on I knew he was there.

The next day I rummaged purposefully through the box of clothes Matt had sent to find something to wear. I was hoping for jeans and a sweatshirt but it would appear my new lifestyle didn't incorporate anything quite that casual. I had to settle instead on a pair of smart black trousers and an emerald green jumper. I checked out my reflection and couldn't argue that the outfit suited me, and if the labels weren't exactly designer, they were certainly from the top end of the high street. Either my new work paid incredibly well or Matt had been responsible for more than just the Gucci handbag. He always had been generous when we were teenagers. I guessed he still was.

I hung up the remaining clothes in the small pine

wardrobe and then picked up a warm sheepskin jacket and scarf. I hadn't been out of the house for days, and I needed to test my stamina if I was going to get Dad to agree to the latest plan I had in mind. However, all intentions of broaching the idea gently were blown out of the water when I descended the stairs at the very moment he was coming through the front door. He must have just been returning from his daily walk to get the morning paper. He was quick, but so was I, and I still had time to see the small red carton that he hastily tried to stuff into his jacket. Diving into his deep pocket like a missile, my fingers closed about the small container and thrust it out.

'What in the hell are these?'

My dad looked shamefaced and said nothing; I could see various explanations trolling through his mind: each one failing to pass muster and be offered up.

'What in God's name are you smoking again for? Don't you know these things will kill you? That they *were* killing you?'

If either of us had stopped to consider the incongruity of the complete parent/child role reversal we were currently acting out, then we would probably have burst out laughing there and then. Only I was too angry to see it and he was too embarrassed.

I crushed the packet in my hand, rendering at least this one pack unsalvageable, and with the breaking of the cigarettes within, my anger too began to crumple.

'Dad, I know what you're doing and why you're doing it, but you have to promise me that you'll stop.'

He didn't apologise, but he did at least try to explain.

'I've just been so worried about you, Rachel. You've been so lost and I feel so useless not being able to help you. It was just a little something to cope with the stress, that's all.'

'Don't, Dad,' I said, tears rolling down my cheeks at hearing my own father sound so broken down with concern. I brushed the salty flow away with the back of my hand – God, when had I become such a cry baby?

I took both his hands in mine and tried to put into my words and eyes all that I had felt when he had first been diagnosed.

'Dad, if you love me, if you *really* love me, please promise me you'll never touch this poison again?' His eyes too began to mist. Now I'd made my own father cry, but if it stopped this happening all over again, then it was worth it. 'You half killed yourself with these from worrying over me once before; I won't let you do it again.'

I walked around for hours and although I had nowhere in particular to go, it still felt good to be back outside after the inactivity of the last week. I'd told Dad not to worry, and I phoned to check in with him after a couple of hours, just so he knew I was OK. It was mid-afternoon by then, and I realised that somehow along the way I had missed lunch. As I wasn't far from the centre of town, I headed towards the small parade where there were a few restaurants and coffee shops.

I was hesitating on the pavement, trying to decide

which one to choose, when a voice behind me spoke softly in my ear.

'The one on the end does the best cheesecake.'

I turned around, and my heartbeat increased. He must have really startled me.

'And what if I don't like cheesecake any more?'

He stopped as though to consider this absurdity.

'No. Never happen. Whatever else you've forgotten, it won't be that. Some things just go too deep.'

Somehow, by mutual agreement, we entered the small coffee house where Jimmy placed an order for coffees and two slices of cake. There was a table set for two towards the back of the shop beside an open log fire, and we headed over to claim it, both unconsciously rejecting several vacant ones by the front windows.

'So how come you're not at work today, Constable Boyd? It's no wonder that crime is rife in this town – none of the policemen are ever on duty.'

'It's actually *Inspector* Boyd, and I am now officially off duty for the day.'

'Inspector, eh, that sounds important. Do you enjoy it? You never said anything about wanting to become a policeman when we were younger.'

The waitress arrived with our order and he waited until she had placed the cups and plates before us and left before replying.

'Yes. I love the job. Joining the force was the best decision I ever made. And as for never saying anything about it . . . Well, I kept a lot of things to myself back then; things that perhaps I should have said out loud.'

My stomach gave a flip. I felt like he was about to tell me something, something big. But something deep inside me resisted. Not knowing how to proceed down that avenue; not even sure if I wanted to, I chose an abrupt change of topic.

'Jimmy, I want to apologise to you for my behaviour the other day. My little outburst.'

He brushed the apology away with a careless hand, but I continued.

'No, really. I know it all seems extremely . . . oh, I don't know . . . unlikely . . . unbalanced . . . unbelievable . . .'

'Pretty much any word starting with "un" then?'

I laughed. He had always been able to make me laugh.

'It's just that what I know to be completely and unequivocally true, keeps being proved to be false. It's very unsettling.'

He took a long sip of his coffee before replying. 'I'm sure it must be. And frustrating too.'

There was something in his voice, something I'd not heard from anyone else, and it made me drop the forkful of cake which was halfway to my mouth.

'Do you *believe* me?' I realised that in all my protestations, I had never asked that precise question of anyone.

His deep blue eyes held mine in a gaze that a person could drown in, if they weren't careful.

'I believe that *you* believe it, wholeheartedly and completely. And I can see what trying to convince the rest of us is doing to you.' He was quiet for a moment and I almost spoke then – thank God I didn't, or I would never have heard him finish in a whisper, 'And it's heart-breaking to see you like this.'

I hadn't realised his words had made me cry until he lifted my face gently with his finger and dabbed at my eyes with the folded serviette. His voice was still soft and low. 'And I've certainly never seen you cry this much, not even when you kept falling off your bike when you were about eight years old.'

I gave a rather unladylike sniff, but his words had done the trick, he'd made me smile.

'Oh, I've certainly cried plenty in the last five years, more than you'll ever know.'

'What about?'

Here it was. The moment to either back right off or plunge in regardless.

'About losing you. When you saved my life, and lost yours. You've no idea what that did to me. You've no idea how much I've missed you.'

And this was his chance to jump in with the *head-injury-amnesia-soon-all-be-fixed* platitude. But he did none of that. This was Jimmy; the boy who had loved me when we were children and the man he had now become. I could trust him with anything. I could trust him with the truth.

'Tell me,' he urged.

And so, in the dwindling afternoon light and by the flickering flames of the fire, I started at the beginning, from the night of the accident, and didn't stop until I had reached the end.

Chapter 8

We were the last two customers to leave the coffee shop. We realised we had overstayed our welcome when the owner had stopped being subtle about it and had swept the floor, upended the chairs on the vacant tables and switched off almost all the lights.

I apologised for keeping them, while Jimmy lifted my coat from the rack and held it out for me to slip on. He settled the jacket upon my shoulders, and somehow it just seemed natural for his arm to remain there as he guided me towards the door.

'My car's just around the corner, I'll drop you back home before your father sends out a search party.'

The cold December air bit sharply against us in a gust of wind as we walked along the quiet streets, but I didn't seem to feel the cold, not with his body walking in sync so closely beside mine. I knew I was in dangerous territory here. A door had opened sometime that afternoon and I'd walked blithely through it without a backward glance. But now I could see that before adding any further complications to the equation, I first needed to resolve the thousand or so unanswered questions that were standing in my way. Although, damn it, it felt so good, so *right* to be walking like this by Jimmy's side. How could I not have seen this before?

The drive back to my house took only five minutes and when we pulled up to the kerb, I noticed the instant responding twitch of the curtain in the front room.

I gave a small laugh in disbelief.

'Can you believe my dad is actually peeking out through the curtains to check up on me? This is just like being a teenager all over again.'

He ducked his head and leaned across me to view the front of my house through the passenger window. I caught the light fragrance of his aftershave, and the clean smell of shampoo, before he straightened back up. I breathed in the tantalising combination more deeply, as though to commit it to memory.

What was I doing here? I had no right to be thinking these thoughts. Jimmy and I had never been romantically involved, not once, not ever, for we had only ever been best friends, and besides, there had always been Matt. And there still *was* Matt, I had to remind myself. I wasn't free to be thinking this way.

'I guess I should get inside.'

'Before your dad comes out with a shotgun?'

I gave a small giggle at the image.

'Yes, that's right. And also Matt will be calling soon from Germany, so . . .' My voice trailed away. It was the worst thing I could have said. The warm air between us immediately froze at my words and the bristle that ran through Jimmy was almost palpable.

'Of course.' And with those two words, the fledgling thing that had fluttered to life between us was shot down dead.

I asked him to join us for dinner but wasn't surprised when he declined. He did walk me to the front door though, taking my arm as the path was even then beginning to ice over. But it was the guiding hand of a friend and nothing more. I couldn't believe a mood could change so instantly and it made me question my own perception of the rest of the afternoon. Had there really been anything new there at all, or had I merely imagined I could feel something more than just an old and treasured friendship?

He took the door key from my fingers and slid it into the lock, but before he rotated it, I placed my hand on his arm to stall him.

'Are we still all right for tomorrow? Because I can go on my own, you know. No problem.'

His eyes gave nothing away.

'Of course it's still OK. Why wouldn't it be?'

Because I'd gone and ruined the moment by conjuring up between us the one obstacle that had always been in our way. The obstacle that I was now engaged to.

'No reason. It's just . . . Well, it doesn't seem a great

way for you to spend your day off: escorting your newly deranged friend around London.'

He pulled me against him then and enveloped me in a brief hard hug; all friendship – nothing else.

'Not newly deranged,' he contradicted and then, clearly unable to resist, 'You've pretty much been this way ever since I've known you!'

He released me then, and turned the key in the lock all in one smooth movement. Giving me a gentle nudge he propelled me into the warm hall.

'And I told you before, I think it's a really good idea. I'm sure it's going to help. Now go inside in the warm and I'll see you in the morning.'

The arguments I thought I'd have to put forward to convince my dad it was a good idea for me to return to London the next day proved to be unnecessary once he knew that Jimmy would be accompanying me. It did make me wonder if he'd have held the same opinion if I had chosen a different travelling companion. Even so, as I waited for Jimmy to collect me the following morning, my father was still clucking around like the proverbial old mother hen.

'You have got your medication with you?'

I tapped the Gucci bag swung over my shoulder.

'And you'll call me if you feel sick or . . . anything? You have your phone, right, and money and . . .'

'Relax, Dad. I'm only going for one night. I'll be back

tomorrow and hopefully I'll have some answers at long last.'

He still looked doubtful, so I reached up to hug him. 'Don't worry about me so much.' I smelt his aftershave then, and it suddenly reminded me of something. 'And stop checking up on me all night long. You must be exhausted by morning – I've lost count of the number of times you keep coming in.'

Jimmy's car pulled up outside, and I was bending to pick up the small soft bag I had at my feet, so I missed the initial look of confusion on my father's face.

'Rachel, I haven't been in your room at night to check up on you. Not even once. You must have been dreaming.'

The journey to London confirmed that Jimmy had also reached a decision in the intervening hours between last night and that morning. Back once more was the warm-hearted, teasing, platonic friend I had known all my life – or at least the bit that had led up to my eighteenth year. The man who had held my hand in the coffee shop, while I stumbled through the story of what my life had become since that time, had completely disappeared.

And if I was disappointed at having let that person slip through my fingers, at least I still had my old friend Jimmy back in my life, and compared to a week or so earlier, that was a vast improvement.

'So where do you want us to head to first? Have you given it any thought?'

I pulled a folded piece of paper from my bag.

'I guess it makes sense to go here first. The other places are all across on the other side of town.'

The paper fluttered in my hand from a light draught from the open window.

'I have the address, but I've no idea where it is exactly. Dad had to write it down for me.'

Jimmy's eyes flickered away from the road for an instant and glanced down at the scrap of lined paper.

'And that would be . . . ?'

I gave a deep sigh and looked at the words on the sheet before me that meant absolutely nothing to me.

'It's where I live' – I paused, as though in court – 'allegedly.'

I tried to appear relaxed, but as the motorway ate up mile after mile I began to get more and more nervous. Going into London, to where I lived and worked, was my last hope of reclaiming my real life. But it was only now that I stopped to contemplate what exactly I would find when I got there. There were keys in my bag that I didn't recognise. Presumably they would fit the door of the address my father had given me that morning. But what of my other home, the flat I lived in above the launderette? What would everyone say when that too proved to be mine? Filled with belongings and paraphernalia from another life entirely. Could they both exist side by side? How could that even be possible?

A word began to whisper in my mind. A word much more scary and unknown than the dreaded amnesia one: *schizophrenia*. Couldn't that take the form of multiple personalities? All at once I was convinced I had read an article quite recently about that very subject. Could that be what I was suffering from? Was I actually mentally ill?

To silence the voice, I grabbed on to any random thought to fill the silence.

'Jimmy, I never thought to ask before now: are you married?'

Our car swerved slightly in its lane, earning an angry beep from the lorry behind us.

'Married? Er, no. Where did that come from? Don't you think you would know by now if I was?'

I shrugged. 'Not necessarily. I didn't know *I* was engaged.'

'Point taken.'

A further mile clicked onto the clock on the dashboard before I pursued it again. 'So, is there anyone on the scene?'

He laughed softly under his breath but said nothing, which only piqued my curiosity more.

'Girlfriend? Lover? Boyfriend?'

'No, no and definitely no, thank you very much.'

'Why not?'

'What are you asking me? Why aren't I gay?'

I gave his arm a gentle nudge. 'You know what I'm asking. Why is there no one? You're a great guy. You'd make a terrific partner for someone. How come you're alone?'

For the first time he looked uncomfortable and it surprised me that I had ventured too far into forbidden territory. There was a time when nowhere was out of bounds. But perhaps it was all different now.

'The job, for one: long hours, weird shifts. It doesn't help a relationship. Or maybe I just prefer it this way.'

I felt there was more to be asked here, more that he wasn't saying, but perhaps this wasn't the time, so I let the subject drop, to his obvious relief.

By then we were winding through the back streets of London, and it took us longer than we had thought to locate the address we were seeking. Eventually, after several wrong turns, we pulled up in front of an ornately porticoed converted Victorian building.

'Here we are,' announced Jimmy, swinging the car into a vacant parking bay in the small courtyard at the front of the building. 'Home.'

'Not mine,' I muttered bleakly, but nevertheless reached for the handle and got out of the car. I stood for a moment in the cold morning air, looking up at the totally unfamiliar building. There was nothing whatsoever about it that looked even remotely familiar.

'Come on then, let's go check it out.' He reached out his hand, and with obvious reluctance I allowed him to lead me towards the building's stone steps.

I thought we were going to be stymied at the first hurdle, for as we neared the entrance we could see that the building had a security door with a keypad entry system to gain access. I halted halfway up the three shallow steps.

'That's that then,' I proclaimed, and knew the relief in my voice was obvious.

'Not so fast,' Jimmy urged, continuing to pull me towards the door. At that precise moment a blue-uniformed nurse appeared on the inside of the glass entrance, clearly hurrying to exit the building. As she opened the door, Jimmy hurried up the steps to catch it before it closed behind her. The nurse eyed him suspiciously for a moment, then saw me and clearly decided not to challenge our entry.

'Thank you,' said Jimmy as we passed the nurse on the threshold.

Automatically I too voiced our gratitude, 'Yes, thanks.'

She was through the doorway and already descending the stone steps before she called out cheerfully over her shoulder.

'No problem, Rachel.'

We were both silent in the lift as it ascended. And the tension followed us out when the doors slid open on the fifth floor. The corridor spread before us, leading both to the left and the right.

'Which way?' asked Jimmy.

'How should I know?' I snapped back.

He walked back to me then, kinder and more patient than I probably deserved.

'I know this is hard, Rachel. I really do. But we knew you'd have to face something like this. Don't give up on it all just yet.'

He was right, of course he was. But I had *so* wanted this all not to be true.

My key opened the door to the flat: of course it did. We wandered through the rooms, like prospective buyers, not really knowing where we were going. When I opened what

I thought was the door to the bedroom and ended up walking into the airing cupboard, we thankfully both found our temporarily lost sense of humour. In the airing cupboard . . . Isn't that always the last place you look for it?

I felt a little like a burglar, rummaging through drawers and closets looking for something of value. I recognised very little, but then every so often I would stumble across an item of clothing, or a piece of jewellery, and my pulse would quicken when I recognised it as one of mine. The passport and tax papers all neatly filed in a metal storage box only served to hammer home even more evidential nails in the coffin. I definitely lived here.

And that would have been far from a tragedy to accept in any other set of circumstances; for the flat was extremely nice, very tastefully decorated and about four times the size of my home above the launderette. Even so, my accommodation upgrade gave me no pleasure at all. If this *was* my home – and how could I refute it when surrounded by such unshakeable evidence – then what possible grounds did that leave me for continuing to insist that this life was not mine?

While I was ransacking the bedroom, Jimmy had made his way to the kitchen, coming out a few minutes later with two steaming mugs of coffee.

'Black, I'm afraid,' he apologised, handing me one of the mugs. 'You're out of milk. Actually you're pretty much out of everything; the cupboards are quite bare. I'm guessing you must eat out a lot.'

That sounded logical and it would certainly fit the lifestyle I imagined Matt would have.

Holding onto the mug very carefully, I lowered myself onto a cream leather sofa. I cautiously shifted my weight, anxious not to spill any hot drink on the expensive-looking surface. I was an extremely nervous visitor in my own home.

'How can I afford all of this?' it suddenly occurred to me to ask. 'I know what London prices are like. This place must cost a bomb; surely my new job doesn't pay that well.'

Jimmy's eyes darkened for a moment and he looked away from my questioning face before replying.

'I believe Matt's family own this flat. Own several, I think, in this building. I guess you get it at a reduced rent, being almost one of the family.'

Ridiculously I felt myself blushing with embarrassment, although I wasn't exactly sure why. It wasn't as if I'd done anything to be ashamed of.

'Oh,' was my only response. For a journalist, I clearly wasn't all that articulate.

We finished our inspection of the flat together. And though I kept on looking for evidence that this was *not* my home, all the clues around me screamed out in contradiction. And if the pile of bills and junk mail in my name weren't conclusive enough proof, there was a single silver-framed photograph on a small coffee table that seemed pretty indisputable.

Jimmy came up behind me, leaning with his chin upon my shoulder to see what I was staring at so intently in my hands. The image looking back at me from behind the glass was of Matt and me by the Eiffel Tower. He was standing behind me, much in the same way as Jimmy was at that precise moment. Matt and I were both laughing into the camera, and although the day must have been cold, for we were bundled up warmly with coats and scarves, there was such a feeling of warmth exuding from our photographed images that I felt temporarily winded by a kick of shock.

We both looked so happy and carefree and so . . . so in love. I realised for the first time that what with everything that had happened since I'd returned to Great Bishopsford, I'd been so busy trying to unearth the past that I'd somehow managed to bury all feelings for Matt in the displaced topsoil.

'I believe that was where he proposed to you.' Jimmy's words were devoid of any betraying emotion.

I couldn't seem to take my eyes off the photo, and a moment later I felt Jimmy step purposefully away from me.

'I've always wanted to go to Paris,' I said reflectively.

Jimmy didn't reply, just bent down to take our empty cups back to the kitchen, so I don't know if he heard me finish saying in a quiet emphatic voice: '. . . *but I've never been there.*'

There was nothing left to hold us in the flat. I rejected Jimmy's suggestion that I take a few more things with me back to my father's. It would have felt too much like stealing.

Once back in the car, I felt I had to say something to break the awful cloud that had descended between us.

'Even though I've seen what I've seen, even now none of it seems real.' I waved my hand in the direction of the Victorian building. 'Logically I can see the proof before me, I have to accept that, but in my mind, in my heart, it still all seems completely and utterly wrong.'

Jimmy also seemed to make a deliberate effort to shake off the suffocating shroud we were under.

'Don't worry. You can't expect it all to come back at once. Let's go and get a bite to eat and then we'll check out the magazine where you work. Perhaps we'll find something there which will give us some answers.'

He had no idea how prophetic his words would turn out to be.

Thankfully Jimmy had suggested we telephone the magazine in advance to warn them we were coming, which was just as well as the place was enormous and we'd never have found our way unaided to the section where I worked. We walked across an ice-rink-shiny reception floor to a large curved desk, behind which sat several receptionists. Everyone around us seemed incredibly smartly dressed and well put together, and while the clothes I was wearing definitely weren't out of place, I certainly felt that I was.

I lost major points in poise, when I forgot the name of the person we were meeting and had to hunt in my handbag for the piece of paper I'd written it down on.

'Miss Rachel Wiltshire to see Mrs Louise Kendall,' provided Jimmy smoothly, whilst I was still scrabbling with an indecent lack of reverence within the cavernous Gucci bag. 'She is expecting us.'

We were instructed to take a seat on an impossibly low red leather settee situated directly opposite the bank of lifts. I fidgeted nervously as we waited to be met, half rising each time the lift doors slid open and a woman came out. This was ridiculous. The building was vast and there was a constant stream of people flowing out into the reception area. My boss could be any one of them.

In fact it was fifteen more minutes before a woman no more than ten years older than me came walking swiftly over to us clad in a designer suit and unbelievably impractical heels.

'Rachel!' she cried out when she was halfway across the foyer. I got to my feet and held out my hand. This she ignored and swooped in like a hawk to air-kiss the space beside my head, enveloping me in a haze of expensive perfume.

'How are you, you poor old thing? We've been *so* worried.'

Something in her voice made me seriously doubt that. She'd wasted no time on further greetings and had already pivoted on her killer heels and was making her way back over to the lifts. As she had completely ignored Jimmy up to that point, I thought it only polite to offer an introduction.

'Mrs Kendall, this is an old friend of mine, Jimmy Boyd. He's brought me into London today to see if anything here might jog my memory.'

She turned to flash the briefest of smiles at the man

beside me, but it was only her mouth that moved, none of it reached her eyes. I'd already seen the top-to-toe appraisal she had raked over him when we had risen to greet her. I only hoped Jimmy hadn't noticed it too.

'Not *Mrs Kendall*, just Louise,' she corrected as she jabbed a perfectly manicured finger on the lift call button. 'Your darling young man Matt called on Monday and explained all about the dreadful mugging. How terrible that must have been. And they got your beautiful ring?' Her eye dropped to my left hand as if to verify it was really gone. 'What a *tragedy*.'

As we followed her into the lift I couldn't help but feel it was losing my diamond that my boss deemed more tragic rather than any physical peril I'd been in. There was something about her that reminded me of Cathy, or how Cathy could turn out to be in another ten years or so.

We exited the lift on the ninth floor and Louise was instantly accosted by a junior member of staff dashing down the corridor carrying a sheaf of papers. As she stopped to sort out the crisis, Jimmy and I both took a polite step backwards and surveyed our surroundings. We were in a large open-plan office, brightly lit by long neon tube lighting. There were innumerable desks to both sides of the lift, divided up into work stations by blue felt-covered partitions. It looked like one of those experimental things you see in laboratories: the ones that rats run around in.

'Nice woman, your boss,' commented Jimmy, whispering low into my ear so he couldn't be overheard. 'Very sincere.'

'Sshh,' I giggled back, but was pleased I wasn't alone in my assessment.

With the problem taken care of, Louise sent the junior on their way and turned back to us saying, 'I'm not quite sure what you want to do next. Would you just like to wander about and say hi to people or do you want to have a poke around at your desk?'

'Er, just the desk, please, I think.'

'All right then. Well, good luck. I'm sure I'll see you again before you leave.' And with that she turned to walk away.

'Um, Louise.'

She turned back and was a fraction too slow in sliding the smile across the look of irritation on her face. The *I'm-a-busy-woman-and-I-really-don't-have-time-for-this* look was just peeking out from beneath.

'Which one *is* my desk?'

A look of almost delighted astonishment filled her face.

'Oh my God. You really *do* have amnesia! How bizarre! Matt said you did . . . But, well, it's just so utterly unusual.'

Her fascination with my condition lasted all the way to my desk as we wove around and between the cubicles of my co-workers. Some dismissed me with a fleeting glance, but many of them looked up and smiled. I smiled at everyone; just in case I knew them well.

Eventually she stopped in front of an area where two desks sat face to face. A young woman sat in one, banging furiously away at the keyboard in front of her.

'Dee, can you spare some time to show Rachel a few things?' And then, as though imparting the most delicious of secrets, she stage whispered, 'She really *does* have amnesia!'

We waited until she had gone, then the young woman got up from her chair and held out her hand in greeting.

'Hi. I'm Dee Ellis and we both joined the magazine at about the same time.'

I nodded, and smiled back at her, unable to think of anything to say.

'And we both can't stand Louise.'

I grasped her extended hand warmly. I didn't know who the heck she was but I felt I had just found a friend.

Dee was extremely patient but I could tell from the surreptitious glances at the wall clock and her computer that we were keeping her from her work.

'Look, I can see you're busy, please don't feel you have to babysit me here.'

She smiled ruefully.

'I'm sorry,' she said apologetically. 'Big deadline coming up. You know how it is.'

I didn't actually.

'Is there anything Rachel can look at while she's here? Perhaps something she was working on last week that might help her to remember anything?'

Dee looked directly at Jimmy and, unlike Louise, I could see that she had warmed to him in an instant. I liked her even more.

'Well, there's nothing that she was in the middle of.' She frowned as though searching for a key to unlock a door. 'You'd been working really hard to get everything done before your friend's wedding. How was that, by the way?'

'I missed it.'

'Bummer.' She bit her lip in concentration. 'Oh I know. Would it be useful if you looked through some of the articles you've worked on in the last few months? Is that the sort of thing that might help?'

'That would be great,' I assured her.

She disappeared from us then, murmuring something about 'archives' and while we waited I sat down at the vacant desk. There were no personal items cluttering up its surface and nothing to be found in either of the two drawers, except the expected stationery. I shut the drawers with a guilty slam when Dee returned carrying a stack of magazines, feeling like I'd been caught snooping.

'Here we are. You can see which ones you were involved with from the indexes. And I've just checked that the conference room is free, so if you like you can browse through them in comfort in there.'

Although constructed of wall-to-wall glass, the conference room at least gave us some degree of privacy from the open-plan office. Jimmy laid the stack of magazines he had taken from Dee's arms down on the polished oak table and pulled out a couple of the comfortably padded chairs. I checked out the dates of the issues, and dragged the earliest one towards me. Jimmy plucked a random one from the pile and when I raised an eyebrow to look at him questioningly, he gave a boyish shrug.

'I thought I could do the quizzes while I'm waiting.'

We sat in silence, reading the back issues for several hours. Twice Jimmy left and returned with Styrofoam cups of something hot and brown from the nearby vending machine. The room was filled with nothing but the sound of turning pages.

'You know, some of my stuff is really quite good,' I observed, closing another magazine and placing it on the completed pile on the table.

'And she's so modest with it,' Jimmy teased.

I felt my cheeks pinken.

'I'm not being big-headed,' I corrected, 'I'm just surprised I was good enough at this to actually achieve my dream.'

He gave my hand a friendly squeeze. 'I never expected anything less.'

Two magazines later my perception of reality exploded in smithereens in front of my face.

I hadn't noticed the title of the article at first. My attention had been drawn to the small colour photograph occupying the top right hand corner of the page.

'Oh my God!' I gasped, feeling the colour draining from my face.

'What? What is it? What's wrong?' exclaimed Jimmy, getting instantly out of his chair to stand beside me.

Unable to find my voice, I pointed with a trembling finger at the photograph. Jimmy bent lower to read the caption out loud.

'Dr James Whittaker of the Hallingford Clinic.' He turned to me, confused. 'So?'

'It's Dr Whittaker,' I said, my thoughts buzzing around my head like angry bees. 'Dr Whittaker is *my* doctor,' I went on, knowing I was sounding increasingly annoyed at his lack of comprehension. 'He's the specialist I was under after the accident. He's the person who has been treating me for my headaches for the past six months!'

We both read the article through twice. It was only when we were done that our eyes met and the silence was broken.

'It doesn't mention that he treats head trauma cases,' Jimmy ventured in a quiet voice.

'I know.'

'In fact, from the sound of it, he doesn't seem to treat patients at all any more.'

'I know.'

'He seems more involved in these clinical trials and research.'

I stayed silent.

'It's a good article,' offered up Jimmy at last, as though that might be some consolation.

'Thanks.'

I turned the magazine towards me as though I wanted to read the title again, but I didn't need to, I had already committed it to memory.

Multiple Personality Disorder: Medical Fact or Fiction?
And there in smaller italicised writing was the byline:
By Rachel Wiltshire.

Chapter 9

I don't remember leaving the building. Jimmy took charge, returning the magazines to Dee and then steering me smoothly towards the bank of lifts. Once inside the carriage and heading back to the ground floor, the other occupants gave us a wide berth when they saw my deathly white complexion and Jimmy's supporting arm hooked around my waist. I guess I did look sick, but not in the way that they imagined.

The cold wind outside took my breath away and I gave a huge gasp as I inhaled it, like a drowning person coming up for air.

'Just breathe slowly,' Jimmy said. 'There's no rush, just take it easy.' He had switched automatically into his professional role of how to deal with someone in shock.

And I guess that 'shock' was a pretty accurate description to cover what I was feeling right then.

The jigsaw pieces were suddenly all fitting together, but instead of the clarification and explanation I had sought, the puzzle was coming together all wrong and the picture it was revealing filled me with terror.

'It's all true. It's all true. How can it all be *true*?' I hadn't realised I was speaking so loudly until I saw the wary stares being cast my way from passers-by. I must have looked more than a little unhinged.

'Come on, hon, let's get out of here,' Jimmy recommended, and I numbly allowed him to lead me to the underground car park where we had left the car.

He settled me in the seat as though I was a child, before shutting the passenger door and walking around to the driver's side. I watched him through the windscreen, wondering how he could appear so calm. Shouldn't he be on the phone to the nearest hospital to have me committed? But he truly didn't look worried. Perhaps he was as insane as I was. He started the car and we slid out into the busy London streets before either of us spoke.

'Well,' he finally broke the ice, 'that was a bit of a surprise.'

'That's the understatement of the century.'

We drove on for a further ten minutes before he spoke again. 'I'm going round in circles here.'

'Welcome to my world,' I replied darkly.

'No, Rach, literally. I'm going round in circles; we've driven round this block half a dozen times. Where do you want to go now? Do you still want to find the other flat and the engineering company?'

I turned to look out the window, hoping to hide the despondency in my eyes.

'What's the point? We both know what we'll find when we get there. I can't be living in two places at once, holding down two jobs simultaneously. I guess it's time I stopped being so pig-headed and started listening to what everyone has been telling me all along.'

He took his eye off the road for a moment to glance at his watch.

'It not all that late yet. Would you like to head back to Great Bishopsford tonight?'

I sighed unhappily and considered the options for a moment. Our original plan had been to spend the night in London, believing that we would need that time to explore both the two locations in the city where I appeared to reside and the two separate places where I was believed to be employed. In my stupid optimism I had envisioned our quest ending with us spending the evening in my small flat, perhaps sharing a bottle of wine and a takeaway, piecing together at last the final mystery of my broken memories. Now there would be no such ending to the day, but the thought of going back and facing my father with this new revelation seemed too hard to bear.

'I don't want to go back tonight.' I spoke in a quiet determined voice. 'I need time to think this all through properly: time to get it all straight in my head, before I'm ready to deal with what will happen next.'

Jimmy gave an understanding nod of his head, and I was pleased he wasn't about to insist on driving me straight back to my father's.

'I think I'd be better off being alone tonight,' I ventured.

He kept his attention on the road as he negotiated our passage through a narrow gap, before he turned to me with a smile.

'Absolutely. Of course. Couldn't agree more. As long as you realise that my definition of "alone" incorporates me staying right by your side. I have absolutely no intention of leaving you by yourself tonight, Rachel.'

We compromised in the end.

Yes, we would stay in London and not attempt the journey back while there was still so much to think through.

And no, we wouldn't be spending the night in the only accommodation in London that seemed to belong to me. I didn't feel anywhere near ready to accept the Victorian apartment as my home yet, and I think the association the place held with Matt easily decided Jimmy against opting for that location. That really only left us with one option: to find a hotel.

It was already after six o'clock on a busy Friday night in central London, so we were lucky to secure accommodation in the first place we tried. We left the car in the hotel's car park, and Jimmy carried both our bags into the reception. I hung back while he went to enquire about availability, staring unseeingly into the hotel gift shop's window.

It was only when he returned to my side several

minutes later that I saw he had been successful in booking us in for the night. For the first time a rather obvious question that I had completely ignored up until then occurred to me: had he booked us into one room or two? The query was answered before I could give it voice, when he pressed one plastic entry card into my palm, retaining a second in his own.

'Adjacent rooms,' he informed, as I turned the plastic card over in my hand.

I smiled back at him but couldn't decide if my predominant feeling was one of relief or disappointment.

At Jimmy's suggestion, we agreed that we would find somewhere to eat; somewhere quiet where we would could talk without interruption. He said he'd seen a small Italian restaurant just around the corner when we approached the hotel, so we settled on that and he gave me fifteen minutes to freshen up before meeting him back out in the corridor.

I used my time alone to splash reviving cold water on my face and attempted to drag a comb through my wind-tangled hair. I hadn't brought much make-up with me, so I just did what little repairs I could, and then sat on the bed until the remainder of the fifteen minutes ticked away. The room, although pleasant enough, was hotel-bland, and there was precious little in it to distract my incoherent thoughts from running wildly away from me.

The restaurant was within easy walking distance, situated on the corner of a side road only a few minutes away from the hotel. As we walked past the large glass frontage to the front entrance, I peered inside and couldn't escape the feeling that the place looked strangely familiar. It really felt like I'd seen it somewhere before. The answer came to me as we waited for the waiter to confirm whether or not they could accommodate us.

'Lady and the Tramp!'

Jimmy looked down at the fresh pair of jeans he had changed into and his crisp white shirt.

'Tramp? That's charming, I must say. I didn't think I looked that bad!'

'Not you, you idiot. This place.' I nodded to indicate the room around us, and it was true, the cartoonist could have used the restaurant as the inspirational blueprint for his design. Here were the chequered cloths on the small intimately grouped tables, each one of which held a flickering red candle trickling its wax down onto an empty Chianti bottle. Lilting violin music, played discreetly through concealed speakers, served only to complete the picture.

Jimmy saw what I meant and grinned back, just as the waiter offered to take us to our table.

'If you think I'm sharing my spaghetti strand with you – forget it. And as for the last meatball . . . that's definitely mine. I don't love you *that* much!'

'Just as long as you don't start singing "Bella Notte", we'll be fine,' I retorted, remembering his complete inability to hold a note.

And even though we were both still smiling at the banter as we walked to our table, I couldn't help but replay his last casual comment in my mind.

But the frivolity between us was only a mask we had

taken up to disguise the real purpose of the evening, and once our order was placed, the reality of what we needed to discuss could be ignored no longer.

'Are things any clearer in your mind now? Now that you've had some time to think about them?'

I took a long sip of my wine before answering as honestly as I could. '"Clear" might not be the right word exactly. If you're asking if I suddenly remember the last five years the way you all say that they happened, then no, I don't. For me, the only reality is still the one I explained to you the other day. The only difference between then and now, is that now I know that none of it could actually have happened the way I thought it did.'

He reached across the table and took both of my hands in his own.

'That in itself is a huge step forward,' he encouraged. 'At least when you meet with the amnesia specialist, you'll be more receptive to hearing how you can get back your true memories.'

'I suppose so.' My voice still sounded heavy with a scepticism I couldn't disguise.

'When is your appointment, anyway?'

'The end of next week.' I wondered if he was going to volunteer to accompany me, then realised that Matt would be back in the country by then, and as my fiancé it would be his place to go with me, rather than Jimmy's. It surprised me that I wasn't at all sure that I wanted it to be Matt. If the choice was entirely mine, which man would I rather have at my side?

Jimmy released my hands as the waiter arrived with

our plates, and I felt strangely bereft at the loss of his grasp. But at least it crystallised the answer to my question.

'You know, many of the things you thought had happened to you are really beginning to make sense now, when you think it all through.'

'They are?'

'Absolutely.' Clearly he had been giving the matter some serious thought. Or perhaps his policeman's mind had been unable to stop itself from seeking out the rational and logical in a situation that seemed to defy either.

As we devoured the deliciously steaming pasta and crisp green salad, not to mention the bottle of surprisingly good house wine, Jimmy, time and time again, found evidence to rationalise and clarify the minutiae of my imagined reality.

'But what about the explicit details that I knew? For instance, how did I know the name and number of that woman in Human Resources at Andersons Engineering?'

'That's simple. You could have applied for a job there at some time in the past. Those details could all have been lodged somewhere in your head. I'm sure I remember hearing once that anything you know is never entirely forgotten.'

I supposed it was feasible, although it seemed highly unlikely. I tried a different track.

'OK then, why would I have conjured up such an awful idea of my father dying of cancer?'

He paused to consider for a moment, before a solution presented itself to him.

'Well you *did* make him stop smoking many, many years ago when we were kids. You were terrified of him dying after seeing some TV ad campaign, or something. So perhaps that fear had never really gone away, it was only buried somewhere in your mind.'

He had a point. I had always had an almost irrational hatred of people smoking.

'And,' Jimmy continued, clearly on a roll now with his theory, 'the idea of people having a second, completely fictitious identity would already have been planted in your head after interviewing Dr Whittaker for your article.'

I gave a humourless laugh. 'It *does* explain why his number was on my mobile.' It also explained why I thought I'd seen an article on that subject. It should have been familiar – after all, I'd written it.

'You see?' encouraged Jimmy. 'Once you start to break it down, detail by detail, almost everything there can be explained.'

I took a moment to absorb his words, and could so far find no hole in his theory. But one question still remained.

'But why was everything I created so terrible? So bleak and tragic? Why did my mind conjure up my father's illness – my own too, for that matter? Why was I alone and lonely? Why hadn't I imagined a second perfectly happy life for myself?'

I stopped, knowing I had omitted to include the largest of all the tragedies I had created in my imagined nightmare world.

'Why did I think that you had been killed?'

He was quiet for a very long time. So long in fact that I thought he wasn't going to reply at all.

'Perhaps your real life *was*, or rather *is*, your perfect reality. You were already living it. So you manufactured something that was the exact opposite. And as for me being . . .' he hesitated before saying the word, 'dead. Maybe that's because I haven't been a part of your life for quite some time.' His voice was full of sadness. 'We grew apart; we hadn't seen each other for a very long time. Perhaps it was more symbolic of the death of our friendship?'

Or perhaps it was more than that, I thought. Perhaps my subconscious mind had realised something that the rest of me had refused to acknowledge. That a life without Jimmy was like a living death and suffering through it was the worst sort of hell I could ever imagine.

The plates had been cleared, and the wine we had drunk had effectively taken the edge off the anxiety that had threaten to overwhelm me when we'd left the magazine offices. Jimmy too, seemed to have allowed the alcohol to relax his guard. I didn't know if he was aware of his hand absently playing with mine as we spoke. But the electric charge I felt as his fingers entwined and circled about my own was a real and physical thing. His hand and mine must have been linked together a thousand times before in our lifetime. Why was his touch only now able to ignite my flesh? Why was I suddenly overcome by these feelings; why now, when I belonged to another man?

'So tell me, Rachel. Now that we think we have sorted out the mystery, what explanation had *you* come up with to explain away your dual past?'

I plucked a breadstick from the container on the table and began to twist it, baton-style, between my fingers.

'Nothing really. Nothing that made much sense.'

The stick rolled and twirled; I kept my eyes upon it, knowing he would probe further.

'Come on then, tell me what you had figured out.'

I rolled the stick back and forth between my thumb and forefinger, so fast I could feel the generated heat.

'It's all a little silly, really.'

'I promise I won't laugh.'

The breadstick rolled faster.

'I thought that something had *happened* on the night of the accident. Something to do with time. I thought that reality had . . .' I hesitated; this was sounding really stupid now I was saying it out loud. 'That reality had somehow split in two.'

There was a snap, as the fragile breadstick broke at that precise moment into two pieces. I didn't dare look at Jimmy to see his reaction. He'd spent the whole of the evening patiently pointing out that I was not, in fact, insane, and I had a feeling that my own theory of what had occurred was going to get him doubting me all over again.

'Split in two?' I couldn't tell from his tone if he was incredulous or horrified at the idea.

'Yes, you know, as though my life, all our lives, had somehow . . . fractured . . . at the moment of the accident.'

'Fractured?'

'Uh-huh. And in one life we were all OK, and everything continued as it should have. But in the other . . . it was the exact opposite. I was maimed, and everything was ruined from that moment on. And you, well, you . . .'

'Died.'

That one word gave it away. I looked up and saw the agony he had been in to suppress his hilarity at my theory. I threw both the breadstick pieces at him as he burst out in laughter so hearty that half the other diners turned to look at us in amazement.

'Shut up,' I hissed, acutely embarrassed at the attention he was drawing upon us. 'It was only a theory.'

Eventually, when the tears had stopped rolling down his cheeks, he managed to control himself long enough to say, as though in dire warning: 'And *that's* what happens when you spend your entire youth reading nothing but Stephen King novels!'

We left the restaurant in good spirits, surprisingly so, considering the emotional traumas of the day. It had just started to snow as we began the short walk back to the hotel, and the soft white sprinkling falling around us, combined with the twinkling Christmas lights laced in the avenue of trees, made everything look somehow magical.

The pavements were already becoming icy and Jimmy took my arm without comment after the second near-slip, which threatened to leave me in a crumpled heap beside the road.

'It's these shoes,' I protested, as his arm reached out with lightning speed, catching and steadying me before I managed to totally embarrass myself. 'My *other* wardrobe was much more sensible.'

Jimmy chose not to remind me that my 'other wardrobe' was in fact, imaginary, but commented instead, 'It's not the shoes. It's you. You're a liability – you need constant looking after.'

'Well, isn't that what policemen are supposed to do? Isn't that your motto: "protect and serve"?'

Jimmy laughed. 'I think you'll find that's just the American police.'

'I stand corrected,' I murmured at the precise moment that I once again lost my footing and almost fell.

'Really? From what I can see, it looks like you can hardly stand at all!'

We were both still laughing when we entered the warm and brightly lit hotel foyer.

We parted company in the hallway outside our adjacent rooms, but before saying goodnight, I reached up to hug him tightly.

'Thank you for being with me today,' I whispered in his ear. 'I was wrong, I couldn't have done this by myself. I'm so glad you came with me.'

His response was the gentlest of smiles, then he bent down and kissed me softly upon the lips. I drew back slightly, a little surprised, but while there was immeasurable warmth in his eyes, there was no fire. It was a kiss which said *you're welcome; don't mention it; any time.* It was wholly appropriate and completely innocent. So why was it that, when we slid our respective pass cards into the locks and entered our rooms, I was left feeling as though I had wanted that kiss to say something else entirely?

I thought it would take me ages to fall asleep. I thought I would be replaying the day and all its outcomes over and over in my mind on an endless spool. But the combination of the wine we had drunk with dinner and sheer nervous exhaustion must have overtaken me, for I drifted off into oblivion within minutes of my head nestling onto the pillow. And for several hours I slept soundly, deeply and untroubled.

The dream began pleasantly enough. I was lying somewhere warm and relaxing, on a beach, I thought, and although I couldn't quite make out his words, I could hear my father talking nearby. In my dream I kept meaning to say something, to ask him something, but I was so overcome by a delicious lassitude that to stir, even an inch, from the warm enveloping sand was all too much of an effort.

And then it all abruptly changed, in that bizarre way that dreams do. The beach was gone, and so too was my father. I was back in time, back to the night of the car accident, only this time it wasn't Matt who had seen the approaching car heading towards us, it was me.

I knew what I had to do but when I opened my mouth

to shout out a warning, no words came out, no sound at all. Frantically I tried to get everyone's attention, but each one of them was deeply engrossed in conversation with someone else at the table, and despite my hysterical gesticulations, still no one but me was aware of the imminent danger. The waiters were laying our plates of food before us, refilling our wine glasses, while death hurtled towards us at around sixty miles an hour.

And it was then I saw that, incongruously, on the wall behind me was a large bright red emergency button. I slammed my hand down hard upon it and the responding beep of the alarm filled the air. Yet still no one moved. I struggled to get out of my chair but I was every bit as much imprisoned by the table as I had been on that actual night. Why couldn't they hear the alarm? To me, the continual piercing bleep was so loud it was almost a deafening klaxon, but my friends remained oblivious as they sat at the table and waited for death to join them.

As the approaching car hurtled towards us, I relived the moment that had haunted so many of my dreams over the past five years, and then, finally, I found my voice. I screamed, not once but several times, and only stopped when the sound of breaking glass exploded all around me.

Only it wasn't glass, it was the china base of the bedside lamp which my thrashing arm had knocked from the nightstand.

I sat up, hearing the thunderous pounding of my heart, waiting for it to slow down. Only the pounding wasn't slowing down at all; if anything it was getting louder, and as I swam to the surface of full consciousness I could hear my name being called out urgently from Jimmy as he all but took the door off its hinges with his frenzied hammering.

Still not entirely awake, I swung my legs off the bed and stood up, only to sit sharply back down again as the sole of my foot encountered one of the broken shards of china. I swore loudly at the shock and pain and clambered over the bed to reach the door before Jimmy succeeded in waking up every other occupant of the floor.

We would have been a peculiar sight to any onlooker who happened to be passing down the corridor at two o'clock in the morning. Fortunately there was no one around to see Jimmy, with his hair awry, standing semi-dressed on the threshold to my room. He had at least taken the time to pull on a pair of jeans, but I noticed that, like me, he too was barefooted.

He strode purposely into my room.

'Are you all right? I heard you screaming.' His eyes raked the room, looking for the cause of my terrified cries, and there was no disguising the alarm in his tone, which struck me as odd, for aren't policeman trained to stay cool in an emergency?

'Nightmare,' I said succinctly, hopping over to the room's only armchair to avoid standing on my damaged foot.

His sigh of relief seemed to empty his body of the tension that had obviously been coursing through it.

'Oh God, is that all? I thought you were being

murdered in here. And then when I heard that crashing sound . . .'

'I had a little argument with the bedside lamp.'

It was then that he noticed the way I was cradling my left foot in my hand, while a slow but persistent trickle of blood oozed from the deep cut on the sole.

'Rachel you're hurt! What happened?'

Not for the first time I wondered if he was really in the right line of work. His powers of deduction seemed flawed, to say the least.

'I stood on one of the broken bits of lamp in my hurry to get to the door before you broke it down.'

I knew that I must have sounded a little ungrateful but the nightmare still had me in its thrall and my foot was actually very sore. Instantly he was by my chair, gently prising my hands away from my injured foot.

'Here, let me take a look.'

Gingerly, I laid my left foot in his outstretched hand, already preparing to wince at his touch, but he was infinitely gentle as he supported my heel in his palm, examining the wound which was still bleeding quite profusely.

'Let's get this cleaned up,' he announced getting to his feet. 'I don't think there is anything in the cut, but we need better light than in here to be sure.'

Before I realised his intention, he had bent and scooped me into his arms and was carrying me towards the bathroom.

'I can walk,' I protested. 'Or hop.'

He ignored my comments and kicked the bathroom door ajar with his foot and flicked on the light. As he looked around for somewhere to deposit me, I was acutely aware of the unfamiliar, although not unpleasant, sensation of being held against his naked chest. Less agreeable was the realisation that my nightdress was incredibly short and, as a result of my nightmare, was clinging revealingly to my sweat-dampened body. I tried to pull down on the hem but only succeeded in displaying even more of my cleavage by doing so. Fortunately, Jimmy's attention was all on my foot.

He lowered me onto the edge of the bath and used the shower attachment to slowly cascade water over my foot and ankle. It stung a little at first, but I didn't dare fidget too much, trying as I was to maintain what little modesty I had left with one leg lifted over the edge of the tub. Never before had I felt in such desperate need of underwear.

Under the soothing rivulets of water and the fluorescent bathroom lighting, Jimmy took careful stock of the wound and when he had determined that it was clean of foreign objects, he pressed firmly down on the cut to staunch the flow of blood. The bathroom was tiny, no doubt designed for single occupancy only, so we were by necessity very close together. So close that I could hear when his breathing, instead of slowing down now the initial panic was over, began to increase in pace. I knew then that it wasn't just me who was aware of the intimacy of the moment. With his thumb still covering the cut, his fingers were moving in slow almost imperceptible circles upon my ankle. I didn't know if he realised what he was doing, whether the caress was intentional or not, but his actions weren't helping my heart to resume its normal rhythm.

Something new was happening here, and the very air in the small enclosed room seemed to pulsate with a heady and unfathomable emotion. Jimmy looked up and there was something in his eyes I had never seen before; he would have recognised it though, for it was reflected back at him on my own face. The moment seemed endless and we remained locked within its intensity, neither daring to speak or move for fear of breaking the fragile cocoon around us.

'Jimmy,' I breathed uncertainly, reaching out a hand to touch his chest. My fingertips rested there only a moment, just long enough to feel the strong pulse of his heartbeat reverberating against them and then, with a determined shake of his head, as though denying what was happening, he got roughly to his feet. He took several moments longer than necessary to return the shower to its stand and shut off the water, but when he turned to look at me once more there was nothing in his face to betray his emotions. The fragile interlude between us might never have been.

'I think it's stopped bleeding now but you should probably put a plaster on it, if you have one.'

'Uh-huh.' Switching from intimacy to practicality in a matter of seconds had done nothing to improve my ability to articulate.

He left me then to dry my foot and dress the wound, while he returned to the bedroom and busied himself methodically clearing the carpet of broken china.

I watched him in silence from the bathroom doorway, fascinated by the display of his muscled arms and back as he bent to his task. I knew then that my feelings for him had strayed off the path of friendship, and I wanted so badly to reach out to him that it felt like a physical ache. But every bit as clearly, I could see that Jimmy did not reciprocate those feelings. Whatever territory we had almost ventured into a few minutes ago, was clearly somewhere Jimmy didn't want to go. If I pushed it, I could lose him for ever and I couldn't cope with that again.

'There,' he said, straightening to his feet. 'I think I've got it all, just watch where you walk.'

'Thank you.' My voice was a little subdued but I don't know if he noticed. What he did notice, however, was my sudden involuntary shiver in the coolness of the bedroom. He came over and put an arm around my shoulders.

'God, Rachel, you're freezing. Have you got a dressing gown or something?'

I shook my head. I'd only packed the bare essentials and I certainly hadn't been expecting company in the middle of the night.

'Well let's get you back into bed before you catch a cold.'

He bent as though to carry me again but I ducked from his grip and hobbled the short distance over to the bed. He gave a small laugh at what he thought was my stubbornness, and I was happy to let him believe it was that. Far better to have him think I was being pig-headed than for him to realise the effect his proximity was suddenly having on me.

I scrambled under the blankets, the coverage they provided being even more welcome than their warmth. To my surprise Jimmy didn't appear to be in any hurry to return to his own room and settled himself down to sit on top of the covers beside me on the bed.

'So what was this nightmare about then, the one that made you decide to trash the room like a rock star?'

I gave a small smile. 'Oh, nothing really.'

'It didn't sound like nothing to me. You really scared me, you know.'

I looked into his face and knew he was telling the truth.

'Sorry,' I apologised, not really knowing if I was saying it for worrying him; for what happened in the bathroom; or for any and all future transgressions. 'The dream was the usual one. Usual for me, that is. I was dreaming about the night of the car accident.'

'Does that happen a lot?'

I nodded sadly.

'Ever since the accident?'

'Ever since you died,' I corrected.

We were both silent then, temporarily lost for words at the improbability of my statement.

'But why are you still dreaming it now?' Jimmy asked suddenly, turning on his side, the better to see my face. 'Why now, when you know it didn't really happen like that?'

I shook my head miserably. 'I don't know.'

But then a thought occurred to me, a really obvious one. For the thing I didn't know, what I was *really* in the dark about, was what had *actually* happened on that fateful night. Because that was when reality had split into two different realms for me. Perhaps when I understood what had actually transpired, the imaginary second life would lose all substance and disappear like the mirage everyone said that it was.

'Tell me everything. Tell me what you remember about that night, from the moment we sat down at that table.'

Jimmy read the need to know in my voice and, as though to protect me from the truth, should it turn out to be painful, he put an arm around my shoulders before beginning.

His story was just as I remembered it being. Even the air of camaraderie and friendship came to life again at his recollections. I didn't interrupt at all until he mentioned the penny he had given me.

'I kept that!' I cried out involuntarily, before correcting myself. 'Or rather, in my other life I did. I kept it in my jewellery box. I couldn't throw it away, it seemed like my last link with you.'

He smiled, but said nothing. And then another thought occurred to me.

'And we'd made arrangements for the following day. I remember that now. You'd asked me to go round the next day to see you and you'd sounded really mysterious about it. I wondered about that for years. What had you wanted to talk about?'

Was it the light, or had his cheeks really deepened in colour at my question?

'Oh I don't know. I can't remember after all this time.'

I let it go without comment, not wanting to divert him from his tale. But I couldn't help wonder why he had just lied to me.

The story continued true to my memories until we reached the point when we had all begun the frantic dash from the table to escape the oncoming car.

'. . . and we all managed to get clear of the window before the guy drove into it.'

'But I was stuck. I couldn't get free, a chair was blocking me in. Didn't it happen that way?'

He was silent for a moment, seeming to almost weigh up what to tell me.

'It all happened so quickly, it's hard to say. Perhaps you *were* the last to get clear.'

There was something he was glossing over here and I wasn't about to let it rest.

'No. I wasn't the last. My dad said that you got hurt, so obviously you were still near the window when the car crashed through. What happened?'

I realised then what he was reluctant to tell me.

'It *is* as I remember it, isn't it? You came back for me. You pulled me clear.'

He looked strangely embarrassed to admit it.

'We all kind of helped each other get away.'

I shook my head. I could still see it so clearly: everyone had moved back, everyone had been safe, everyone but me. But one of them had come back to rescue me.

'You saved my life.'

For a moment it looked like he was going to continue to deny it, but then he heard the certainty in my voice and went instead for humour.

'I couldn't let you die and take my lucky penny with you.'

But I wasn't going to let him divert me.

'You saved my life.'

His answer this time lost all flippancy, and with desperate honesty he replied, 'How could I do anything else?'

I didn't know what to say. There are no words to cover that sort of gratitude; to repay that kind of debt.

'And you got hurt.'

I raised my hand and lifted the hair away from his forehead, revealing a small white jagged scar that ran down from his hairline to the level of his eye.

'It's so like mine,' I breathed in wonder. 'The one I thought I had,' I corrected. 'Except mine was deeper, longer.' I let my finger trace the line of his scar. 'Mine went down here,' my finger ran over his cheek, catching slightly on the roughness of bristle, 'and then went to here.' My finger continued to etch the blueprint of the remembered scar, but instead of stilling where my disfigurement had ended, I continued to trace a pathway to his mouth, coming to rest upon his slightly parted lips.

Electricity crackled between us. The moment in the bathroom suddenly paled into insignificance compared to the potently charged atmosphere.

Gently, oh so gently, he drew the tips of my fingers in between his parted lips, flicking against the sensitive pads with his tongue. My entire body shuddered with a frisson of excitement.

And then I was in his arms. I truly cannot say who made the first move, it could have been either of us. All I knew was the force of the passion in his kiss and the feel of his long, hard body pressed against mine.

Time became suspended as our kisses deepened; the heat of our passion welding my body to his with an intensity that astounded me. His hand trembled slightly as he slid the nightgown from my shoulders, but he had no need to be hesitant. I wanted this to happen just as much as he did, maybe even more. And in a sobering revelation of clarity, I finally acknowledged that I had been waiting for and wanting this very moment for years but had been too blind to see it.

As his lips and hands travelled over my exposed flesh I heard a low throaty murmur of pleasure escape me. I couldn't believe how wantonly and readily I was responding to his touch. It was like nothing I had ever experienced before.

The bed covers were kicked aside and I felt no embarrassment to be naked in front of him. Given our long friendship I would have expected this to feel wrong, maybe even vaguely incestuous, but nothing before had ever felt so right. Our ragged breathing tore into the silence of the room and the trembling that coursed through Jimmy's body as he covered mine shook me with its intensity.

I don't remember when he first began to pull back. One minute we were fused together, our mouths and hands exploring and delighting and then, all at once, it was just me. The hands that held my shoulders, arching me closer to him were now gently, but insistently, pushing me away.

Embarrassingly it took me several moments to realise what was occurring. My fumbling fingers were still struggling with the buckle of his jeans when his hand came down to encircle my wrist and move it away. The red mist of passion began to lift enough for me to see his face. The fire was almost gone and had been replaced by a darkly determined, steely strength. Stupidly I refused to acknowledge what he doing and reached up to kiss him once again, opening my lips against his, sure I could elicit his response and reignite the flame.

But it was gone. Doused in sanity, where surely no sanity should belong. I didn't care what his reasons were in stopping, I only knew I didn't want to.

'Oh God, don't stop, please don't stop,' I begged, all pride abandoned. I kept my eyes riveted to his and actually caught the moment when the last ember of desire was extinguished in their blue depths.

He lifted himself off me in a quick and decisive move, half turning away to sit upon the edge of the bed.

'I have to, Rachel. Don't you see that?'

Clearly I did not see, and still refusing to acknowledge his withdrawal I shamelessly reached out to try to pull him back to me, but he was like a rock: cold, hard and totally immovable.

Without turning to look at me he picked up my discarded nightdress and tossed it back in my direction.

'Cover yourself up.'

And those three words finally sliced through my desire, carving into my very core. I grasped the cotton garment and quickly struggled into it, feeling humiliated and strangely dirty at the same time. I had thrown myself at him, there was no other way to describe it; I had virtually begged him to take me and he had rejected me. How much clearer did he have to make it? Oh sure, he had responded at first, but I realised now that it had just been a natural male response to a woman so obviously trying to seduce him. A physical knee-jerk reaction, nothing more.

But even physical desire hadn't been sufficient to allow him to follow through. It was a cold and undeniable fact: Jimmy had never wanted me in that way; neither in the past nor now, and I had just made the biggest idiot of myself by launching myself at him like some third-rate seductress in a tacky novel.

'I think you should leave now,' I said in a quiet voice that trembled enough for me to realise that tears were only moments away. The speed with which he complied told me the truth: he couldn't get out of there fast enough. He paused just once at the door, turning to give me a long hard look.

'I'm so sorry, Rachel, please forgive me.' His voice sounded truly tortured, but before I could even think of a response he had opened the door and left.

Sorry? *He* was sorry? What in hell's name did he have

to be sorry about? I was the one who should have apologised. I was the one who was apparently incapable of controlling her emotions and had to be told that what she was doing was completely out of order.

What was Jimmy guilty of? Nothing, except of not wanting me. And I could hardly blame him for that; for at that moment I felt like the most loathsome and disgusting creature that had ever walked the face of the earth.

Another night of crying myself to sleep. It was almost becoming a habit. If Jimmy noticed my red-rimmed eyes the following morning, he was too polite to comment on them. I had to admit that he didn't look so great himself when we met in the corridor at the time that we'd arranged the night before. Of course, that had been during the civilised portion of the evening; before the madness had overtaken me in the middle of the night, when I had acted in such a way that had probably killed our friendship for ever.

On waking I had even harboured the pathetic hope that I had dreamt the entire episode, that none of it had really happened and that nothing had been irretrievably broken or damaged. But when I'd turned my head I could see the remains of the broken lamp and knew it was as irrevocably damaged as my relationship with Jimmy.

When I saw him waiting for me in the corridor I hesitated at the threshold of my room. I had no idea what to say. But fortunately it appeared that neither did he.

'Do you want to stop for breakfast or just head back?' were his opening words.

'I'd just like to go back,' I answered quickly.

Some response flickered in his eyes but he just nodded, as though this was what he had been expecting. He lifted the bag from my fingers and turned in the direction of the lifts.

'Let's go then.'

There may have been more uncomfortable car journeys in my life, but that one was right up there with the worst of them. There was a tension that couldn't be ignored. It sat between us like a third passenger all the way from London to Great Bishopsford. In the end we both abandoned conversation, preferring instead to pretend that the silence we were travelling in was companionable, rather than strained and awkward. But we were just fooling ourselves. For the first time in . . . well, actually in for ever . . . I couldn't speak freely or easily with Jimmy. The strain of not talking about the topic we both couldn't avoid thinking about was monumental. And yet, as mile followed mile, neither of us dared to voice the subject and when finally we passed the sign that announced we were now in our home town there was, thankfully, no time left.

As we manoeuvred through the familiar side streets and turnings, I was itching to get out of the car, desperately hoping that by exiting the vehicle I could somehow leave behind the debris of last night. And then, just when

I thought that the day couldn't possibly get any worse, it just did.

We rounded the last bend and there, parked directly in front of my house, was a low sleek car.

'Terrific,' muttered Jimmy, pulling in to the kerb to park behind it.

I looked up in confusion at the unfamiliar vehicle and then my eye fell upon the registration plate: MR 10. Matt's car.

Jimmy switched off the engine and turned to look at me, properly at me, for the first time since last night.

'Rachel, I wanted to say . . . to explain . . .'

I shook my head. 'Please, don't say anything, it's not necessary.'

He reached out and took my hand, and part of me wanted to jerk back from his touch and an even greater part wanted to hold him against me for ever. He saw my hand judder under his and misinterpreted the reaction.

'I know you must hate me right now,' he continued, 'but please give me a chance to—'

I never heard what he wanted the chance to do or say, for at that moment the passenger door was swung widely open by a rather impatient-looking Matt.

He saw my hand in Jimmy's, even though I had yanked it away as speedily as if it were caught in a flame. Forestalling any comment, I quickly scrambled out of the car.

'Matt, what are you doing here? I thought you were in Germany for another three days?'

Matt drew me into an enveloping embrace, which I

think was more for Jimmy's benefit than mine. By the time I was released, Jimmy had also climbed out of the car.

'I wound things up really quickly; thought you might need me more back here. But I see you managed to make . . . alternative arrangements.'

God, here it was again. That old revisited teenage rivalry that had so fascinated me in the hospital, only now it was just petty and irritating.

'Jimmy very kindly gave up his day off to take me into London. I had a lot of things I needed to sort out and he offered to take me.'

Matt raised his gaze to meet Jimmy's over the roof of the car that stood between them.

'And his night, of course. He gave up his night too.'

I could see where this was going and I didn't like it one little bit. So far, Jimmy hadn't risen to the bait, but I could feel the testosterone-infused tension eddying around me like a miniature tornado.

'It was too late to come back last night, so we found a hotel and stayed in town. Dad knew what our plans were.'

Matt nodded, and I wondered what his reaction had been when he had arrived here and learnt from my father that Jimmy and I had been away together overnight.

'We were lucky to find somewhere that had two rooms available at such short notice,' I supplied, clumsily attempting to let Matt know that everything had been above board. I was babbling, I could hear that even to my own ears. And I was also annoyed at my compulsion to explain our movements, knowing all the time that as my fiancé, Matt was perfectly entitled to ask where I had been. I was also embarrassed at the need to lie.

'It *was* all perfectly respectable,' I assured Matt, moving away from Jimmy's car and turning to walk up the path.

'I'm sure it was,' replied Matt, and while his words implied he had never doubted it for a minute, the look he gave Jimmy said something different entirely. 'You not coming in?' he asked, as Jimmy walked towards him, passing over my small overnight bag. I stopped then, halfway to door; I had assumed they were both following me inside.

'No, not this time. I've got some things I have to do. And I'm sure you want to spend some time alone with Rachel. She has a lot to tell you.'

I felt the betraying colour begin to warm my cheeks. Don't blush, don't blush, oh please, God, don't let me blush.

Matt looked from Jimmy to me, the suspicion on his face only just managing to masquerade as curiosity.

'About the magazine,' Jimmy provided, already half back into the car. 'G'bye, Rachel.'

I wanted to run to him then, to launch into his arms and beg him not to go. Ridiculous. Completely and utterly ridiculous. And of course I did nothing of the sort, my feet remaining rooted to the path as though fixed there in cement. But I didn't like the permanent tone of Jimmy's goodbye: I didn't like it at all.

As Matt walked past the open driver's door to join me on the path, Jimmy's hand reached out to stall him.

His voice was low, and he probably never intended me to hear what he had to say, but the street was suddenly quiet and I clearly heard his low entreaty.

'Take good care of her, Matt. She's had quite a tough twenty-four hours.'

To say my father looked relieved to see me walk through the door was an understatement. And although I knew that a large part of that was due to his natural instinct to worry about me, I realised too that an even greater part was that the burden of entertaining a less-than-good-humoured Matt could now be handed over to me. I correctly guessed it had been a pretty tough several hours since his arrival while they awaited our return.

'He's been pacing up and down the living room like a caged lion,' whispered Dad as we stood together in the welcoming kitchen, making a fresh round of teas and some toast. I wasn't really hungry but it had been a welcome excuse to escape to the kitchen and find out what exactly had happened when Matt had turned up and found us gone.

'Sorry you had to deal with that. I don't know what he's so wound up about.'

My dad stopped placing mugs and spoons on the tray and turned to give me a long appraising look. No words, just a look.

'What?' I asked, playing dumb. 'What?'

My attempt at nonchalance was ruined by the warm flush that suffused my cheeks. And the more my dad continued to stare at me in that knowing parental fashion, the hotter they grew. I don't know what he knew exactly, or guessed, but I don't think he was that far off the mark.

'Just be careful, Rachel, or someone will get hurt.' And then he softened the entreaty by wrapping his arm around me and pulling me tight to his side. 'And I don't want it to be you.'

By the time the tea and toast were consumed, a little good humour seemed to have been restored and naturally enough they both wanted to hear about everything that had happened in London. It took quite a while to regale the entire account of the last twenty-four hours, obviously omitting all that had occurred the previous evening from my narrative. I was pretty certain no one in the room wanted to hear that sorry tale – especially me.

There was a long pause when I eventually finished, while they both absorbed what I had told them.

'So do you remember everything now?' pressed Matt hopefully.

'No, not really. Well, not at all, if I'm being totally honest. But at least now I guess I know what *hasn't* happened.'

The disappointment on Matt's face was obvious, and I couldn't help but think that some of it was aimed at me personally, rather than the situation. It was almost as if he suspected that I just wasn't trying hard enough to remember: and that if I put a little more effort into it, everything would come flooding back.

'Never mind, love,' supplied Dad, reaching over to squeeze my hand reassuringly. 'It's still early days yet. At least now you have somewhere positive to start from when you meet the amnesia guy this week.'

'Yeah, that's what Jimmy said.'

Matt's face stiffened in irritation at the name, but fortunately he let the comment pass unchallenged.

'And in the meantime, I've sorted out anything I could find around here from the last five years that could help you remember.'

He sounded so delighted that it was hard to suppress a groan when several hefty-looking albums and a box of selected memorabilia were produced from the side of the settee and laid onto the coffee table before me.

'Now, I've just got to go into town for a while, so you two can browse through these. I'm sure Matt will be able to answer any questions you have – probably far better than me. I don't suppose you tell me the half of what's really going on in your life!'

Considering recent events, that was probably just as well.

I was several pages into the first album when the front door clicked shut at my father's departure. Moving closer to my side on the settee, Matt gently removed the album from my hands and slid his arms about me, drawing me towards him.

'Let's leave the old photos for now, huh? I think I can find a much better way of helping you to remember.'

And before I could say anything to stop him, or even consider if I wanted to stop him at all, his mouth was on mine, powerfully and persuasively commanding me to respond. And after a moment of immobility, I did. Perhaps this was the very thing I needed to jolt my memory back. Maybe it wasn't just in fairy tales that the prince could kiss the sleeping princess back to life. And Matt, with his sexy good looks and masterful self-confidence, was accomplished enough to elicit a response from a shop mannequin – let alone the woman who'd been on the receiving end of those kisses for the past seven years.

And as his lips moved in sync with mine and his hands travelled possessively up and down my back, suddenly I *did* remember. I remembered how deeply I had fallen in love with him as a teenager; how much he had meant to me back then. I remembered him, as women do the world over, in the way they never forget their first love. But I also remembered how I'd brutally severed him from my life when Jimmy died, cutting away all vestiges of memory of our relationship. And what I remembered most of all, was that while ending things with Matt had caused me pain, it had been insignificant weighed up against the incomparable agony of my grief. And if it *did* transpire that those events had only ever existed in my imagination – and the evidence for that was now pretty compelling – well, you didn't need a degree in psychology to work out the message my subconscious had been trying to get across.

I didn't push him away from me, but my lack of response eventually filtered through.

'Rachel?' he murmured into my ear, pausing to nip

gently upon my neck, making me shiver in spite of myself. He drew back to survey my face, his own a clear portrait of passion and desire.

'Too much for now? Do you want me to stop?'

I nodded silently, and thankfully he understood. I could see the effort it took him to regain his composure and I felt horribly guilty at having led him on, knowing all the while that this was probably something I shouldn't be doing. I wondered if this was exactly how Jimmy had felt the night before. The thread that wound the tapestry of our lives together suddenly seemed heavily laced in irony.

'Maybe we could just look through the stuff Dad left out?' I suggested lamely.

'If that's what you want,' he agreed, but vowed softly, 'Don't think I'm giving up on you that easily.'

I'm certain he meant it as a pledge of things to come, so why couldn't I shake the feeling his words sounded more like a threat than a promise?

Three albums and several hours later I was no closer to remembering anything and I was totally bored with looking at pictures of me with people I never knew, in places I had never been. Although Matt could supply a large proportion of the missing data, a whole host of photographs taken during my university days remained a mystery.

'Looks like I had a good time,' I proclaimed, plucking a photograph from the pile, which captured me with my arms flung around the shoulders of several friends, beer bottles in hand, all smiling broadly, and somewhat drunkenly, at the camera.

'Uni was good,' Matt proclaimed, then breached my defences by leaning over and planting a kiss upon my lips. 'But now is better.'

You couldn't help but admire the man's unshakeable confidence. Still, I didn't want things to progress any further down that road, so I quickly stumbled down a conversational side-track.

'And we managed to survive the long-distance relationship thing?'

Was there something that flashed quickly through his eyes, some small hesitation?

'Well, we're still together, so we must have done something right.'

There *was* something there in his voice that didn't sound quite so sure, and this was confirmed when he tried to divert me with a little side-tracking of his own.

'And now we are engaged,' he declared, undeniable satisfaction in his voice.

'And now we are engaged,' I echoed, my own voice full of another emotion entirely.

'Are you sure you don't want to join us, Tony? You're more than welcome.'

The words were polite enough, and I wondered if my dad could hear that the sentiment wasn't entirely heartfelt. I saw the twinkle in my father's eye and knew he understood perfectly.

'No, no, you two run along and enjoy yourselves. You don't want me tagging along and ruining your dinner. And besides, I have to make up the spare room for Matt.'

Touché, Dad, excellently done.

Matt said nothing until we were safely inside the leather cocoon of his car.

'So I'm to be banished to the spare room again, am I?'

I tried not to smile but I could feel my quivering lips beginning to betray me.

'I'm sure he thinks we're still teenagers,' he complained, softly gunning the engine with unnecessary vigour before pulling away from the kerb. 'He's still got that old "not under my roof" thing going on. What does he think we get up to in London?'

As I actually didn't *know* what we got up to in London, I thought it best not to respond.

'Anyway,' said Matt, turning to me with an irreverent wink and a grin, 'I still remember which of the floorboards in the hall creak, so just remember to leave your door unlatched.'

I laughed nervously, not sure if he was joking, but made a mental note to secure my door when we got back.

We had a surprisingly good time that evening, all things considered. Once away from the house and my father's watchful eye, Matt seemed more himself, or the self I remembered from years gone by. He was attentive and charming, and it was impossible to ignore the envious glances directed towards me from several females in the pub-restaurant where we had chosen to eat.

'That's something I had happily forgotten,' I informed

him, after yet another very obvious *what-does-he-see-in-her* appraisal.

Matt must have seen the look the woman had given me but he dismissed it with a shrug.

'Don't let it worry you.'

'It doesn't worry me, it's just annoying, that's all. And rude.'

He got to his feet then. 'I'm just going to see where they've got to with the bill.' But before leaving he dropped a light kiss on my head. 'Just remember, I've only got eyes for you.'

Less than two minutes later, something happened to make me wonder just how true that statement actually was.

I could still see him crossing the restaurant in the direction of the bar when a small humming sound erupted from the edge of the table. Matt's mobile phone lay beside our empty plates, its slim shape vibrating persistently against the crockery to indicate an incoming call. I glanced up to summon him back but some instinct made me check the phone first. On the small square screen the caller's identity was displayed in bold green neon like a billboard. I could read it quite clearly upside down, but nevertheless swivelled the phone with my index finger until it faced me the right way up. Cathy. Five harmless letters, but something about them rang a warning bell that had nothing to do with the incoming call.

What was Cathy doing calling Matt? The phone was still ringing with urgent insistence. Should I answer it? Undecided, I allowed my hand to creep towards the small device, but some instinct stayed me from taking the call. Several diners from nearby tables had turned around at the ringing, the sound clearly interrupting their evening. I met their gazes with an apologetic smile but still didn't answer the phone. Eventually it stopped.

A minute or two later Matt returned, carrying my coat. Now was the time to tell him about the missed call. To ask why Cathy, who he claimed he hadn't seen in years until the night of my accident, was phoning him on his mobile phone, the number of which I clearly recalled him saying was only given out to his closest friends and family.

It rang again on the way home. We were stationary at traffic lights and he smoothly extracted the phone from his pocket to check the display. An unreadable expression crossed his features as his fingers moved rapidly to disconnect the call without answering it. Intuition told me it was Cathy again, even before I heard the lie in his voice.

'Who was that?'

'Just someone from work. It can wait until tomorrow.'

The lights were still on downstairs when we returned, so Matt took advantage of our last moments of privacy on the doorstep as I hunted in my bag for my key.

'I had a very nice time tonight, Miss Wiltshire.'

I tried to smile but all I could think about was the strange look that had been on his face when the phone had rung in the car.

'Do you think your dad will come after me with a shotgun if I try for a goodnight kiss on the doorstep?'

And without waiting for my reply, he pulled me against

him firmly and gave the sort of kiss that in other circumstances might have left me weak at the knees. His eyes were dark with desire when we drew apart and he didn't appear to have noticed that my mind had been on other things during the embrace.

I reached into my bag and successfully extracted the key. Walking close behind me as we entered the hall to greet my father, Matt whispered mischievously in my ear. 'Don't forget what I said earlier about your bedroom door.'

I hadn't realised the huge knot of tension I had been holding in check all day, until I was finally alone in my room. I kicked off my shoes and sank down heavily upon the old single bed. Then, alone for the first time, I could feel the edges of the seal begin to weaken, and knew the thoughts and feelings I had tried to bury so deeply in the vault of my mind now refused to be silenced. But there was so much to deal with; so many conflicting emotions, that I literally felt overwhelmed by the deluge. Having to launch straight from the pain and humiliation of Jimmy's rejection, to fending off Matt, who was understandably bewildered at his fiancée's tepid response, was too much for a mind to cope with. Let alone a mind, it had to be said, that still believed it owned a totally different past. It was little wonder I couldn't cope with the present.

To quieten my chaotic thoughts, as though the source of all my problems was merely due to inactivity, I began to frenziedly straighten and tidy my room and belongings, finally bending to pick up the case I had taken to London the night before. I unzipped the holdall and allowed the contents to fall in an untidy heap upon the bed covers.

It took only moments to put away the smaller items, which left only the cotton nightdress I had worn at the hotel. I reached out to the garment, fully intending to wear it again that night, but the moment I touched the soft fabric, a violent and vivid snapshot filled my vision. I could no longer see my own bedroom and was suddenly transported back to the hotel. I could feel the heat of Jimmy's lips on mine, feel them as strongly as if he were there beside me. I had never believed in psychometry – didn't believe in anything psychic really – but the sensation of Jimmy removing the nightdress slowly from my body was replayed in excruciatingly exquisite detail. Convulsively my fingers held tightly onto the folds of cotton, reliving the moment when I had finally opened my heart to a truth I had denied for so long, and then the moment too that followed, when all hope was taken away.

I gave an angry cry and threw the nightdress away from me across the bed. It lay in a crumpled heap, an innocuous scrap of material, but I could almost see the heat of Jimmy's fingerprints burned into the fabric. To me the garment would be for ever branded and I knew I could not wear it this night, not with my fiancé sleeping fifteen feet away down the corridor. In fact, I didn't think I'd ever be able to wear it again.

I dreamt vividly again that night, my subconscious still in as much turmoil as my waking mind. In my dream I was bizarrely asleep – not here in my own bedroom, but somewhere strange I didn't recognise. But I guessed I must live there, because my dad was there too, close enough for me to hear his voice, but not so near that I could make out the words. And in my dream I knew I had an important appointment to keep. The nature of the assignation wasn't clear – it might have been with the amnesia specialist, or it could have been something else altogether – all I knew was that my dream was filled with a dire foreboding that I would oversleep and miss the very important meeting.

I had had similar dreams before, when something important was looming, like examinations, or a holiday, and while this dream was similar to those in the past, it felt altogether far more urgent and imperative that I did not oversleep. In my dream I knew there would be catastrophic consequences in missing the appointment; that this was not something that could merely be rescheduled for another date. It was crucial that I didn't oversleep, and as if to further endorse this, I could hear my father whispering to my dreaming self.

'Time to wake up, Rachel, it's time to wake up now.'

I wanted to answer him, to let him know I *was* awake, but sleep held me down in its grip and I couldn't shake off the manacles of slumber to reply. The impotence of not waking up and getting to the appointment on time was beginning to frighten me now, and I could feel my heart start to quicken in frustration.

The beeping began slowly, filtering into the dream like small sharp stabs from a needle. It pierced through the cloak of sleep, its sharp insistent tone commanding that it not be ignored. What *was* that sound? In my dream I could hear it really clearly, and as the tentacles of sleep began to weaken their hold, I realised it was an alarm. As I blinked myself awake I could still hear the beeping. Dazed, I reached out my hand to the bedside table. It must be an alarm clock, which I had inadvertently set before going to sleep. But my groping hand found no such clock beside the bed.

I lifted my head from the pillows. The fog of sleep lifted a little more and I realised the beeping was getting fainter and fainter and a moment later was gone. I blinked stupidly in the darkness, totally confused by the dream, and then, as though carried on a small eddy of breeze, I caught the familiar odour of my father's favourite after-shave. That brought me more awake than even the imaginary alarm clock had done. This wasn't the first time I had detected this fragrance in the night, and as my father was nowhere to be seen it clearly proved that he hadn't been checking up on me when this had previously occurred. But what did it mean? Was it even possible to hallucinate a smell?

My jumbled thoughts were suddenly interrupted by a small noise coming from the direction of the corridor. I froze, straining my ears to catch the sound. After a moment I heard it again: the faint creak of old floorboards giving up the presence of an intruder. My first frantic thought was 'burglar'. And I can only blame the fact I was still half asleep on the crazy illogicality that made this my initial conclusion.

Another creak, one further footstep on the betraying beams and then, in the filtered moonlight coming through the flimsy curtains, I saw the handle on my door begin to depress slowly. When the small arc had been completed, I heard the door groan softly as weight was gently applied to open it. The door resisted. The handle was released and depressed again, and this time enough force was applied to make the door grind against its hinges in protest. Still the lock held.

I waited, my breath stilling in my lungs. Scared to stir upon the mattress in case my movements could be heard from the hallway, I bit my lip nervously, wondering how many more times he would try and how sturdy the lock was. It was crazy to feel it might actually have been preferable if it really *was* a thief invading the house, instead of my fiancé.

'Rachel?' Matt's voice was a low whisper, spoken close to the hinge of the door. 'Rachel, are you awake? Rachel?'

Time seemed to be suspended for ever. I couldn't hold my breath for much longer, and if he didn't abandon his quest soon, he would surely hear the loud expulsion when I either drew breath or passed out from lack of oxygen. Fortunately, neither of those events occurred, for after another anxious minute I heard the retreat of his footsteps down the hallway back to the guest room.

He was dressed and seated at the kitchen table when I

went down the following morning. An empty coffee cup and an open newspaper were both before him.

'Good morning,' I greeted him lightly, in what I hoped was the appropriate tone for a woman who had locked her fiancé out of her room the night before. For good measure, I bent to place a grazing kiss upon his cheek.

'Sleep well?' he enquired politely. My back was to him then, as I poured a large cup of coffee into a mug. I was glad he couldn't see my face as I replied.

'Yes. Really, really well, in fact. I went out like a light; dead to the world the minute my head touched the pillow.'

Stop, Rachel, a little voice inside me screamed; that was way too much overemphasis to sound believable.

Apparently he thought so too. 'So you didn't hear me at your door in the night?'

I didn't meet his eyes, and concentrated on stirring my cup so vigorously I was in danger of removing the ceramic.

'No. Why, was there something wrong?'

He was silent for so long, he forced me to look up. 'I came to be with you.'

'Oh.' And when he seemed to want more from me than that, I added, 'I thought you were only joking when you said that.'

Clearly not the right response. His look spoke volumes and his silence forced me into saying more.

'But we couldn't do anything. Not here. Not with my father just in the next room.'

'That never stopped us before.'

He was right. I could recall several teenage forays down the corridor, the risk-taking and fear of getting caught only adding to our excitement.

'Well, it's different now. We're older. And besides, you know things are still very mixed up for me right now. You said you understood. You said you'd be patient.'

If he'd looked just a little abashed then, I would probably have softened my tone. After all, he didn't know for sure that I was awake when he came knocking at my door. He took up the paper, folding it neatly in half before continuing.

'I think I'm being extremely patient, Rachel. But I'm only human. One minute we have a full and complete adult relationship and the next you don't remember anything about us and you're hiding in the dark from me behind a locked door.'

Damn. He *had* known I was awake. And he'd still let me walk right into his trap, letting me make a complete fool out of myself. I was suddenly angry.

'Well, I'm very sorry that my getting mugged has been such a terrible inconvenience to your life plan. It certainly wasn't my intention. Do you want me to apologise for the amnesia too, while I'm at it, or should I just say sorry for not wanting to have sex with someone it feels like I just re-met a few days ago?'

He came to me then, and although I was still mad I let him put his arms around me, but I didn't relax in his hold, and I'm sure he could feel the tension rippling through me in waves.

'I'm sorry,' he whispered into my hair. 'It's just so hard, seeing you, loving you and wanting you and knowing you just don't feel the same way.'

He sounded so genuine that I felt most of my anger wash away on a tide of remorse. I didn't remember loving him as a grown woman, but that wasn't his fault. Quite unbidden, the image of the two of us taken at the Eiffel Tower flashed into my mind. I might not remember the feeling, but there could be no doubt that at the moment that photograph had been taken, I had been completely and utterly in love with the man I was now holding at arm's length. I gave a small groan and allowed my body to relax completely against him, even putting my arms about his steely torso to hold him close.

'I'm sorry, Matt. I will try harder. Really I will. Just give me a little longer. Just give me time to get . . . well again.' My heart gave a little trip hammer. I had almost said *to get over Jimmy*!

His fingers lifted my chin, holding my face towards his in a long-ago remembered way.

'Just don't take too long, huh?'

And then he kissed me, long and passionately, as if to show me what I was missing out on. And I kissed him back, because I felt guilty; because I used to love him very much indeed and because . . . and because he was Matt.

He dropped his bombshell a few minutes after my father had walked into the kitchen, unsubtly interrupting our embrace by announcing his arrival at the threshold with a small 'Hrrumph'.

'I'm really sorry, Rachel, but I'm going to have to head back to London today instead of tomorrow.'

I was still feeling guilty about how I had reacted, so I sounded genuinely regretful when I replied, 'Do you have to? I thought we were planning to spend the day together.'

His look was remorseful but his determination didn't waver.

'I'm sorry, something important has come up at work and I have to sort it out today.'

'On a Sunday?'

'You know I often have to work at weekends.'

'Actually, I don't know that. Amnesia. Remember?'

I could have dropped it then but something in his eyes had trip-wired my feminine intuition.

'Does it have something to do with that call you got from work last night?'

For a moment he looked blank, then in quick succession another expression fell across his handsome face, followed swiftly by a look of regret.

'Yes, it does actually. There's some crisis I have to deal with that just can't wait until Monday. You just have a relaxing day with your dad and I'll call you tonight, OK?'

He left some ten minutes later, kissing me goodbye in the hall and shaking my father's hand. We stood at the open doorway watching his car pull away from the kerb in a gleam of chrome and a squeal of rubber.

'What a shame he had to leave so soon,' said my father at last, when the car had finally disappeared from sight. I knew he wasn't sorry at all and gave him a long look which spoke volumes. But it did make me wonder how many more lies I was going to be told that day.

The rest of the day passed uneventfully enough. I spent an hour or so trying, and failing, to get my father's cat to like me, another hour wondering what urgent Cathy-related crisis had suddenly required Matt's presence in London, and the rest of the time trying very hard, and also failing, not to think about Jimmy at all. The only bright point of the day had been an unexpected telephone call from Sarah who had just returned from her honey-moon. She and David were spending the night with her parents, but we made arrangements to meet for lunch the following day before she and her new husband returned to Harrogate.

I fell asleep that night with something pleasant to look forward to and, for once, was not disturbed by dreams.

Chapter 10

We'd arranged to meet by a small bistro in the high street, and as usual I was there long before Sarah arrived. The weather had turned even colder overnight and although wrapped in warm scarf and gloves I could feel the December air, heavy with the threat of snow, taking vicious swipes at my face and legs.

And then Sarah arrived, spilling out of the taxi in a tumble of warmth and sunshine that instantly transported me back to memories of our youth. She enveloped me in the most rib-breaking hug, quite a feat for someone a good six inches smaller than me, and it was some time before either of us felt able to break apart.

When we did, the tears that were in my eyes matched those sparkling in her own and we both erupted into laughter, which was the only way we could stop ourselves from crying.

'How are you, my lovely?'

It took a while to reply, for the old greeting had brought a huge lump to my throat, and my face was still deeply buried into her shoulder. We were getting some pretty curious stares from passers-by too, but neither us could care less about that.

'Still alive, but slightly insane.' I felt that was a pretty accurate précis of my current situation.

'No change at all there then,' she replied, linking her arm into mine and steering us both towards the restaurant. 'Let's get out of the cold and you can tell me all about it.' Adding impishly as we went, 'Do you know, it's really much colder here than it is in St Lucia at the moment?'

We waited until we were seated and had ordered drinks before speaking properly. And then, when we did, we both began at once.

'So how are things really, have you got your memory back yet?'

'So tell me all about your honeymoon.'

We both laughed and waited for the other to back down.

'I'm sorry,' said Sarah, 'I do believe my head wound and amnesia inquiry trumps your honeymoon trivia.'

'OK,' I said with a smile. 'What do you want to hear about first? The mugging I don't remember or all the juicy stuff that came next?'

Sarah's suntanned face lit up with obvious delight. 'The juicy stuff, obviously.' But before I could commence she changed her mind. 'You know what, I want to hear it all, every last detail.'

'That might take some time,' I cautioned. 'Don't you and David have a train to catch this afternoon?'

She gave a shrug, as though such a trifling detail was of absolutely no importance.

'If I'm not there, he'll just have to leave without me. We've only been married for five minutes – he probably won't even miss me!'

I doubted that very much but took a long and steadying sip of wine and began to fill her in on what had happened to me since the night of her hen party.

She listened intently as I spoke, taking it all in, interrupting now and then when she wanted further clarification about something. She was also much more fascinated than anyone else had previously been by my alternate reality.

'So what am *I* like in your other past? Please say I'm tall, thin and beautiful. Oh no, better yet, please tell me that Cathy has got fat and ugly. Now that really would be something.'

I laughed. 'Sorry to disappoint you, but Cathy was even more gorgeous than she'd been when we were younger. Although a good deal nastier, I have to say.'

Sarah pursed her lips wryly. 'No trouble imagining that.'

I looked at her carefully. Sarah had never been once to mince her words where Cathy was concerned. I was relaying events as they happened, so I hadn't yet told her about the call I had intercepted to Matt's mobile. I was pretty certain she was going to have something quite colourful to say about that.

'So really, this other life you thought you were living was the total pits? Correct? Everyone was sick, or horribly scarred or dead? And all the good stuff that has gone on in your life just didn't happen at all? Have I got that right?'

'In a nutshell, yes.'

'And yet you still went around trying to prove to everyone that you needed to get back to that place?'

'Well, yes.' I could see where she was heading with this.

'Everyone's right. You *are* crazy. Did no one ever tell you that when you conjure up a fantasy world it's meant to be better than the real one – not a hundred times worse.'

Only she could pronounce me insane as though it were merely a charming quirk of character.

'I do know what you're saying. But even so, I still wanted to "go back", if that's the right way to put it, to what felt like my proper reality. But now I don't. Well, not since the other night.'

'Oohh, did something happen with Matt?'

I paused for a long second before replying, knowing my answer would register off the scale in terms of shock and astonishment.

'No, Jimmy.'

I swear the suntan literally paled for a moment as her eyes widened in disbelief at my words.

'Excuse me.' She snagged the arm of a passing waiter.

'Do you think you can bring us another bottle of this?' She indicated our almost empty bottle of wine. 'I have a feeling we're going to need it.'

I didn't know what I expected her to say when I finally finished telling her about the hotel incident. Perhaps I was expecting shock, even disappointment, at learning how readily I had been willing to cheat on Matt. What I *wasn't* expecting was her unequivocal approval.

'About bloody time.'

'What?'

'You heard me.'

'Yes I did. But did *you* hear me? He turned me down. He just wasn't interested. And the following day he could hardly bear to look at me. Now call me crazy, but in any of my previous lives that's a pretty clear message of "I don't want to do this".'

'Phah,' Sarah retorted. 'That means nothing. You're the only person in the world who exists, as far as Jimmy is concerned. It's the way it has always been.'

'You weren't there, Sarah. You didn't see how disgusted he looked. He couldn't get away from me fast enough.'

'And did you ask him about it the next day, when you were coming home?'

'No,' I replied miserably, remembering the awkward car journey. 'Neither of us dared to bring it up. It was just too embarrassing. Too humiliating.'

Sarah shook her head. 'There's more to this than you

realise. There has to be. Jimmy wouldn't act like that with anyone, let alone *you*. I know you haven't seen much of him over the last few years, but trust me on this one. He's still every bit as much in love with you as he was in high school.'

'You're wrong,' I corrected glumly.

'We'll see.'

We'd reached an impasse. There was nothing more to say about that night. So we finally – and thankfully, on my part – moved on to the much less complicated topic of Sarah's wedding and honeymoon. She had stopped off on the way to the restaurant to collect the proofs of her wedding photos, and once our plates had been cleared, she spread the large album on the table.

Never had I seen a bride look more beautiful and glowing with happiness than Sarah had on that day. As I turned the heavy embossed pages of the album, I couldn't help but feel overwhelmed with sadness that I hadn't been there to share that incredible moment with her. She must have known what I was thinking, and seen the regret in my smile, as my fingers hovered beside a photograph of her and David laughing happily under a falling cloud of confetti.

'I wanted to postpone the wedding, you know,' she said softly, 'when we knew what had happened to you, but your dad and Matt wouldn't hear of it.'

'They were quite right. I'd have been furious if you'd done that.'

I carried on turning page after page. Here now were photographs of the reception, the tables beautifully decorated with deep red floral displays that perfectly matched the crimson bows cinched around the back of the chairs.

'It all looks so beautiful,' I murmured.

Another page, and here were photographs of the guests, randomly taken after the meal. Matt's handsome face looked up at me from several group photographs. Jimmy was there too, but always more in the background, not smiling directly towards the camera like my fiancé. I also couldn't help noticing that in many of the photographs, Cathy was also present, never far away from Matt's side. I paused to study her exquisite face and caught Sarah watching me.

'She looked amazing, of course. That dress of hers was so tight she must have been sewn into it!'

I laughed. The deep red gown Cathy wore did indeed look as though it was moulded to her body like a second skin.

'I think she was trying to upstage me.'

'Never happen,' I assured her, but after turning yet another page and seeing Cathy once more cosied up to Matt, this time on the dance floor, I just had to ask, 'Did she stick by him like this all night?'

Sarah shrugged as though to say she didn't know, but I could read her better than that. 'God, she doesn't miss a trick, does she?'

'You know Cathy,' Sarah pronounced.

And I was quiet for a moment. Yes, I did know Cathy; but perhaps it was Matt who apparently I might not know that well.

'And anyway,' Sarah said, taking the album from me and firmly closing it. 'It doesn't matter how much eye-fluttering and cleavage-flashing she tries, you're still the one he's engaged to; still the one he's been with for ever.'

I nodded, but I wasn't sure a little detail like that would stop Cathy, not if she really set her mind to it.

'I know you two have been going through a sticky patch in the last few months, but you keep assuring me that's only about work stuff – not anything serious, not like what happened when you were at uni.'

I sat up sharply in my seat. 'What? What happened when we were at uni? What are you talking about?'

She jumped guiltily then, and I could see the thought process flashing through her eyes as she considered a means of bluffing her way out of the gaffe she had just made. I repeated the question, trying to keep my voice even and calm.

'What happened when we were at uni, Sarah? Tell me. It's not fair that I don't know.'

The laughter was gone from her voice but I could see that my plea had convinced her to tell me.

'You and Matt had a major row and broke up for about four months or so in our second year.'

This was indeed news to me. Certainly Matt hadn't thought to mention it, despite the fact there'd been every opportunity for him to do so when we had been talking about our relationship recently.

'We broke up? But why? What happened?'

'I can't tell you.'

'Don't be daft, of course you can tell me,' I cajoled.

'I'm not going to get upset, or anything, I just want to know.'

'No. It's not that. I mean, I can't tell you, because I don't know.'

This was very strange indeed. How was it possible that Sarah didn't know the details of something that must have been such a major event in my life? We'd always shared everything. Surely I would have told her all about it? But apparently not, she reported. Oh she'd certainly tried to get the story out of me on many occasions, but apparently I had refused to tell her anything.

'Was I really upset about it?' I queried.

'Yes. Very. But you still wouldn't give me any of the details. And believe me, I tried to get them out of you!'

I laughed then, imagining the third-degree tactics she had probably employed, all – apparently – without success.

She wagged her finger at me in warning, 'And this is precisely why you should never keep secrets from your best friend. Because you never know when one day you're going to get amnesia and need her to fill in the blanks!'

The restaurant was beginning to empty around us by then. And when I looked out the window I could see the day had darkened under a slate-coloured sky. There was still so much I wanted to talk to Sarah about but we'd simply run out of time. We settled the bill, and in order to eke out our last few minutes together, I said I'd walk with her to the taxi rank.

We were standing by the crossing, waiting for the

lights to change, when it happened. The pedestrian lights had just turned to green and Sarah had already taken one step into the road when I first heard the siren. Strangely it didn't sound far away and distant, but was instantly loud and strident, as though its arrival were imminent. My head darted up as I looked left and right for the approaching emergency vehicle. But the long grey road appeared clear in both directions: nothing was heading towards us. Yet the sound was everywhere, the discordant two-tone klaxon reverberating off the buildings and pavements. I looked around in confusion as other pedestrians began to traverse the road, surely walking blindly into the path of a speeding vehicle. Later it would occur to me how similar the situation was to my recent dream; the one where only I could see there was impending danger and everyone else was oblivious. But for now I had only one thought in mind, to snatch Sarah back from the looming threat. The siren was now so loud I could scarcely hear my own cry of warning as I reached out and grabbed her coat sleeve, literally snatching her backwards onto the kerb. I fully expected the thunder of the vehicle to cover the space where a moment earlier my friend had stood, but nothing came whistling past us in a blaze of flashing lights. The road remained empty.

The other pedestrians, those who had been crossing the road with Sarah, had by then all successfully made it safely to the other side, never once realising how close they had been to disaster.

'Where did it go?' I asked Sarah, unaware that

my strange behaviour was now the object of some attention by the gaggle of 'survivors' on the other side of the street.

Sarah, to her credit, only looked a little shaky; as though being plucked from the path of invisible non-existent jeopardy was something she regularly contended with.

'Where did *what* go?'

'The siren.' And when she continued to look at me blankly, 'You *must* have heard it? It was heading right towards us!' My voice trailed off as it slowly began to penetrate through my panic that the sound of the siren was actually not there any more. A horrible feeling of déjà vu came over me.

'You didn't hear it, did you?'

She shook her head.

'But it was so deafening, as though it was almost on top of us.'

Another slow shake of the head.

I didn't need her to tell me that no one had heard the sound but me, I could already see it in her eyes.

'Has this happened before?' she asked gently.

I thought of the alarm clock that wasn't there, beeping in the night, and the numerous times my father's aftershave had surrounded me like a cloud.

'There've been a couple of times,' I admitted slowly, 'where I've heard things, smelt things even . . .' My words died away.

'You have to tell the doctor about this when you see him this week,' she urged, and I knew she was right, even though I was loath to add another inexplicable symptom to my ever-increasing accumulation.

'It might be something that's really common with amnesia cases,' she suggested, then seeing my gloomy response she tried a different tack altogether. 'Or maybe, since you bumped your head, you now have these incredibly acute senses, and can hear and smell things the rest of us can't.'

'What, like a dog, you mean?'

She laughed then and gave me a hug. 'Yeah, but a really pretty pedigree one.'

The doctor's words stayed with me all the way down the marble flight of steps of the clinic, down the length of the exclusive London road, reserved primarily for offices of the medical profession, and into the busy bustling shopping street, heaving as it was with Christmas shoppers. It had been too much to anticipate a simple solution to my problems from the one consultation. But I had hoped for some answers at the very least; only what I had actually ended up with were a hundred more questions.

Nothing about the session had gone entirely as I had imagined, I mused, as I allowed myself to be carried along on a wave of shoppers and tourists, all busily trying to seize whatever bargains there were to be had in the days before Christmas. The clinic itself had been far more elegant and exclusive than I had expected, while the doctor's offices had been far less intimidating; no scary leather consultation couch, no men in white jackets waiting in the wings to escort me to some secure facility if my story sounded just too outlandish to allow me to continue to live among 'normal' people.

Even the doctor had been unexpected: female, when I had been expecting male, and far more maternal and warm than the Freudian-like physician I'd been anticipating. She had been professional enough to get me to open up completely about my bizarre misconception of the past five years, and kind enough to make me feel that nothing I said was even remotely weird enough for her to press the panic alarm, which must surely be hidden somewhere in her office.

What I hadn't been expecting was that this would only be the first of many sessions we would have to share in order to piece together my lost past. Medically, I had already undergone all the tests and procedures that were necessary to diagnose any physiological problem, but I was still crushingly disappointed that there would be no quick-fix solution. I suppose I had secretly been harbouring hopes that some form of medication or treatment could be offered to dispel my illusions and make my new reality feel . . . well, feel real. Dr Andrews had been kind but firm when clearing up that particular delusion.

And when I asked the final question, the one whose response followed me now like a shadow on the busy London pavements, she had at least been honest.

'Rachel, I cannot tell you when your memory will return. It could be tomorrow, or next week, or indeed it may take a good deal longer. And, although it is rare,

I do have to be honest and tell you that in some very exceptional cases, the lost period of time remains just that, for ever lost.'

For ever lost. The words haunted me as I walked, echoing hollowly as my feet trod the glistening thoroughfares of the capital.

Not that the entire consultation session had been all doom and gloom. Dr Andrews had at least made me feel slightly better about the weird imagined sensations that I had been experiencing. Apparently auditory and olfactory hallucinations were by no means uncommon for those who had undergone head trauma, and when I questioned why the things I could smell and hear were so specific, she even had a reasonable theory for that too. The fragrance of my father's aftershave would have very specific connotations of safety and security for me, and as the sense of smell is particularly evocative in taking us back to somewhere in our past, the doctor guessed that the hallucination probably mirrored feelings of physical safety I had felt as a child, when held by my parent. Her reasoning about the imagined sirens was even more prosaic – for she guessed that when I was taken to hospital after the mugging, I had not been entirely unconscious and the ambulance's siren had somehow implanted itself into my memory, and was now being arbitrarily replayed as my confused mind struggled for a foothold in reality.

She was a little less sure of why I was also hearing alarms that were not there, but assured me that in time we would uncover all of the mysteries. In time. And there it was in a nutshell. I would have to be patient and let the truth uncover itself one fact at a time, and she assured me that with each emerging element I would then be able to let go of a comparable piece of my imagined history, until at last only the real past would remain.

It sounded like a very slow business to me, and I still couldn't help but think it would have been so much better if I could have been given some short sharp treatment – however horrible – to make it all happen much more speedily.

The one thing I did like very much about Dr Andrews was the way she hadn't laughed when I'd answered her question of why *I* thought I had two entirely different past lives. Her reaction was nothing like Jimmy's had been when I offered up my earlier theory of parallel worlds. At least *she* didn't laugh out loud and blame it all on my somewhat fantastical literary choices. I hastily slammed the door shut on that line of thought. I had resolutely not allowed myself to think of Jimmy all week, and now, in the offices of a psychiatrist who was skilled at probing out a person's innermost secrets, was definitely not the time to journey down that path again.

And even though I hadn't spoken to Jimmy myself, I did know he had been in daily contact with my dad, for I'd overheard several whispered conversations behind doors which hadn't been as securely closed as my secretive parent thought they'd been. So, despite the fact that he clearly wasn't anxious to speak to me, Jimmy still wanted to know how I was on a daily basis. And while part of me was pleased to know he cared enough to call, the other part was becoming increasingly angry that it was my father he chose to speak to and not me. It confirmed my worst suspicions: that he was still so uncomfortable with what had happened between us at the hotel that he could neither face nor forgive me. I wondered if he would ever be able to do either again.

Tired of being buffeted by the determined holiday shoppers, I slipped inside a small coffee shop and found an empty table. At the last moment my doctor's appointment had been rescheduled from late in the afternoon to early morning. I hadn't minded having to get the early fast train into London, but it did leave me now with many hours to kill before the time I was supposed to meet up with Matt for dinner and a lift back home to Great Bishopsford. It had been too late to reach Matt the previous day to let him know of the change of plans, and while I had thought the extra time in London could be spent Christmas shopping, the doctor's appointment had taken more out of me mentally than I'd expected, and I'd now lost any appetite for pushing and shoving through hordes of people in the department stores.

I glanced at my watch. It was only late morning but there was a possibility that Matt might be free for an early lunch. It would be good to explain to him some of the things Dr Andrews had said while they were still fresh in my mind. Perhaps it would help him to understand why I was finding it so hard to fall straight back into my role as his fiancée, as I know he had been expecting. Acting on impulse, I pulled out my mobile phone and scrolled down the address book until I reached *Matt Office.*

His secretary answered the call on the second ring, her cool professional tone warming considerably as she recognised my voice. Which was more than I did for hers.

'Oh, Rachel, I'm sorry, you've just missed him. He left about ten minutes ago for his flat, but you're meeting him there for lunch anyway, aren't you?'

'Umm . . .' I never knew why I didn't immediately correct her assumption but some small warning voice told me not to. And I listened to it.

'He should be back there really soon, traffic permitting. And could you let him know I've managed to cancel those meetings he had this afternoon, like he asked?'

'Oh . . . good. I'll tell him.'

'It was nice speaking to you again. I do hope you enjoy your lunch today. We're all so glad to hear you're getting better.'

'Thank you . . .' I struggled for her name, but obviously nothing was forthcoming, so I just repeated again, 'Thank you.'

I sat looking at my phone for a long time before finally flipping the lid back into position and replacing it in my handbag. I don't recall finishing my coffee, or paying the bill, but as no one ran after me yelling 'thief' as I left the coffee shop, I guessed I must have taken care of it.

There were a hundred different reasons why Matt's secretary could have misunderstood what he'd told her about his plans. We had, after all, been intending to meet for dinner that night, and when he asked her to cancel his appointments this afternoon, she might have become confused and believed we were meeting instead for lunch.

And yet she had sounded so positive he was on his way to meet me at his flat. How could she possibly have misinterpreted that?

But perhaps I was ignoring the even bigger question. What was so pressing that it was enough to make a workaholic like Matt cancel his entire schedule in the middle of the day? Because it certainly wasn't to have lunch with his fiancée.

It was easy enough to hail a cab, although I did have to consult my address book for the precise location of Matt's flat. As the taxi crawled through the midday traffic I tried to keep my mind deliberately blank and completely refused to listen to the voice in my head that was screaming out a prediction of the outcome of this surprise visit. I kept reminding myself that I knew so little of Matt's working practices that disappearing like this in the middle of the day might be perfectly usual behaviour on his part. *Yeah right*, said the voice.

Eventually, the cab pulled up in front of an exclusive-looking apartment block.

'Here you are, love, Hanbury Mansions.'

I tried a smile that felt a little too stiff to be natural and reached into my wallet to extract a note for the driver. I saw then that my hand had begun to tremble, ever so slightly. This is ridiculous, I chided myself. Why was I getting so worked up about something that no doubt would have the simplest of explanations? I was seeing mysteries where there were none, and surely I had enough real drama going on in my life that I didn't need to be inventing a whole new episode?

I almost told the cabbie then that I'd changed my mind, but that was before I looked out through the rain-speckled window and saw Matt's car discreetly parked to one side of the forecourt in a private bay. OK, so he *was* here. That still meant absolutely nothing. Nevertheless, my hand, which had been hesitating over the door latch, pressed down on the lever and I climbed out of the cab.

My resolve wavered slightly as I looked up at the tall, red-brick and glass building. How stupid was I going to look when all this turned out to be nothing more than a wild goose chase? Not to mention paranoid. No doubt this would give me something else to have to work on with Dr Andrews at our next session.

Yet still my feet continued to walk towards the building. Even knowing that Matt could have any one of a hundred valid reasons for going home in the middle of the day, reasons he chose not to share with his secretary, I still couldn't ignore the impulse that had set me off on this journey after that phone call to his office.

But for the first time it occurred to me to question if I really wanted to go through with this. Even though I had tried not to listen to the warning voice in my head, I wasn't completely stupid. I knew that whatever was about to follow from this point on could very well end badly. But the secretary's words had planted a question in my mind, which screamed out now for an answer. The taxi gunned into life behind me and sped quickly away from the forecourt, eliminating my last chance of escape. I took a deep breath, squared my shoulders, and walked up to the building.

The large glass-fronted entrance was manned by a uniformed doorman, who politely held open the plate-glass doors to allow me to enter the building. It wasn't until I was inside that it occurred to me that I didn't have the slightest idea which flat was Matt's. The only details I had were the address of the building. The bank of locked mailboxes to the left of the foyer showed that there were twenty or so flats in this block: Matt could live in any one of them. The obvious solution would be to ask the uniformed concierge at the reception desk which apartment was Mr Matt Randall's. But if I did that, the protocol would probably be to call up to the apartment and let the owner know they had a visitor; it stands to reason that you don't have this kind of security on the ground and let any old person simply walk in off the street. Clearly, if I went via the doorman I would lose the element of surprise, so the only solution was to somehow get past him and then try to locate which flat was Matt's.

In a flash of inspiration I pulled a blank piece of paper from my bag and pretended to consult it as though it was confirming my validity to be there at that time. If I just walked past the security man with confidence, perhaps I could pull this off. Luckily, the telephone on the reception desk rang at that moment, and as he busied himself in answering the call, I seized my opportunity. Keeping my eyes firmly fixed on the bank of lifts at the rear of the foyer, I strode purposefully past the desk. I was quick, but not quick enough.

'Excuse me.'

I ignored the voice. Walk with purpose, as though you

DANI ATKINS

have every right to be here, I told myself, not allowing my stride to falter.

'Miss, excuse me.' His voice was louder that time, and despite myself I hesitated. There was no one else in the foyer. His comment was clearly directed at me. I considered proceeding regardless but it was impossible to ignore the sudden unwanted image of me being frogmarched from the building between two burly security guards. I turned towards the desk with what I hoped was an innocent-looking smile. A second security guard, who I hadn't even noticed until then, looked up with interest from the pile of paperwork that was before him: the forthcoming interlude clearly promising to be more diverting than his current task.

The first man, the one who had hailed me, made a small beckoning motion with his finger for me to approach the desk. Oh, this was beyond embarrassing. I gave a quick glance towards the entranceway, still being securely guarded by doorman number three. The possibility of making a run for it was clearly not an option. Feeling guilty, and hoping I looked anything but that, I tried to keep smiling as I walked towards the reception desk on legs that felt like jelly. As I got closer I could see that what I had taken for an angry glower was actually a fairly pleasant smile.

'Yes?' I enquired, hoping no one but me could hear the wobble in my voice.

'Have you forgotten something?' the man prompted.

I blinked back at him stupidly. Forgotten what exactly? Forgotten to report to reception? Forgotten that I don't live in this building? Hell, I could do way better than that: I'd actually forgotten the last five years.

'Your key?' the man continued, as though coaxing the answer out of a child in class.

'Um, oh, of course, my key,' I replied, and opened my bag to pretend to look for a key I didn't have.

The guard's smile widened a little as he reached across the desk and handed me a front door key, attached to which was a large silver fob. His voice was kindly as he continued, 'You always ask us to keep your key to Mr Randall's apartment for you at reception, Miss Wiltshire,' he explained, in a gentle paternal tone. 'You say it saves you having to carry it around with you all the time.'

I reached out to take the proffered key, noting thankfully there was a number engraved in the silver-plated fob.

The guard hesitated as though unsure as to whether his next comment was entirely appropriate. 'We all hope you're feeling better now, Miss Wiltshire. We've missed seeing you around here recently.'

'Umm, thank you. That's very kind of you.'

My fingers fastened around the key and I smiled at both men, realising for the first time that the younger of the two appeared somewhat agitated. His eyes kept darting from me to the key and then back towards his older colleague. Something was bothering him about letting me have the key but I didn't intend to hang around long enough for him to voice his concern.

I turned and began to head back towards the lifts once

more, hearing as I did some hurriedly whispered comment and responding exclamation from the men at the desk.

I pressed the call button on the lift.

More urgent whispering; they were clearly in a quandary about something. An instruction was given, followed swiftly by the sound of a telephone keypad being sharply punched. Another exclamation and a quickly heated muttering between the two.

Where was the damn lift? I heard them try the phone again at the precise moment that the carriage pinged to announce its arrival. I just caught the words 'still engaged' as the doors slid open and I entered the lift.

'Miss Wiltshire,' hailed the older man, getting up from his seat and beginning to leave his desk. But he wasn't fast enough and the doors glided to a close before he was even halfway across the foyer.

Matt's flat turned out to be on the top floor, and I could only hope that his phone line had remained engaged throughout the time it took me to reach his doorway. I think I knew by then what had been worrying the security men in reception and why they had not wanted me to reach his flat without alerting him first.

Luck was clearly with me, for when I reached the front door there was no sign that my visit had been announced. From within the apartment I could hear the vague strains of music, but no voices at all in conversation.

I drew in a deep breath to steady my nerves, momentarily deafened by the loud beating of my heart, and slid the key into the lock. The door opened onto a vast, wooden-floored loft-style apartment, elegantly decorated in black and white leather. The source of the music lay to my left; the slow seductive strains of jazz emitting from an expensive hi-fi system.

On a large, low, rectangular glass table stood an open bottle of wine, beside which were two half-empty glasses. To one side of the huge leather settee was the telephone, lying off the hook beside its base. *Good luck with making that warning call, guys,* I thought wryly, surprised at the bitter taste suddenly in my throat. The room was empty of all occupants.

For several moments I stood rooted to the spot, then from far away at the rear of the apartment I heard a voice, followed by what sounded like a soft peal of laughter. I didn't move. I knew the answer to the question now. Knew it from the evidence before me in the room. Had known it, if I were being completely honest, even before I left the café and hailed the cab. Did I really need to pursue it further to its inevitable and ugly conclusion?

My feet began to take me in the direction of the voices. Apparently I did.

The door was open, well, why wouldn't it be? They thought they had the place to themselves. I entered the room silently, seeing more than I wanted to of their entwined bodies, before some latent sense alerted them both to my presence. Their reactions were completely different: Matt jerked back as though electrocuted, immediately disengaging his hold on the woman in his arms. Cathy, on the other hand, moved with precise deliberation, her eyes unreadable as she slowly reached down to pull up a sheet to cover her naked breasts.

We remained motionless in that way for what could only have been a second or two, but it felt like an eternity, frozen in a hideously tawdry tableau.

I had thought I would say something but all speech was momentarily stolen from me. It was, surprisingly, Cathy who was first to break the silence.

'Well, this is all horribly familiar.'

Matt shot her an angry look before reaching for the trousers he had obviously carelessly discarded beside the bed. His eyes were locked to mine as he fumbled to struggle into the garment. I'd seen enough, quite literally, in every sense of the word.

I turned away from the bedroom then and quickly began to cross the large living space. I was moving fast but everything appeared strangely dream-like, as though it were all happening in slow motion. From behind me I could hear Cathy say something, which was followed swiftly by some angry barked retort from Matt. I was almost at the door before I heard him cry out.

'Rachel, wait! Please wait!'

Walking even faster, I got to the door and hurriedly opened it. His next words were silenced by the shutting, *not slamming*, of the front door.

In the corridor once more, with the dreadful pathetic scene shut firmly away in the flat behind me, I finally drew breath. I hadn't even realised I'd forgotten to inhale from the moment I'd interrupted my fiancé in bed with another woman. The dizzy feeling that had begun to blur my senses was instantly washed away on a tide of oxygen, and with it too came the pain, and even worse than that, the humiliation. In fact, the only emotion that didn't assault me was surprise. Wasn't this, after all, exactly what I'd been expecting to see?

I didn't wait for the lift but followed the signs for the emergency stairs, only just slipping through the fire door as Matt burst into the corridor, hastily buttoning a shirt over a torso still glistening with sweat from his activities.

Unfortunately he either heard the door, or guessed where I had headed, for he wasted no time in summoning the lift and ran instead down the hallway towards the staircase. I heard the click of the door opening and the call of my name ricocheting down the concrete stairwell. His flat was on the fifth floor: that meant ten half-flights of stairs. I still had a head start. I could do it, if I ran.

He caught up with me before I was even halfway down, my progress slowed by the height of my heels and my blurred vision. Strangely I hadn't even realised I'd been crying until then. Even so, he must have all but flown down the concrete stairs, his bare feet pounding each tread to catch up with me so quickly. His hand reached out to stop me, with such force that I almost fell, only his quick reactions pulling me back against him preventing me from plummeting down the remainder of the flight. I felt the heat and damp from his body through the thin material of his shirt and recoiled in disgust. It was the heat from her.

'Rachel, please, for God's sake slow down before you fall.'

I turned on him then, my anger thankfully hot enough to have dried the tears in an instant. 'Like you care! As if that wouldn't be the perfect solution!'

Oddly, a truly stricken look contorted his face.

'Of course I care. How can you even say that?'

Venom, dark and poisonous flooded through me.

'Well, I don't know, let me think . . . Could it be the fact that less than five minutes ago you were busy screwing someone else?'

His face spasmed at my words and he reached out for me, but I backed away repulsed.

'Please, Rachel, let me—'

I cut him off. 'What, Matt? What is it you want to do? Explain? Is that the word? Because don't bother. I saw enough of your dirty little movie that no explanations are necessary at all. I understand *perfectly* what's going on!'

'Nothing is *going on*!' he cried.

'Really?' I snapped. 'That's not what it looked like from where I was standing! And remember, I just got a ringside seat. I might have amnesia but even *I* can remember that what you and Cathy were up to is definitely not *nothing*!'

He ran his hand through his hair in frustration. 'No, I didn't mean that. What I meant is that it means nothing to me. *She* means nothing to me. It was just sex. That's all it was.'

I feigned a look of enlightenment before rounding on him angrily like a tiger. 'And that's supposed to make me feel *better*?' He looked helpless, struggling for words and

I took advantage of the moment. 'You know what, Matt? I don't care.'

'No, Rachel, don't say that. You have to let me explain. You have to let me make this right.'

It was hard not to lash out then, not at his words, but at his failure to understand exactly what he had done.

'There is no "making this right", Matt. Don't you get that? Whatever your reason was, it doesn't matter. Nothing can make this right again.'

'You can't mean that,' he pleaded, and there was genuine anguish in his voice. Not that I'd have weakened then, but his next words sealed his fate completely. 'And then, last week, when you locked your door on me—'

He never got to finish. Fury like molten lava flowed through my veins. 'What? Is that it? It's been like three weeks since my accident so that justifies you sleeping with someone else? Is that what you're saying to me? Well, is it?'

He looked worried then, knowing of all things that should never have been voiced, that was possibly the worst thing he could ever have said.

And that's when Cathy's words came back to me. The words she'd spoken when I first came upon them.

'And what did Cathy mean up there, when she said this was "horribly familiar"?' A slow red flush suffused his cheeks, while conversely I felt the blood drain from mine. 'What? This has happened before? Have you been having an affair with her behind my back? Is that it?'

'No, no. Of course not. I told you, this thing today, it was a one-off. It just . . . happened.'

There was more going on here than he was admitting to, I could feel it.

'But you've been with her before, haven't you?'

I saw the dull look of confession in his eyes.

Inspiration dawned then, as the nasty little puzzle pieces all came together. 'Oh my God! I found you with her once before, didn't I? When we were at uni?'

For one insane moment he actually looked pleased that I'd got my memory back. 'You *remember* that?'

'Not entirely,' I hissed. 'But that *is* what happened, isn't it? I found her with you and we broke up?'

He nodded miserably. 'But then you forgave me.'

And I saw then the entreaty in his eyes. I killed that hope before it could even draw breath, crushing and grinding it underfoot to extinguish all life.

'But not this time, Matt. You don't get any more chances to do this to me. Not ever again.'

Chapter 11

I walked for a long time; walked until the boiling rage had cooled and the humiliation only stung instead of seared through me like a lance. Unfortunately, however far I went I couldn't seem to erase the image that had greeted me in Matt's room; of their two perfect bodies enmeshed together like some exotic piece of art. I didn't think anything was going to spare me from having that vision stencilled on my memory for a long time to come. Ironic really, that that would be sticking with me when so much of my life these days was all about the forgetting.

Eventually the cold and sheer exhaustion stopped my restless feet. I looked up at the corner of a busy junction, read a street name I'd never heard of, and realised I had absolutely no idea where I was. I'd been walking mindlessly for several hours and, for the first time since bolting out of Matt's building and into the street, I made myself stop to consider what I was going to do next. The answer came surprisingly easily.

I hailed a cab within a few minutes and gave him the address of the London flat I'd visited with Jimmy just one week earlier. I asked the driver to stop off once on the way so I could make a few essential purchases. My mobile was ringing continually as we drove through the capital, but I resolutely ignored it, as I had done in the hours since I'd finally torn away from Matt on the stairwell. Eventually he stopped calling, perhaps at last realising that all words were superfluous, for there really was nothing left to say.

The driver certainly earned his tip by assisting me into my building with the flat-packed storage boxes I had purchased en route. Once inside my own apartment, although it wasn't going to be that for much longer, I propped the cardboard containers up against the wall, together with the reels of packing tape, scissors and string I had also bought.

The telephone call to my father was a difficult one. There was no easy way to dress up the situation, and even though I played down the explicit nature of what had happened, his paternal instincts went straight into overdrive. It took almost every last ounce of my powers of persuasion to prevent him from getting on the next train up to London.

'I don't like the idea of you being there all alone tonight. You're just going to dwell on what's happened.'

'No I'm not,' I assured him, hoping the answer wasn't a lie. 'I'm going to be far too busy packing to dwell, anyhow.'

Eventually, something in my voice must have convinced him that I was neither manically depressed nor suicidal, for he stopped trying to get me to change my mind and asked only that I call him in the morning. I hung up the phone, feeling certain that the fact that I'd broken off my engagement and was quitting my London flat to return home was not exactly bad news as far as he was concerned. It was too early for me to say if I felt the same way.

I began assembling the storage boxes, distributing them in each room of the flat. I worked methodically, emptying cupboards, drawers and wardrobes as dispassionately as a professional remover; packing up the belongings I didn't recognise, from a flat I didn't remember.

I kept very little for the two containers that were returning with me to Great Bishopsford, filling them only with important-looking documentation or old items I recognised from many years before. The charity shops and the local dump could have the rest. I wanted to take as little as possible from this unremembered place with me.

The packing was strangely cathartic, and as box after box was filled and taped shut, it felt as though I was doing more here than just getting rid of possessions. Here at last I'd found the one and only benefit from having amnesia: there was no pain in packing up a life you didn't remember, no regrets when you were leaving no memories behind.

I lingered only once, over the picture of Matt and me in Paris. Somehow it didn't seem to belong in any of the boxes, so I created a new pile of items that I thought might have been gifts from him – all too expensive to discard. They could be parcelled up and returned to him sometime soon.

Four hours later I was done. My back was aching, and I was more than a little grubby from my task, but even so I felt for the first time that, despite its horrific revelations, today was the first day I had actually taken a step towards the future and away from the past.

I leaned back against the side of the bed, too exhausted even to get up from the bedroom floor. I just needed to close my eyes for a moment.

Heavy hammering and shouting rumbled from somewhere close by, not near enough to wake me completely. But when the door burst open, with enough force to buckle one of the hinges, that *did* wake me. From my prone position on the floor I looked up, blinking like a myopic owl in the suddenly blazing bedroom light. I tried to focus on the large shape filling the bedroom doorway, silhouetted by the host of lights from the rest of the flat: lights I knew I hadn't left on.

'Thank God!'

My ears recognised the voice, even though my eyes were still too sleep-filled to focus.

'*Jimmy?* What on earth are you doing here?'

But he never answered my question, turning instead to a person I had just noticed was standing slightly behind him. The short, middle-aged stranger looked from me to

Jimmy, before asking hesitantly: 'Is everything all right, officer?'

I struggled to my feet, rubbing my eyes as though this were all a crazy dream I could brush away with the movement. I lowered my hands. No, they were both still here.

Jimmy, with a firmly guiding hand, was leading the man back out through the flat to the front door, thanking him all the time for his cooperation.

The man allowed himself to be led away, looking both awed and a touch disappointed at being so speedily written out of a potential drama.

'If you need me to make a statement or anything . . .' His voice trailed off.

'That won't be necessary at this time, sir. But I'm extremely grateful to you once again for your assistance.'

I waited until Jimmy had shut the door behind the man and walked slowly into the living room. I said nothing as I watched him return his police ID to his jacket pocket, but the inclination of my head and raised eyebrows said it all.

He looked vaguely embarrassed, but not entirely repentant.

'Is that even legal?'

'Is *what* even legal?'

'Using your ID to break into someone's private accommodation?'

His eyes met mine but I couldn't read his expression.

'I didn't break in,' he corrected, 'I got the supervisor to open your door.'

'By telling him what, exactly? That I'm an international terrorist? A dangerous bank robber? An escaped lunatic?'

He look chagrined at the last of my suggestions, before covering the distance between us in two short strides and answering in a low voice. 'That no one could reach you . . . That you'd had a recent trauma and then some very bad news. And that you might be . . . hurt.'

His arms came around me then, and I felt the tremor in his strong hold as he pulled me against him. I saw it all then, through different eyes than mine: understanding why concern had flared so quickly into panic.

'I take it you've spoken to my dad?' I asked into his shirt-front where my face was still pressed.

'I did.'

'Didn't he tell you I just wanted to stay up here to clear up the flat? That I was coming home tomorrow?'

He sighed deeply, and his voice sounded a little hoarse when he replied. 'I just needed to speak to you. To check you were OK. And then, when I tried – God knows how many times – to get through to you on your phone . . .'

'I've been ignoring it. I thought it was Matt.'

He leaned back from me then and studied my face, as though trying to see what it had cost me to speak his name.

Clearly my features were unfathomable, for he questioned haltingly, 'Your dad did mention something about that: that you'd had a disagreement.'

I gave a small wry laugh that held very little actual humour. 'Yeah, you could call it that. He thought it was all right to be having sex with Cathy in his flat today, and strangely I disagreed.'

A fleet of emotions crossed Jimmy's face, too swiftly for me to differentiate one from the other, but I thought I'd glimpsed barely restrained fury as well as something much more gentle and hopeful.

'Your dad never said that!'

'He got the edited version.'

Taking hold of my hand, Jimmy gently led me over to the settee and settled himself beside me. I thought about taking back my hand but he seemed in no hurry to relinquish it, so I left it encased in his own.

'Tell me all about it,' he urged. His voice was soft and encouraging, once again my confidant and friend, but there was something in his eyes, something I scarcely recognised, that was having a disturbing effect on my pulse.

He stayed completely silent as I recounted my entire day: from the doctor's appointment, to the discovery of Matt's betrayal. He was so motionless as I spoke, I had to watch his face extremely closely to glean even a hint of a reaction to my words. The tightening of his jaw when I reached the part when I walked in on Matt and Cathy was the only indication of a fury I knew he was struggling to hold in check.

When at last I was finished, he turned my hand over within his, seeming to take a good deal of time to select exactly the right words.

'I'm so sorry, Rachel; sorry he did that to you. Sorry he's hurt you like this. I know how much you . . . love . . . him. But you deserve so much better than that.'

His face was very close to mine, merely inches apart. I raised my eyes, hoping he could read in them all that I hadn't been able to say. I saw his head begin to lower, and my lips parted as I half closed my eyes in anticipation. They flew open again moments later as he leant in and gently grazed my forehead with the lightest of kisses.

He got smoothly to his feet then, the atmosphere changing as abruptly as though a switch had been pulled. Not meeting my gaze, which I knew must still be registering confusion, he made a deliberate show of consulting his watch.

'Look, it's getting fairly late. Why don't I go and get us a takeaway or something? I'm sure you've not eaten all day, have you?'

I shook my head, not entirely trusting that I'd be able to keep what I was feeling from my voice.

'OK, I'll go and get us something to eat. I won't be long.'

His departure was so overly hasty it was almost comical. How many more times was I going to misread the signals, and have to watch him all but run from me, before I accepted that whatever feelings I had buried deep inside for him should be allowed to rest in peace? There clearly was no chance at all of them ever being reciprocated.

It didn't take him very long to find a nearby takeaway, and I'd only just finished washing some of the grime of packing from my face and hands before he returned, heavily laden with numerous cartons of Chinese food and two bottles of wine.

'Are we expecting company?' I asked, eyeing the array

of fragrant containers he was busily opening on the coffee table.

'Let's hope not,' he replied darkly, and it didn't take a genius to work out who he thought might be planning on joining us. I didn't think that was even remotely likely; feeling sure Matt would realise that turning up at my door that night was not exactly in his best interests. However, the thought of what might happen between the two men if Matt *were* foolish enough to put in an appearance made me shudder involuntarily.

I was actually surprisingly hungry and managed to do reasonable justice to our impromptu dinner. As I battled on determinedly, chasing the last morsel from a container with a pair of chopsticks, I noticed Jimmy regarding my healthy appetite with poorly concealed approval.

'You don't have to do that, you know.'

'Do what?' he asked, clearly unaware that I'd caught him watching me.

'Check up on me. Make sure I'm all right all the time. That I'm not about to pine away, or starve myself to death, or do anything . . . stupid . . . in a fit of depression.'

'I don't do any of that,' he denied, his voice full of bluster, which didn't fool me at all. I had, after all, known this man for a long long time.

'So what was that all about earlier on tonight, when you came storming in here?'

He met my eyes, but didn't reply.

'I don't need another parent looking out for me, you know,' I declared. I was in danger of sounding ungrateful here, but I still needed to be certain he understood. 'It's not your job to keep rescuing me.'

His eyes were unreadable, but he finally answered quietly. 'I know that. It's just I feel . . .' His voice trailed away intriguingly.

'Yes?' I prompted softly.

'I feel . . . partly responsible for what's happened to you and Matt.'

That was definitely *not* what I'd either been expecting – or hoping – to hear.

'How on *earth* do you figure that out?'

He sighed deeply and sat down in the armchair opposite me, putting the large expanse of coffee table between us.

'Matt and I have never really got on that well . . .'

'That's hardly breaking news.'

He ignored my sarcasm and continued. 'And I guess in the weeks since your attack, you and I have spent quite a bit of time together. I've certainly seen more of you than Matt has.'

An unbidden image flashed up at his unintentional double-entendre; an image I quickly rammed to the back of my mind.

'So that can't have helped the situation between you two.'

I started to interrupt then, but he put up a hand to stall me.

'And what happened today, at his place . . . I guess I must take some responsibility for that too.'

I stared at him incredulously. 'Not unless you paid

Cathy to take her clothes off and climb into bed with someone else's fiancé, you don't!'

He ran his hands through his hair, clearly exasperated by something I was failing to grasp. 'God, Rachel. Don't be so glib. Don't you think that at least some of the reason he did that today was in retaliation for what nearly happened between us?'

I felt like I'd just been kicked, very hard, in the stomach.

'What? Do you think I told him about that? Just dropped it casually into the conversation? Why would you think I'd do that?'

He searched my face for an answer, surely able to read the feelings I didn't have the courage to voice. But whatever he saw did not elicit the kind of reaction I'd been hoping for, as there was a tightness and control to his tone when he finally replied. 'No reason. No reason at all.'

We cleared away in silence then, each lost in our own thoughts. After waiting so long for him to finally acknowledge our interlude at the hotel, I now wished the subject had never been raised at all. It was obvious to me that Jimmy deeply regretted the whole incident and apparently assumed I felt the same way. The weight of the day and all its many revelations was suddenly too much to cope with, and I wasn't feigning my over-exaggerated yawn when I announced, 'I'm feeling pretty exhausted, so I'm going to turn in now. Are you sure you'll be all right on the couch with those blankets?'

As we both knew the only other alternative was to share my bed, there was no surprise at hearing his hasty confirmation.

'No. That will be perfect.' I was almost at the door before I heard his final softly voiced utterance. 'Sleep well, Rachel.'

Surprisingly I did. No dreams. No mysterious alarms, strange aftershave, nothing. Jimmy had clearly been up and dressed for some time, as there was coffee gurgling in the filter pot and a plate of golden croissants waiting for me on the kitchen counter. I grabbed one and began nibbling on the light buttery flakes as he poured me coffee – with milk.

'I see you've been shopping.'

He smiled, and the awkwardness of last night was, thankfully, nowhere to be seen. I figured we would be all right as long as we just confined everything to neutral territory.

He pulled out one of the high kitchen stools and tried not to smile as I struggled to get onto the seat.

'It's easier with heels on,' I muttered.

Before I could stop him he had taken hold of me by the waist and lifted me effortlessly onto the high wooden seat. His hands lingered only fleetingly upon me as I settled in place, but even that brief contact made me shiver.

'Are you cold?' he inquired, taking in the sleeveless vest and cotton jogging bottoms I had slept in. It was hardly my most alluring look, especially not with a face devoid of any make-up and my hair pulled back in a swinging pony tail. Without waiting for me to answer, he shrugged out of his jacket and laid it around my shoulders, enveloping me both in warmth and the irresistible smell of him.

He looked down on me, and his eyes were warm. Suddenly I wasn't cold at all. His gaze travelled from my head down to my bare feet, dangling some ten inches off the floor. I thought I could see appreciation in his look, I swear I didn't imagine that, but then his lips curled in a grin I had seen a thousand times before.

'What's so funny?' I asked, taking a large sip of coffee to hide the blush I could feel beginning to form from his scrutiny.

'You. Just sitting there like that, you look just like you did when you were thirteen years old.'

'Wow. It's compliments like that which have kept you single,' I confirmed, reaching for another croissant.

It took over an hour to carry out all the boxes and load them in the back of Jimmy's car. We were in the lift, halfway back up to my floor to collect the next load, when my mobile phone began to ring once again: as it had been doing at regular intervals for the past few hours. I pulled it from the pocket of my jeans, checked the identity on the backlit display, and pressed the button to disconnect the call.

'Matt again?' Jimmy asked succinctly.

I nodded, sliding the phone back into my pocket. 'He'll give up eventually,' I pronounced.

'You think so?' Jimmy asked obliquely, as we reached our floor. He had his back to me as the doors opened, so I couldn't read his expression when he added softly, 'I wouldn't.'

Interesting. Very interesting.

I pulled the door shut on the flat for the last time a little while later. I supposed I would have to come back here at some point in time to sort out the lease and utilities, but to all intents and purposes I had now officially moved out.

'You OK?' Jimmy asked, giving my shoulder a comforting squeeze.

'Surprisingly, yes,' I answered.

'Good,' he declared. 'Because if you get your memory back and want this stuff all moved in again, you'll have to find someone else to do it!'

I laughed, but something of what he said lingered with me as we made our way back to his car. What if I did regret the decisions I was making now when my memory returned? The picture of Matt and Cathy drifted back to me – it really *was* going to take some time to get rid of that one. No, some decisions would hold up whatever Dr Andrews helped me to remember.

The traffic was fairly light considering how close we were to Christmas; perhaps the darkening sky and gusting wind were keeping people away from London. Either way, it was warm and safe in Jimmy's car, or was that just the way he made me feel when we were together?

'Have you given any thought to what you're going to do about your magazine job?'

I frowned. I had thought about it. A lot. It was actually a much harder prospect to give that up than almost anything else. That particular career had been my dream for so many years, it was ironic that it should now feel vaguely wrong and fraudulent that it was mine without having earned it.

'That's daft,' said Jimmy, when I tried to explain my hesitancy in staying there. 'You saw those articles you wrote. You are *good*. You deserve that job.' I basked a little in his praise, and gave a wistful sigh.

'Maybe. I don't know. I can probably drag out making a final decision for a few more weeks yet.'

'Of course,' Jimmy said speculatively, another alternative just occurring to him, 'you might be able to get your old job back on the paper. Your dad once said they'd welcome you back anytime.'

That idea hadn't even occurred to me and I was still considering the suggestion when he added, 'And it would be good to have you closer to home.'

I turned to look out through the rain-splattered passenger window, so he wouldn't see the ridiculous little smile his words had plastered on my face.

And that's when the axis of my world tipped once again and the craziness came back.

'Turn left here!'

Jimmy took his eyes off the road, clearly startled by the urgency in my voice.

'What? Why? That's the wrong way.'

Something in my face told him to question no further, and in a move that probably deserved the blaring horn from the taxi he cut up, Jimmy swerved from one lane to another and turned left.

'Straight ahead at these lights,' I commanded.

Again he looked at me questioningly, but I just shook my head, and he didn't probe further. A busy junction approached.

'Which way?' he asked.

'Take a right here and then follow the road down to the end. It bends sharply to the left.'

He never once questioned me; never tried to get me to stop or explain where I was directing him. He never even flinched at the curtly barked out instructions, except for once commenting softly, 'You know, the satnav lady is much more courteous.'

I nearly smiled then, nearly relaxed a little, which would have been a welcome relief, for my heart was pounding erratically and my stomach felt twisted in knots as we wound our way through countless side streets and back turns. I felt like I was being dragged back by some irresistible and unstoppable force that was drawing me like a magnet to our destination.

Gradually we left behind the more desirable residences and at last arrived in a street of rather shabby shops boasting one of London's less enviable postcodes.

'Can you pull in over there?' I pointed at a parking space that had just opened up. 'Behind that van.'

He did as I asked, parking efficiently and switching off the engine before turning to me.

The panic I had felt during our fifteen-minute detour had begun to lessen, but in its place was a familiar dread.

What I was about to say was going to ruin everything: was going to have everyone looking at me like I was some sort of lunatic again.

Jimmy took hold of my hands, which were twisting convulsively together in my lap.

'Which one?'

'Which one what?' I replied, keeping my eyes upon his large hands, which had gently curled around mine, steadying them.

'Which one is your flat?'

I looked up then, but I couldn't see him properly through the diamond jewelled tears that threatened to spill over. I nodded my head slightly to indicate the properties on the other side of the street.

'The one on the end, above the launderette.'

He looked over at the property for a moment or two, before unbuckling his seatbelt.

'Come on then.'

I looked up, perplexed.

'We have to check it out.'

He came around to my side of the car and took my arm, firmly tucking it under his. My death-white pallor and stony expression must have worried him, for he tried to defuse the moment with humour.

'By the way, remind me never to go rally driving with you. You're far too grumpy a navigator.'

We waited to cross the road, which I had crossed a thousand times before during the time I lived there. There was a resolve and determination to Jimmy's stride as he guided me through the traffic. I knew he was probably wondering how to deal with my reaction when I found out that the flat was not, and never had been, mine. But I had an altogether different worry. I turned to him, and hoped my voice sounded steadier than it felt.

'What are we going to do if that flat turns out to be full of my stuff?'

We were outside the launderette by then, and mindless of the captive audience of those waiting in the steamy interior by the machines, he pulled me into his arms and held me fiercely against him, as though the strong circle of his embrace could keep out the demons.

'We'll deal with it. Whatever it is, we'll deal with it.'

It was a vow, an oath, a promise. It gave me the strength to step out of his hold and lead him slowly towards my other home.

The entrance to the cluster of flats above the shops was just around the corner. I halted before making the turn, allowing Jimmy to reach the door first.

He looked at me curiously.

'Do you see, there's a push-button entry panel beside you?'

He glanced to the left-hand side of the front door.

'I do, but most flats have—'

'Winter. Hunt. Webb. Freeman.'

I watched his frown deepen in confusion as I correctly listed the names on the cardboard tags beside each individual buzzer. Names I couldn't possibly read from where I was standing.

'And the top one is mine. Wiltshire.'

He looked from me, back to the panel, and then at me again.

'Four out of five,' he announced. 'The top card is blank.'

I stepped around the corner and saw he was right. The last time I'd seen this device, my name had been clearly printed by the top button. Doubt began to inch into the certainty that had drawn me to this place.

'This flat could belong to a friend of yours. Someone you don't remember,' he suggested gently. It was a reasonable enough conclusion: except for one thing.

'And do you memorise the names of your friends' neighbours?'

He had no answer, but I could see his policeman's mind was already struggling with the evidence.

I pressed the second buzzer on the entrance system, saying as I did, 'Mrs Hunt. She lets everyone in, without asking who they are. It's a real crime hazard.'

Sure enough, the clicking of the front door mechanism came almost immediately in response to the buzzer, and the front door swung slowly open.

Jimmy took the first step over the threshold into the darkened hallway, which always smelled vaguely of detergent from the launderette. The familiar aroma rocked my assurance for a minute and my steps faltered slightly as I began to climb the threadbare stairs in front of us. Jimmy took my hand and I gripped it like a lifeline as we began to ascend the well-worn treads.

We passed the first and second landings without incident, but as we turned to climb the next flight, a large middle-aged woman with ebony black hair swept past us. She was clearly preoccupied with some paperwork she was reading, and jumped in surprise when I greeted her.

'Good morning, Mrs Keyworth.'

She stopped in her tracks, her automatic smile of greeting wavering as she took in the two strangers standing before her.

'Good morning,' she replied automatically, even as her eyes were narrowing in confusion. 'I'm sorry . . . do I know you?'

That indeed was an interesting question. I stood silently as her gaze travelled blankly over my face, before she turned both her attention and questioning smile upon Jimmy. I almost smiled myself then at the familiar response from my landlady. She always *had* favoured her male tenants, especially the younger ones.

'You probably don't remember us,' supplied Jimmy smoothly. That clearly was true enough. 'We're friends of someone who lives here.' And that was a lie.

Mrs Keyworth's smile was still a little uncertain, as she replied, 'Ah yes. Of course. Nice to see you again.'

She moved past us then, continuing on her descent, but twice she paused to look back questioningly at us on the landing above her, as though something was vaguely troubling her. She would probably spend the rest of the morning trying to remember where and when she had previously met Jimmy. Me, she had already forgotten.

When we were alone once more on the stairwell, I looked to see how Jimmy was processing this latest revelation.

'That was my landlady, Mrs Keyworth. She's a nice enough woman. A bit overly chatty sometimes. And she has quite a thing for younger men.'

Jimmy said nothing, not even smiling at my final comment. He looked preoccupied, as though something here was beginning to chip away at the foundation of his belief.

'I think she took quite a shine to you,' I teased.

Again he gave no responding light-hearted rejoinder, replying only in a slightly distracted tone, 'But she didn't recognise you.'

We were silent for the rest of the climb until we finally reached the top floor, on which the last flat was located. I hadn't been expecting the jolt of recognition that assaulted me the moment we stood by the apartment.

'And here we are. Home sweet home.'

Jimmy surveyed our surroundings: the front door with layers of paint curling off in thick flakes; the walls sadly in need of redecorating and the grimy hallway window, too flecked with dirt to let in much light on a dark December morning.

'Quite frankly, I prefer your other place.'

I gave a small shrug.

'Well . . .' he prompted, standing back slightly to allow me access to the front door. 'Are you going to knock?'

I took a small step forward, feeling knocking was surely unnecessary: whoever was inside my flat could probably already hear my heart hammering out like a drum.

I realised that the flat wasn't mine even before I raised

my hand to tap upon the wooden panel. There was a bright shiny new Yale lock on the door, which definitely hadn't been there when I was the occupant.

The rapping of knuckles against timber echoed down the length of the empty corridor. Minutes ticked by before I tried again, banging even more firmly on the familiar door.

'Doesn't look like anyone is home,' Jimmy eventually declared. 'Perhaps it's not even occupied. There wasn't a name on the doorbell downstairs.'

I was surprised at the disappointment that filled me at his words. To have come this far without finally being able to access the flat was beyond frustrating. Even though the evidence we had already uncovered told me what to expect, I still needed to see the proof with my own eyes. If I was ever to have any peace of mind, I needed to get inside the flat and verify there were no hidden traces within of my missing life.

And then I remembered something. Abandoning the front door, I crossed swiftly over to the window, which was a short distance away down the corridor. I ran my fingers around the faded wooden sill, seeking a handhold. Gripping the yellowed wood firmly in both hands I began to pull, thrusting up against the sill with my knee when it resisted my efforts.

'Er, what are you doing?' queried Jimmy, coming quickly to my side.

I gave a grunt at my efforts but just kept trying to release the sill from the window cavity. Jimmy put his hands over mine, stilling my attempts to lift it.

'Rachel, if you don't want me to arrest you for vandalism, would you please explain what you're up to?'

I sighed and straightened up.

'The guy who had the flat before me, an American chap, told me about this dodgy sill when I moved in. Apparently he was always locking himself out, so he found this neat place to keep a spare key. If it's still there, we can let ourselves into the flat and check it out.'

'Now that *is* breaking and entering,' Jimmy confirmed. 'Not exactly the best career move on my part, do you not think?'

I looked up at him. He was right. This could get him in serious trouble with his bosses. I couldn't be responsible for that. I couldn't jeopardise his career.

'OK. You wait for me down in the car. I'll do this by myself. It won't take long.'

He sighed deeply.

'You really are hell-bent on a life of crime, aren't you?'

Then, despite his words, he gently pushed me to one side and took hold of the sill. It lifted easily from its resting place in one smooth move. Little flurries of plaster dust puffed up at the removal of the wooden base, which for a second or two obscured the bricks upon which the sill had sat. As the dust settled, we both leant forward as though to take a closer look. But really there was no need. A front door key, safely encased in a clear plastic bag, was plainly visible, nestled in a gap between two bricks. Jimmy gave a small exclamation of surprise.

My hand was already halfway towards the key when behind us came the unmistakable sound of a latch being released and the rattling of several door chains. In one hurried manoeuvre Jimmy replaced the sill upon the bricks, thumping down firmly on the wood to secure it in position, just as the front door to my old flat opened behind us.

'Hello there,' trilled a male voice. I spun around, hoping my features were devoid of guilt, to face the tall, slimly built man standing in my doorway. 'Sorry I couldn't get to the door straight away. I was on the phone. Can I help you?' He was smiling engagingly but I noticed it was being directed at Jimmy and not me. He really was proving to be a big hit today.

'Good morning, sir,' began Jimmy, his voice adopting a smooth professional tone. 'I'm sorry to disturb you but I wondered if we could have a moment or two of your time.' As he spoke, Jimmy slipped his hand into his jacket pocket and produced his warrant card for the young man to peruse.

His reaction was interesting to observe, for his face paled a little under the expensive fake tan, and he ran his hand nervously through his immaculately highlighted hair. I wondered what he might have been involved with to make him so uncomfortable at finding a policeman at his door.

'May we come in for a moment?' Jimmy asked, still the consummate officer of the law.

'Oh yes, of course, of course,' flustered the flat's new occupant. 'Please excuse the mess. I wasn't expecting visitors; the place is an absolute tip!'

We followed him through the hallway which I had

painted bright yellow to lighten it. It was now covered in smart blue and white striped wallpaper. The lounge too was far from being the disgrace its owner had described, being stylishly and minimalistically furnished in sleek white and navy blue. It really did look so much bigger with all my furniture removed.

'Please, sit, sit,' flapped the man. 'Can I get you something to drink? Or eat?'

'No, thank you, sir. This really won't take more than a few minutes.'

The man was beginning to relax slightly now at Jimmy's encouraging smile. He was really quite good at this policeman stuff. If he *had* been here to question the man about some misdemeanour, he would totally have lulled him into a false sense of security.

'Could I have your name please?' asked Jimmy smoothly, even withdrawing a small notebook to complete the illusion of an investigation. God, he was *really* good.

'Maximilian MacRae,' informed the man, perching on the edge of a white settee which contrasted strikingly with his black leather trousers. He leaned towards Jimmy with a twinkle. 'But everyone just calls me Max.'

Could he *be* any more blatant? I bit my lip, which was threatening to quiver slightly. Jimmy, on the other hand, seemed impervious to anything inappropriate.

'Mr MacRae,' he began, putting the interview back on a more formal footing, 'we are making enquiries today about a missing person. Do you know anything of a Miss Rachel Wiltshire?'

My head flew up at my name.

'Nooo. I've never heard of her, I'm afraid. Why, has something happened to her?'

There was an almost ghoulish curiosity to his tone; a desire to hear every last grisly detail. If I really *was* missing, this guy would be high up on my list of suspects!

'We hope not. We're just trying to trace her whereabouts. We have this flat listed as her last known address.'

I almost applauded then at the skilful way Jimmy had manipulated the conversation to find out what we wanted to know.

'Really? That's very odd. You see, I've lived here for three years now, and before me there was some young American man, who'd been here for even longer. So if this – what was her name? – Rachel girl *did* live here, it must have been a really long time ago.'

'I see,' Jimmy replied. He looked over to me with a question in his eyes. *Have you seen enough?* I looked around the room that was mine, and not mine at all. I was everywhere and nowhere. I gave a small nod.

Jimmy got to his feet and I followed suit.

'Well, thank you very much, Mr MacRae. I apologise again for disturbing you.'

'Please, just Max.'

'Thank you, Max,' corrected Jimmy already heading towards the hallway. 'You've been extremely helpful.'

Max smiled doubtfully at Jimmy's words.

'I do hope you find this missing girl. And please, if you have any more questions, anything at all, just pop in anytime. I'm always here.'

The invitation was directed totally at Jimmy; I was so

completely excluded from that one, I might as well have been invisible. I turned away and pretended to be examining my shoes, afraid it wasn't going to take much more before I was actually laughing out loud. I glanced briefly at Jimmy and saw the hint of a tremor to his shoulders.

Max followed us both all the way to the hallway and stood lingering by his open door as we began to walk away.

'By the way . . .' began Jimmy, turning back towards Max when we had taken only a few steps, 'that key you have hidden under the window sill: it's really not such a good idea.'

It was highly amusing to see the change in Max's expression from coy flirtatiousness to absolute astonishment.

'How did you know . . . No one else . . . How . . . ?'

'First place a burglar looks,' assured Jimmy, taking my arm to guide us towards the stairs. 'Good day to you, sir.'

We held it together until we were safely out of earshot, then the laughter came, a blissful and welcome temporary escape from the tension. I actually had tears rolling down my cheeks when we opened the main door and tumbled out of the house into the cold December day.

'Boy, you're on fire today, aren't you?' I said at last, when my ability to speak had returned.

Jimmy gave a self-effacing shrug. 'What can I say? When you're hot, you're hot.'

Back inside his car once again, his mood sobered a little.

'Do you know exactly how many laws I broke just then?'

I bit my lip guiltily. 'Quite a few?' I hazarded.

'Yeah.'

'Sorry,' I murmured.

He reached over to pick up my hand, sliding it comfortingly within his own. I looked down at his fingers laced so easily around mine, knowing I shouldn't keep misinterpreting his intentions, but it was so hard not to. Perhaps it was time for a reality check.

'Come on then. Let me have it. Give me your explanation for what just happened in there.'

'Ah well, Maximilian naturally fell under the spell of my not inconsiderable charms and—'

I gave a very unladylike response, before steering him away from humour.

'You know what I'm talking about. Explain to me how I knew everything that I did: how to get here; the names of the landlady, the tenants, past and present – not to mention the hidden key.'

He was silent for so long I almost thought he wasn't going to answer. When he did, his words came out on a long sigh.

'I can't.'

I swivelled in my seat then, to study his expression more clearly. I wasn't used to him sounding so uncertain. I almost felt sorry for the dilemma I was putting him in, knowing how his logical policeman's mind must be struggling with something that made no sense at all.

He turned the engine on then, finally releasing my hand from his.

'Can you try directing me a little less aggressively this time?'

'Directing you where?'

He looked at me as though I was being deliberately dumb.

'Andersons Engineering. That *was* the name of the place you worked, wasn't it?'

I nodded, unable to help a smile of pure gratitude being my response. Not only had he remembered the name, but more importantly he knew and understood that I needed his help in this impossible quest, without my having to ask for it. And suddenly the journey to seek out the answers didn't seem nearly so daunting and scary, not now I realised I wasn't facing it alone.

Forty-five minutes later we were back in central London.

'There's a small car park tucked away down this side street,' I indicated.

Jimmy followed my directions and no longer looked surprised when the small compound was exactly where I had said it would be.

I scoured the faces of passers-by as we walked the short distance to the engineering company, looking out for any of my colleagues, but I saw no one I recognised; nor, more importantly, did anyone recognise me.

The building's access was at the top of a broad flight

of concrete steps, and I hesitated for a moment on the pavement before turning to Jimmy.

'Thank you,' I murmured quietly, my words almost whipped away on the December wind.

His responding smile was all the encouragement I needed to begin to climb the steps to the large plate-glass entrance door.

When we reached the top, Jimmy went to press the doorbell which was sited beneath a sign reading *Visitors please ring for admittance.*

'Wait,' I urged, nodding my head in the direction of a small silver keypad set into the aluminium frame. My fingers were chilled by the cold weather, but they still flew without hesitation over the buttons, punching in the eight-numbered entry code for staff.

Behind me I heard Jimmy's sharp intake of breath as the door responded to the command and opened for me.

I looked at him then, unable to keep from my expression the gauntlet of challenge I was throwing down in the face of all logical explanations.

His face was still a picture of doubts and questions as we entered the building, but once inside the foyer I was the one who drew to a hesitant halt.

'Rachel?' Jimmy queried. 'Are you OK?' I looked around at my familiar work place and gave a helpless sigh.

'What are we doing here? What am I going to do now? Go up to my desk and haul whoever is sitting there out of my chair? Keep insisting I belong here until someone calls security and throws us out?'

It was as if my words had actually summoned them up, for we were both taken by surprise by the arrival of a security guard, who'd walked over to us with such speed and stealth neither of us had seen him coming.

'Can I help you?' the man enquired, his tone sounding anything but helpful. I could only guess that he had seen us access the building, and failing to recognise us as employees he'd wasted no time leaving his work station to challenge our entry.

I tried to give a small guileless smile, which didn't work at all at thawing out the frostiness in his eyes. I recognised the man vaguely, but could see no reciprocation in his slightly hostile stare. I could only hope he hadn't already pressed some hidden alert button.

'Oh, hello there. I wonder if you *can* help us, actually. We're meeting a friend of mine for lunch; she works here. It was a bit too cold to wait outside. I do hope it was OK to come in?'

The guard's attitude relaxed the merest fraction, his body language turning down the aggression from boil to simmer. Clearly he now believed my 'friend' had given out the company's entry code to random non-employee members of the public. I think I'd just got my new imaginary friend in a whole heap of trouble.

The guard gave a small non-committal grunt, which could possibly have been his response or just him clearing his throat. I continued to smile broadly at him, thinking if he didn't stop scrutinising us in that suspicious way very soon, my jaw might actually break from the effort.

Fortunately Jimmy interjected at that moment, adding plausibility to our charade.

'Is it possible to call up and let our friend know we are here?' He really lied most convincingly for an officer of the law, which was somewhat alarming. However his comment seemed to add enough validity to our story that the guard turned to walk back to reception, motioning that we follow him.

Behind his desk once more, with visitors separated by the appropriate barrier, he clearly felt that order had been restored, for he was far more civil when he inquired, 'Your friend who works here, could I have her name, please?'

Without even thinking I interjected, 'Rachel Wiltshire.'

I saw Jimmy's eyes close briefly in disbelief, even as the guard began running his finger down the W section of the staff list, looking for a name that no longer belonged on that particular sheet. Too late I realised the stupidity of my comment.

With his stubby index finger coming to rest at the foot of the directory, the guard looked up at us both, his distrust instantly returning.

'Rachel Wiltshire, you said? We don't have anyone of that name working here.'

I looked at Jimmy to see if he was going to extricate me from the mess I had just made, but he just flashed me the merest flicker of a smile, which clearly said *you dug this hole – now get out of it!*

I narrowed my eyes meaningfully at my companion, and resigned myself to having to play the blonde card.

'Oh, sorry, that's *my* name!' The guard's look spoke

volumes. 'My friend is called Emily. Emily Frost.' I plucked the first name I could think of from one of my colleagues. 'But, actually, you know what, I think we'll just wait outside after all and then we can . . . surprise her. Sorry to have bothered you.' I grabbed Jimmy's coat sleeve and began to drag him towards the exit.

'Smooth,' pronounced Jimmy, allowing himself to be steered towards the doorway. 'That certainly didn't make him suspicious, did it?'

I could still feel the guard's eyes following us all the way across the foyer. As we reached the door I heard him speak, and thought at first he was about to call us back, but he was only bidding goodbye to a fellow guard who was going to lunch.

'See you later, Joe.'

Hand already on the door handle, I turned back to see a second security guard crossing the foyer, also heading for the exit. He was a man of about my father's age, with greying hair and a deeply ruddy complexion. My mouth automatically turned up to greet him with a warm smile.

'Hi, Joe. How are you?'

Bafflement was his first emotion, but neither Jimmy nor I had expected how that would change to disbelief, when I made my next remark. 'And how is your wife doing? Is she out of hospital yet?'

All colour drained from Joe's face as his eyes flew from Jimmy and me and then back over his shoulder at his colleague. He bustled through the door, forcing us along with him. It wasn't until all three of us had crossed the threshold and were out of the building that he turned sharply to me, questioning almost belligerently, 'Excuse me. What did you just ask me?'

I wasn't used to hearing him speak to me in that way, forgetting for a moment that to him I was a complete stranger.

'I just asked how Muriel was doing. Her latest round of chemo must be finished now, mustn't it? You said you were hoping she would be out of hospital by Christmas.'

Jimmy had taken a small step back, standing to one side and watching our strange interplay with curiosity.

Joe, on the other hand, seemed totally shaken by my words.

'I don't understand . . . who *are* you?'

'I'm Rachel. Rachel Wiltshire.' If I was hoping for anything resembling recognition, I was going to be waiting a very long time.

'I don't know you,' Joe announced, shaking his head from side to side. It was a familiar chorus: everyone appeared to be singing it these days. I couldn't think what to say to him that wouldn't sound completely deranged.

'But what I *really* want to know,' Joe continued urgently, 'is how the hell you know about Muriel. I've not told anybody here at all about her illness. Not one word.'

I think Jimmy got Joe to the pub on false pretences. Telling him that if he joined us for a drink we would explain everything was stretching the truth by anyone's definition. However, when I suggested that we get out of the biting wind and move our discussion to the King George pub, where most of the staff went each day for lunch, Joe reluctantly agreed to go with us.

It was a little disconcerting to see the way he kept darting sidelong glances at me as we walked the few hundred yards to the popular watering hole; as though I might be some sort of weird clairvoyant or worse.

The pub was crowded, as it usually was at that time of day, and we struggled to find a table for the three of us. All around us were small groups of my work colleagues and I had to bite my lip to stop greeting everyone I passed. Eventually I spotted a vacant table towards the back of the pub and hurried to claim it, with a clearly reluctant Joe following in my wake.

I smiled at him tentatively as we took our seats. There was no answering response, which was sad, because I had always liked this man, long before I realised we had so much in common. Eventually Jimmy returned with a round of drinks, informing us that he had ordered three ploughman's lunches which they would bring over shortly. Somehow I doubted that anyone was going to have much of an appetite before this meeting was over.

'So who told you about Muriel?' was Joe's first question, fired out at speed.

I shook my head, thinking I had better not answer that particular question first. Joe was clearly extremely defensive, which was apparent by his next comment.

'I don't know what your game is but I don't want anyone making any trouble for me at work about any of this.'

He was clearly exceedingly rattled that his most private secret was known by someone he had never met before. I reached out to pat his hand comfortingly and stopped only when I saw the look of horror on his face.

'We're not trying to make any trouble for you, Joe,' assured Jimmy in a very soothing tone.

'I don't have any money, you know,' Joe advised.

'Of course you don't,' I agreed without thinking. 'Not after putting two kids through university and keeping your mother in that retirement home.'

Half of Joe's pint of beer slopped over the table as his shaking hand almost dropped his glass.

'That's it! How do you know all this? Who *are* you people?'

There was no easy way to begin, but all I could do was tell the truth as I knew it.

'I know you might find it a little hard to believe, but actually, Joe, I'm your friend.'

Joe fixed me with a long hard stare. He then turned a similar look upon Jimmy.

'Ah no,' Jimmy corrected, 'I *am* a total stranger. Rachel's the one who knows you.'

Once again Joe looked back at me, still so openly confused that I felt sorry we had dragged him into this. He had enough to cope with already.

'If we are friends then how come I don't know you? I've a good memory; you need it in my job. And I don't forget a face and I would most definitely remember spilling the details of my private life to some stranger.'

I smiled to soften my words, hoping he wouldn't misinterpret the baring of teeth as an act of aggression.

'I know this sounds crazy. But we *are* friends. Good ones. And the reason I know so much about you and your family, especially about Muriel's illness, is because I have been going through something similar myself, with my dad.'

For the first time Joe's expression softened, revealing the kindly man who had been such a support to me as we swapped concerns and worries over loved ones who were battling the same illness.

'I'm sorry to hear that,' he mumbled, and at last realising that we meant no malice here, he continued, 'But I still don't know how you could possibly know the details that you know. I've had to be so careful about not letting anyone at work find out. There've been so many redundancies recently, I couldn't risk giving them a reason to let me go.'

'I know,' I said softly. This worry had been a familiar theme to many of our conversations. As had the progress of our respective family members in their fight for life. We had bonded together and both gained strength from it. It was sad that in this new version of the world, Joe didn't have anyone he could share his burden with.

'But *how* do you know all this?' Joe asked once again. 'Who was it who told you?'

I couldn't evade the question a second time.

'You did.'

*

I don't know if we ever managed to convince Joe that we were sincere. All I know is that when I recounted detail after detail of his wife's battle, which had so closely matched my father's, he could no longer refute that I was in possession of facts he thought no one else had been told. In the end he struggled to find a solution he could live with, one that wouldn't keep him awake at night for years to come.

'It must be the stress that has done this,' he pronounced at last.

'Done what?' Jimmy queried.

'Made it so I don't remember. Yes, that's it. All the worry has given me a sort of . . . amnesia.'

There was a long silence at his words. I looked at Jimmy meaningfully for a moment, before replying solemnly, 'There's a lot of that going around.'

We didn't stay in the pub for long after our food had arrived. Jimmy seemed to be the only one with any sort of appetite, although I thought Joe might eat more comfortably after we had gone.

I did have one bizarre encounter in the Ladies, when I emerged from a cubicle to see Emily Frost standing at the mirrored sink unit.

'Hi there,' I greeted, smiling at her warmly, forgetting she knew nothing about our supposed lunch date or indeed who the hell I was. She looked back at me warily in the reflected glass. Suddenly I was tired of being an outsider among people I had known for so long. It was time to go.

Jimmy held out his hand to Joe.

'It's been very nice meeting you.'

No one was entirely surprised when Joe didn't return the comment. His parting to me was slightly warmer after I offered, 'I'm sorry if we've upset you today. I really *do* hope everything goes well with Muriel. I'll be thinking of you both.'

We turned to go then, Jimmy's hand securely guiding me away from the table.

'Er . . . Rachel?' called out Joe, startling us both.

As one we turned around to face the man we had so confounded that day.

'Your dad, Rachel. How is he? How is he doing now?'

I smiled slowly at my old friend and his concern.

'He got better, Joe.'

Chapter 12

'Joe seemed like a nice guy.'

I said nothing, keeping my eyes fixed out of the window at the disappearing London suburbs.

Jimmy tried again. 'I think we eventually convinced him we weren't total crackpots.'

Again I gave no reply.

'You OK?' asked Jimmy kindly, taking his hand briefly off the wheel to give mine a reassuring squeeze.

'He didn't know me.' My voice was dull and toneless, but Jimmy's ears still discerned the pain.

'I know.' There was compassion and understanding in his tone.

'I don't know why I'm surprised, I should have been expecting it. But he was the first person who I've met who I know well; who I really care about. He's my friend, for God's sake and he didn't know who the hell I was!' I thought of the pub full of familiar faces, none of whom had recognised me. 'No one does.'

I couldn't blame Jimmy for failing to come up with some soothing rejoinder. What on earth could he say that could offer any comfort?

'It's almost as though it's not *me* with amnesia . . . it's them! I've literally been erased from their memories.'

'Hey, you're not going all sci-fi on me here, are you?' Clearly his mind was going back to the theory I had first put forward when we were last in London: the one about a parallel world, where everyone still existed, leading a similar but subtly different life than this one.

'It is a theory . . .' I offered tentatively.

'A crazy one.'

'But what if it were real: crazy or not? What if something happened to me when I hit my head during the mugging? What if I actually did somehow swap places with another version of me?'

Jimmy laughed. But when I didn't join in, the amusement quickly died.

'Rachel, you really cannot be serious about this,' he began gently. 'I know there are loads of unanswered questions here, but I really don't believe that people can go zipping about in time and drop in on their *other lives*.'

'I'm not talking about time *travel*. Maybe something happened on that night, and it created . . . I don't know . . . some sort of anomaly in the space-time continuum?'

'Do you even *know* what a space-time continuum is?'

'No. But maybe we could find an expert or a scientist in this field. Someone who *would* have some of the answers.' *Someone who wouldn't think I was totally insane*, I finished silently in my head.

'Rachel, honey, that stuff only happens in books and movies. In real life you can't find Weird Scientist Guy actually listed in Yellow Pages. Where would we even begin?'

'I don't know,' I replied mulishly. I knew what he was saying was right. I just didn't want to hear it.

'Do you want to hear what I think?'

I turned in my seat to see him more clearly.

'Go on.'

'What I think is that something *did* happen to you when you hit your head. Something very unusual and unique. Something that is allowing you to . . . I don't know, maybe read minds, pick up some sort of psychic energy and interpret it into memories . . . I don't know.'

'And why would none of this neurological damage have shown up on the multitude of tests they've run on me?'

He shook his head. 'I don't know. Like I said, I think that it must be incredibly rare. Perhaps it *is* on the tests but the doctors don't even know what they're looking at. You might be the only person this has ever happened to.'

His suggestion did have a degree of rational credibility, I had to grant him that. But it didn't seem to fit, not in the way my own idea did.

I could go two ways with this: keep on insisting there

was something more supernatural – for want of a better word – going on here, and risk losing his support completely, or be the bigger person and let it go. I chose wisely.

'So I'm unique then, am I?' I said with the beginnings of a smile. 'One of a kind?'

'I've never doubted that for a single minute of my life.'

I couldn't help it: my smile just kept getting broader and broader, until I was in danger of resembling some demented version of the Cheshire Cat. I also couldn't help noticing that he looked more than a little pleased by my response.

A few more miles down the grey ribbon of motorway, I brought up the topic again. 'But what if we never get to the bottom of it? If we *never* find out the answers? What do we do then?'

Jimmy was quiet for a long moment. 'Well,' he said finally on a long and considering tone, 'you remember the first eighteen years of your life just fine, don't you?'

'Yes. Right up to the night of the car accident.'

'So, in the grand scheme of things, we're really only talking about having inexplicably . . . *lost* . . . a small piece of your past. I guess what you have to ask yourself is how much time and energy you want to spend on looking backwards.' His voice changed then, the timbre becoming softer and lower. 'But speaking personally, it's not your past that interests me so much as your future.'

And those were the words that I kept replaying in my head for the rest of the journey back home.

*

My father's eyes lit up with pleasure as I crossed the threshold with the large packing boxes and a suitcase full of my belongings.

'You don't mind if I wind up staying here with you for a little bit longer, do you?' I asked as I entered the house. An unnecessary question really, but even I was surprised to see his eyes glisten unexpectedly at my request.

'Are you feeling OK, Dad?'

He rubbed his hand roughly over his eyes. 'Just getting a cold, I think,' he muttered brusquely, bending to pick up the boxes. 'I'll just take these upstairs for you. And of course I don't mind. You stay here as long as you want.'

I watched his retreating back as he climbed the stairs, suddenly overcome by a wave of love for the only parent I had ever known, mixed with an enormous gratitude that here and now he was so fit and well. Perhaps it had been talking to Joe once more about his wife's illness that suddenly made me really appreciate that life here was in many ways a great deal better than the one I remembered. Well, aside from the unfortunate incident with Matt. But maybe that too would turn out to be not such a bad thing either. Better to know now that he couldn't remain faithful and get out while I could, before making the mistake of marrying him.

The following day I finally got around to answering one

of his numerous phone calls. I had to really; he'd been continually calling both my mobile and the house phone, so I didn't have much of a choice in the matter. It wasn't a pleasant conversation, and I said some things that I'm not particularly proud of. Not that he didn't deserve it, perhaps, but I had hoped we might at least have been able to remain civil. But any phone conversation that ends with one of you yelling at the other 'Have a nice life!' can't exactly be deemed a success.

The next few days should have been pleasant enough, Christmas was almost upon us and although I didn't seem to have my normal enthusiasm for the holiday season, I tried to put on a good show for my father's sake. Not that I think I fooled him much, not when my first question upon returning home from a walk or a visit to the shops was 'Did anyone drop by or phone while I was out?'

I guess he thought I might be waiting to hear from Matt again, and I didn't bother correcting that assumption. But it wasn't the absence of contact from my ex-fiancé that was troubling me, it was not hearing from Jimmy. From the things that had been said recently, I'd thought, well, hoped really, that he was going to be a more frequent visitor to our house, but in reality I hadn't seen or heard anything at all of him since he'd driven me back from London.

Of course he could just be busy at work, but *really*, how long does it take to pick up a phone? Could he already be regretting having spent so much of his spare time with me? Or had I once again totally misinterpreted the words and actions of a close friend for something else entirely?

To fill the hours, I made a concerted effort to keep myself really busy each day, finding that physical exhaustion gave me far less thinking and brooding time. So I reorganised my old bedroom. Twice. And even cleaned the house to never-before-seen perfection. I also took up baking – which was a dubious pursuit, given the fact I had scarcely baked anything before in my life. As I produced tray after tray of food in varying degrees of edibility I saw the question in my father's eyes, even though it was never voiced. And he was right. What was I doing baking enough food to feed an army when it would just be the two of us on Christmas Day?

Each night I fell into bed totally shattered, hoping I would be so worn out that I could ignore both Jimmy's silence as well as the reccurrence of the strange dreams and night-time hallucinations that had returned to haunt me.

A few evenings before Christmas Eve my father came into the lounge, dragging behind him an overly large pine tree.

I looked up from my place at the fireside, where I had been making small but steady progress with my father's aloof cat. At least she now tolerated me touching her for as long as five seconds at a time before bolting away at speed.

'I thought we weren't going to bother with a tree this year?'

'I know,' he said, struggling to drag the giant redwood wannabe across the carpet. 'But I thought we could do with a little brightening up in here. Make it nice and festive.'

I hurried to clear a space in the corner, ducking out of the way of the approaching branches that looked sharp enough to take out an eye or two if you weren't careful. The tree was actually so big its topmost branches bowed over heavily against the ceiling, and it was roughly as wide as it was tall.

'Couldn't you find a bigger one?' I teased.

'It looked much smaller at the garden centre,' Dad explained.

'Leave your poor dad alone. You should have seen him struggling up the hill to carry it back.'

I swivelled around with enough speed to actually crick my neck. I'd been so busy examining the tree, I hadn't seen Jimmy walk into the lounge.

'Thanks for the lift, lad,' said my father. 'I knew I should have taken the car.'

'Don't mention it,' Jimmy assured, his words directed to my father but his eyes never leaving my face.

There was a long moment of silence, which was just this side of awkward.

'Anyone fancy a cup of tea?' asked my father, already half out the door to make it.

I waited until we were alone before speaking. 'Hello,

stranger. I was beginning to wonder if we'd ever see you again.'

He had the grace to look abashed. 'I'm sorry I've not been in touch. I got your texts, I've been meaning to call but . . .' His voice trailed off.

'You've been busy. I get that.'

'No. It's not that. It's just . . .'

This was getting tiresome. Was he *ever* going to finish a sentence?

'Nice tree,' he commented instead, studying the conifer with unwarranted concentration.

If I didn't know better I would have thought he was nervous. But I couldn't for the life of me think why.

As my Dad passed out the tea, I took the opportunity to study Jimmy unobserved. It looked as though I might not be the only one who hadn't been sleeping well recently, not if the dark smudges beneath his eyes were anything to go by.

'Do you have any decorations for this tree then?' Jimmy asked, after draining his cup.

'Are you volunteering to help us?'

'Oh no,' interjected my father. 'I've done my bit as far as the tree is concerned. You two can take over from here.'

I got to my feet.

'I'll get the box, it's still in the attic, right?'

I had expected one or both of them to get up at that point and offer to get the box of decorations for me, but strangely when my dad looked just about to do that,

Jimmy stopped him with a meaningful look, which I probably wasn't meant to see. But I did.

'You can manage that by yourself, can't you?' Jimmy asked confidently.

'Sure,' I replied, taking the very obvious hint and leaving the room.

I wasn't aware I was muttering under my breath as I pulled down the loft ladder and began clicking the struts in place, until I observed Kizzy staring at me curiously from the top of the banisters.

'And you're just as bad,' I said to the disdainful feline, who took off from her vantage point in a flurry of indignant fur.

Jimmy had obviously wanted to get rid of me so he could speak to my father alone. No doubt he was, even at that moment, recounting to him my own slightly eccentric theory. Proving that Rachel was still far from well. This really was great. My dad had just started treating me normally again, now he believed my 'amnesia' might soon be cured, but if Jimmy told him everything I had said in the car the other day, I'd be right back to square one.

I felt angry and more than a little betrayed, and though I'd never actually told Jimmy I didn't want my dad to know what I was thinking, I'd just assumed he knew me well enough to understand that information had been for his ears only.

Typically it took much longer than it should have done to find the blasted box of decorations, and by the time I had eventually located them and packed away the ladder, whatever discussion Jimmy and my father had been engaged upon was clearly finished.

And if I needed further proof that there was something funny going on, there it was when I walked back into the lounge and found both men deeply involved in some pseudo-conversation about football, a subject neither of them was particularly interested in.

Even as I began to rip the sealing tape from the box, Dad got to his feet and gave a huge exaggerated yawn.

'I think I might just turn in now.'

I looked at the clock above the fireplace in amazement.

'It's not even nine o'clock!'

Was that a blush on his cheeks, or was he just flushed from the heat of the fire?

'It isn't? Oh well. Never mind. It never hurts to get an early night every so often. G'night, Rachel. See you soon, Jimmy.'

I waited until I had safely heard the creak of the stairs as he climbed them, before rounding angrily on Jimmy.

'I know what you two were discussing when I was out of the room!'

And that's when everything got weird, because instead of replying, Jimmy just looked strangely uncomfortable, and was that . . . yes, it was . . . the colour in his cheeks was clearly heightened. I actually took my eyes from his face to glance over at the fire burning merrily in the grate. Either it was really *really* hot in here, or something highly suspicious was going on.

'You told him. Didn't you?' I continued, when it seemed unlikely Jimmy was going to say anything in his own defence. 'You told him what I thought had happened to me?'

Relief flooded over his features as swiftly as the raised colour had done. 'Is that what you think? No, of course I didn't. I wouldn't *do* that.'

He was so earnest in his denial that I knew instantly he was telling the truth.

'Then why did you send me out the room?'

His eyes gave a flicker, which betrayed his discomfort, but his voice was smooth enough as he replied. 'No one sent you out the room. You went to get the decorations.'

I gave him a long narrowed-eyed stare, which I knew he would remember from our past. It was the look I had always given him when I was unhappy with something he had said. However, Jimmy wasn't going to let me go any further with this one.

'Come on then. Let's get started. It's a big tree and we haven't got all night.'

It's impossible to stay in a bad mood when you're decorating a Christmas tree. There's something about the twinkling of fairy lights and the glint of fragile glass baubles reflected in the light from the fire that simply sucks all feelings of negativity from you, however hard you try to hold on to them.

At Jimmy's request I had even found a CD of Christmas tunes in my dad's collection and had them playing softly in the background as we worked together, mostly in silence, dressing the tree. It was comfortable and companionable; our heads bent low over the box of decorations, sometimes fingers colliding as we both reached for a particular ornament at exactly the same instant. Either we shared the same taste in gaudy baubles or it was another confirmation of just how in tune we were with each other.

The tree was starting to look really good. Nothing refined and understated here; this was a real Las Vegas-style tree! It just needed the tinsel to finish it off. Careful of the spiky pine needles, I wriggled halfway behind the main trunk and asked Jimmy to pass me the long strand of sparkling decoration so I could thread it through the branches. I held out my hand through the dense foliage, waiting to take the glittering streamer. But instead of passing me the tinsel, I felt Jimmy's fingertips lightly graze my own.

'I can't do this any more.'

His voice sounded almost desperate, as though the words had been torn out of him against his will.

The tree branches obscured my view of him, so I directed my voice in his general direction.

'That's all right. We're almost done here. I can finish it off myself.'

'I'm not talking about the damned tree!' There was no mistaking the tone this time; there was genuine anguish there.

I struggled to get out from the imprisoning branches, but stopped as he went on to add, 'I'm talking about us. You and me. Our friendship.'

I felt my heart freeze over. Every last fear I'd ever had in my life was crystallised in that one moment. It was as devastating to hear now as it would have been when I was five years old. Jimmy didn't want to be my friend any more. Suddenly I was in no hurry to emerge from the tree's protective cover. He shouldn't see the effect his words had on me. I'd brought this on myself. I'd neglected something precious for far too long and then tried to lean on him more than I should have. I deserved whatever was coming.

'I understand,' I said on a voice that was beginning to tremble. 'You have to step back from being my friend right now, I understand that.'

He gave a sound that was almost a groan. 'That's not it. Well, maybe that's partly it; I *do* want to step back from being your friend . . .' It was the worst thing I had ever heard, until he continued, 'but only because I want to be so much more.'

The hand that I hadn't realised I still had protruding through the branches, was suddenly gripped in his warm and steady clasp.

'And you had to wait until I was embedded in a Christmas tree to say this to me?' I asked in a voice too dazed to really take in his words.

The branches were suddenly swept back in one swift move and I stared up in wonder at the man who had just changed my entire view of the future.

'I had to make sure you couldn't run away,' he said, gently pulling me out of the tree and towards him.

'That is the last thing on my mind,' I assured him. 'In fact—'

But I never got to finish that sentence as his head was lowering towards mine, even as he was pulling me towards and against him. In a perfect blend, the soft contours of my body moulded up against the firm hardness of his. Two halves, complementing and blending, and it was as though nothing in the world had ever really been right until this single perfect moment. I felt the thundering of his heart echoing against mine as he held my trembling body against him. I looked into his eyes, and found all I'd been searching for and an expression of love so open and naked, it robbed me of what little breath I had left. And then his mouth was on mine, and his hands were arching me closer and he was holding me while I fell even more in love with the man I was always destined to be with.

The fire dimmed long before our passion did. We lay on the faded old settee, limbs entwined, our bodies in contact wherever they could be. Beneath my head I could hear the resounding and comforting beat of his heart, while his fingers traced small circles upon the nape of my neck. I had never known a moment of such complete contentment in my entire life.

I struggled to sit up but his strong arms wouldn't release me.

'Don't move,' he urged, covering my mouth with his own to ensure that for several more minutes moving away wasn't even the remotest possibility.

I was a little breathless when we eventually separated. 'Jimmy, can we talk for a minute?'

His blue eyes darkened for a second.

'I'd much rather do this,' he suggested, pulling me from his side until I lay completely on top of the long length of his body. My new location did nothing at all for my concentration and several more minutes were completely lost to me as I gave in to the racing passion that was coursing through my veins.

'Enough!' I said, sitting up so abruptly that I would have toppled from the settee if he hadn't caught me.

He must have recognised my determination, for he reluctantly rose from the cushions and swung his legs to the floor, allowing me to slide onto the seat beside him. I could see the effort it had cost him, both physical and emotional, to separate from me, and I felt a flutter deep within me, to know he wanted me as much as I did him.

'You have five minutes,' he warned, 'before I have to start kissing you again, so you'd better talk fast.'

His words and his proximity were doing funny things with my pulse rate. It could easily take me all of my allotted time just to get a single sentence out. But there *were* things I needed to ask.

'This . . . between us . . . I'm confused . . . I thought you didn't . . .' Oh God, he *had* robbed me of the art of coherent speech.

'You thought what?' he prompted gently, taking my hand in his, tenderly lacing our fingers together.

'That you didn't want me . . . well, not in *that* way.'

My words must have been so unexpected that they erased the loving smile from his face, replacing it with a look of incredulity. 'Why on earth would you think that?'

'Well, after what happened at the hotel . . .' My voice trailed away.

Realisation began to dawn in his eyes.

'You made it pretty clear that night that you didn't want me.' My voice was hushed, the memory and embarrassment still raw.

'Is that what you thought?' He ran his hand distractedly through his hair. 'I wanted you so much that night I could hardly breathe. You'll never know how hard it was for me to leave your room that night.'

'Then why did you?'

He pulled me towards him then, cradling me against his chest and drawing my head against his neck. His soft breath fanned my forehead as he spoke. 'Because it was wrong of me to take advantage of you then. It probably still is now.'

I gasped out the beginnings of a protest but he silenced me with a finger against my lips.

'You were so confused that night, nothing made sense to you, and you needed me as a friend then, more than a lover. And besides, you *were* still engaged to Matt.'

The last doubts of uncertainty began to crumble as he spoke. The strength of what he felt for me was even more apparent by him leaving my bed that night than if he had stayed. Sarah had been right, Jimmy would never have rejected me unless he had truly thought he was doing the right thing.

'About Matt . . .' I began, and he groaned softly.

'Do we really have to talk about him?'

I raised my eyes to his, allowing all the love I felt for

him to shine through them like a beacon, letting him know there was nothing I could say that would hurt him here.

'I just want to let you know that I understand now why you've been holding back. And I know you think I still need time to get over breaking up with him, but really I don't.'

He looked doubtful at my words.

'As far as I'm concerned, Matt and I broke up over five years ago. It was finding myself engaged to him now that I was having trouble dealing with, not losing him.'

I looked over at the clock on the mantelpiece.

'OK, my five minutes are up.' I leant over to kiss his mouth but this time he was the one who drew back.

'Before I totally lose myself here, can I just say one thing, Rachel?'

He sounded so earnest that I was suddenly afraid of what I would hear.

'Tonight. Us. This isn't just some spur of the moment thing. I need you to know that. What I feel for you . . . I should have told you a very long time ago. I almost did, in fact.'

Suddenly the pieces were sliding into place.

'I knew you were with Matt, but I promised myself that before we all left for university I would tell you how I felt – how I've always felt – about you. We even arranged to meet, but that was the night . . .'

'. . . of the accident,' I finished.

'And after that there never seemed to be the right time

to say anything. And then after uni you two were still together, so I thought I'd lost my chance.'

It broke my heart to think of the pain it must have caused him over the years to see me with someone else and never be able to say anything about it. If I lived to be a hundred I could never make up for what I had done.

'Thank you for waiting for me,' I whispered softly.

His answering smile was all I needed in the world right then.

'My pleasure.'

The fire crackled quietly in the grate, the fairy lights twinkled in the darkened room, but we saw and heard nothing. Just each other.

I realised my father must have guessed what had happened between Jimmy and me by the stupid grin he wore as he greeted me in the kitchen the following morning.

'You look happy,' was his opening comment.

Apparently we were wearing matching grins.

'What time did Jimmy leave last night?'

Oh Lord, the man had no subtlety at all.

'Late,' I confirmed, reaching for the cup of coffee he was handing me. 'You know, don't you?'

He nodded in confirmation. 'Jimmy told me that he wanted to tell you how he felt.'

So that was what they had been talking about when I was out of the room!

'Did he actually ask your *permission*?' I queried,

astounded at the unexpected nineteenth-century element of the situation.

'No. Not my permission exactly. He just wanted to know if I thought you were ready to hear what he had to say, if you were strong enough yet, or if I thought you needed more time.'

'And you said?' I prompted.

'I told him he had already wasted the last twenty years or so and that he should go right on ahead.'

'I'm not sure if I was entirely ready to hear it when I was three years old.'

'But you are now?'

Did he really need to ask? Wasn't it written all over my face?

'Now everything is absolutely perfect.'

I didn't know it then, but things were about to get even better.

Midnight mass on Christmas Eve. I hadn't been for years, but suddenly it seemed I had a lot to be grateful for. Although Jimmy was on a late shift, he would finish in enough time to join us for the service.

I sat by the lounge window and watched the soft snowflakes falling on the road and pavements, waiting for him. Before my eyes the familiar street was transformed into a Christmas card idyll. I smiled as even the mundane and boring took on a white shroud of beauty.

I'd been smiling quite a lot these past few days. Every minute spent with Jimmy filled me with such joy and happiness that he felt more necessary to my existence than the air I breathed. Every minute apart was spent either thinking of him or in heady anticipation of when his familiar knock would sound on the door.

I could have been a nauseating daughter, wreathed in smiles and wistful glances, if my dad hadn't been so patently delighted at the turn of events. He was even continuing his mission to give us as much private time together as he could, and was going to bed at night at an ever-increasingly early hour. There were six-year-olds who stayed up later than him these days.

My father entered the room, already dressed for the weather in heavy topcoat and hat.

'Is he here yet?'

'He will be soon,' I assured, unaware of the serenity in my tone, which brought a responding smile to my parent's face.

Bright headlights cut through the falling flakes as Jimmy's car rounded the bend and pulled up beside our house. I snatched up my coat from the chair and hurried to the door, heart already beating faster. It was like being a teenager all over again.

I stood in the open doorway as he climbed out of the car, mindless of the snow buffeting against me as I waited for him. The intensity of my feelings had taken me by surprise. Having known each other for all our lives, I had expected our relationship would be more of a slow burn, and not the raging inferno that we were both happy to be consumed by.

'You look like a snow queen,' he murmured, when he

stood before me, kissing the crystal flakes from my face. 'And you haven't got your coat on,' he chided, noticing that I still held it in my hands. 'You'll get cold.'

'Not with you here, I won't,' I said dreamily, but nevertheless slid my arms into the garment he had taken from me and was now holding out. I particularly liked the way he used the wrapping of the long scarf around my neck as a means of drawing me against him for a lingering kiss.

'Ahem,' came from behind us. We broke apart, not guiltily, but with obvious reluctance. 'I hope you two can behave yourself for an hour or so in the church,' my father warned.

'We'll do our best, Tony,' promised Jimmy.

'Don't worry, Dad,' I assured him, tucking my arm under his as we walked down the path to Jimmy's car. 'I'm not going to embarrass you in front of the vicar!'

The pathway leading up to the church was lined with flickering tea lights in glass jars. The church doors were open and inside the choir was singing a familiar carol to greet the large congregation. I paused for a moment on the path, taking it all in: the church spire covered in snow, the glowing candles, the music and, of course, the man at my side.

'So incredibly beautiful,' I breathed in wonderment.

His eyes ignored our surroundings and everyone else, they were only upon me.

'Incredibly beautiful,' he echoed.

The service seemed unbelievably touching. I even cried at the reading delivered by children from the local primary school. And when I went to reach surreptitiously into my bag for a tissue, Jimmy already had one out and ready for me. I dabbed at my eyes, not ashamed by the emotion I couldn't contain. Tears of happiness were nothing to be embarrassed about.

As we filed back out into the night, Jimmy drew me to one side of the path, out of the way of the emerging congregation, who were hurrying back to their cars to escape the falling snow. My father had been waylaid by an old friend inside the church and neither of us had realised he wasn't behind us until we were already outside.

The temperature had dropped several degrees during the service and despite my warm coat and scarf I shivered violently. Jimmy drew me into the circle of his arms, pulling me against his body, whispering teasingly as he did so, 'I think we're all right with this, as long as we claim it was only to keep you warm.'

I don't know if it was my lack of response or the stiffening of my body that alerted him that something was wrong. From my position in his embrace, I was now facing away from the church and was looking directly at the graveyard. Unbidden, the awful memories of standing beside Jimmy's grave suddenly assailed me, so horribly vivid and real, that I forgot for a moment that Jimmy was actually still very much alive.

He carefully held me away from him, saw the pain in my face and in puzzlement turned to make out what I'd seen that had distressed me so.

He was intuitive enough to realise exactly what I was thinking as I stared in fixed anguish at the cemetery.

'Is that where . . . ?'

I nodded dumbly.

He threw a glance at the church doors and saw that my father had still not appeared. He took my hand and gave me a gentle tug. 'Come on then.'

My feet remained rooted on the path, causing him to stop. 'Are you serious?'

There was love and understanding in his eyes. 'You need to see it.'

I shuddered. 'I've already visited your gravesite, it's not something I ever went to see again.'

But, as ever, his patient persistence was hard to resist. 'There is nothing there, Rachel. Come and see.'

It wasn't a long walk to the cemetery, but it was long enough for me to conjure up all manner of horrible outcomes. The one that fought for supremacy, and won by a mile, was what if I got to the plot and actually found his grave there? Would I then turn to look at the man beside me and find him gone? A chill ran through me that had nothing to do with the weather. Wouldn't that just be the perfect Christmas ghost story?

The idea that each step over the crunchy turf of the cemetery was leading me into peril was impossible to ignore.

'Where was it?' Jimmy asked softly; possibly the only person in the world to ask someone for directions to his own grave.

'Over there,' I indicated, pointing with a finger that visibly trembled. 'Beyond that group of headstones.'

He led me gently but determinedly in the direction I

had identified. I caught familiar inscriptions from the surrounding tombstones as we passed. I shouldn't know what they said, but I remembered each one vividly: *Dearest husband, Beloved grandmother, Much loved father.*

My feet were leaden as I walked to the spot where the man I loved had been laid to rest, after giving up his life to save mine.

Jimmy's hand was firmly gripping mine as I haltingly looked up. For a moment I could see it; I really could, the sparkling white marble tombstone was for an instant so real I felt I could almost reach out and touch it. I blinked my eyes and then saw nothing but an empty area of undisturbed grass.

'So it was here,' Jimmy said, his voice strangely humbled.

I nodded, closer to tears than I had realised, as suddenly all the pain of that night threatened to overcome me.

'The inscription was so sad,' I whispered. '"Lost too soon at 18 years. Cherished son and loyal friend. Our love for you will live on for ever."'

I hadn't realised the words had etched themselves into my mind every bit as much as they had been engraved in the marble.

'It was awful, I felt like my heart was breaking, standing there, missing you, loving you . . . I just sort of dropped to the ground beside you.'

He moved swiftly then close to me, and for a bizarre moment I thought he was re-enacting my memories by falling to his knees, just as I had done. And then I realised it wasn't *both* knees he was on . . . but *one*.

He still had hold of my hand.

Snow fell around us in magical swirls. There was a look on his face that I knew would remain with me until the end of time.

'Rachel,' he began, his voice not entirely steady.

'Oh my God,' I breathed.

'Will you marry me?'

The remembered horror of the location disintegrated under the power of his love. The force of his feelings pulling me back from the dangerous memories. Saving me all over again.

'I can't believe,' I began, my voice a mixture of laughter and tears, 'that someday I'll be telling our grandchildren that their grandfather actually proposed to me in a cemetery!'

If there had been even the tiniest glimmer of uncertainty in his eyes, my words removed it in an instant.

'Is that a yes?'

I got down on the frozen ground before him, and whispered softly against his lips.

'Oh yes.'

Chapter 13

Six weeks later

I descended the stairs slowly and carefully, holding up the hem of my long ivory-coloured dress.

My father was waiting at the bottom tread, trying very hard to hold on to his smile.

As his hand reached out to take mine, a single tear escaped his eye and trickled like a lost diamond down his cheek.

'Your mum should be here to see this. She would be so proud of you.'

I reached up to kiss him, breathing in the familiar clean smell of his aftershave.

'Hush now, Dad, you'll make me cry and undo all of Sarah's hard work.'

I looked around the hall and living room; from upstairs

it had sounded as though there had to be at least a hundred people here.

'Has everyone left already?'

His glance swept the empty house.

'They have, my love. It's just you and me. The car is waiting outside.'

I drew in a steadying sigh. It was time.

'Nervous?' questioned my father, handing me my bouquet of deep red roses that the florist had delivered.

I shook my head with a smile. 'Just excited.'

He took my hand again and led me towards the front door.

'Time to go, Rachel.'

The six-week engagement had been swallowed up by wedding preparations. I guess there would be some curious glances at my waistline today to see if that would explain our unseemly haste. They would be wrong, of course, but if challenged it was an easier explanation to give than the truth. How would they react if they had heard the conversation between Jimmy and myself on this matter?

'I don't want to wait,' he had confessed, only a few days after Christmas. 'I've already waited far too long for you.'

His words had filled me with a warm glow, but I still had a major concern.

'I know you think I'm talking nonsense here,' I began, 'but let me just say this once and then I promise never to speak of it again.'

He gave a small nod. I suppose he guessed what I was going to say.

'This thing that happened to me . . . whatever it was . . . I think it started when I hurt my head in that car accident, and then got totally crazy after I was mugged and got injured again . . .'

'Go on,' he urged, as I frowned, struggling to formulate what I was trying to say.

'What if something happens to me again? What if I somehow *go back*? What if something happens and everything changes again?'

He pulled me to him then, kissing me slowly and thoroughly as though to chase the ridiculous notion away.

'Nothing like that is going to happen,' he promised. 'You're not going anywhere, not without me. I won't let you.' It was a beautiful declaration but he could see I was still troubled.

'There are no guarantees about anything in life, Rachel. Accidents and illnesses happen, we can't do anything about that. My job can be dangerous sometimes, and God knows you can get into serious trouble just getting out of bed! But we can't let it rule our lives.'

He was right. Hadn't the last two months taught me how important it was to grasp any chance at happiness and hang on to it for dear life?

'Although to be on the safe side, I may just get you a hard hat for a wedding present.'

'That'll look nice with a veil!'

'What *I'm* more worried about,' he said in a different tone, 'is what might happen if your memory *does* suddenly come back and you wake up and find yourself married to the wrong man. What if you realise it was Matt you really wanted to be with?'

There was a vulnerability in his eyes I don't think I had ever seen before.

'So the amnesia is cured but for some reason I'm going to go completely stupid?'

He tried a smile, but it didn't reach his eyes.

'I guess we're both worrying about something so ludicrous it's never going to happen.'

The long silver car, decorated with white ribbons, was waiting by the kerb. Some neighbours were watching from their front doors and gardens as my father and I emerged from the house. From somewhere nearby a small child cried out in delight, and someone started to clap, which rippled around the street.

In the back seat of the car, my father reached up to brush away a long strand of hair, which had blown across my face.

'My beautiful daughter,' he said with a smile, as the car pulled away from the house and began the short journey to the church.

The nurse made very little noise as she entered the small side room. Nevertheless her entry startled the man seated beside the bed. He looked up in concern but seeing she was alone he relaxed a little.

'Can I get you anything?' she asked kindly, her hands busy straightening the bed covers that never needed tidying at all.

'No, thank you,' he replied politely.

She looked down on him sympathetically. He looked so frail and weak, as though he should be the one occupying the bed. He hadn't missed a single day, holding vigil by her bedside. They said he wasn't even going for his own treatments any more. It was so heartbreaking for the nursing staff to see. They all felt so utterly useless.

She crossed over to the column of machinery located beside the bed, her hand reaching for a dial.

'I'll turn this down for you, shall I? It can be a bit irritating.'

'No, please don't,' pleaded the man brokenly. 'I like to hear it. The louder the better. It proves to me she's still with us.'

The nurse swallowed hard against the lump in her throat, but did as he requested and turned the dial up instead of down.

The sound of the loud persistent beeping of the life support alarm filled the room.

The car swept up to the entrance of the church. Waiting by the lich-gate was Sarah, resplendent in her deep red maid-of-honour dress. My dad offered me his hand as I climbed from the car. Sarah immediately swooped in and began to busy herself straightening out non-existent creases from my dress. I looked down at my old friend, busy at my feet, a question in my eyes.

She reached for my hand and gave it a squeeze.

'Of course he's here.'

I gave a small smile of pure relief.

'He's waited his whole life for this moment, Rachel. Where else would he be?'

The nurse left them alone, understanding the man wanted every last precious moment of privacy. He looked down lovingly on his beloved daughter lying immobile in her hospital bed. He didn't see the tubes and pipes linking her to the machine keeping her alive. He just saw his only child, lying lost in a sleep so deep she couldn't wake up.

'Daddy's here,' he murmured softly, as tears fell once again down his cheeks.

He reached out to touch her face, scarcely noticing the old white forked-lightning scar that ran from forehead to cheek. With trembling fingers he reached up to brush away a long strand of hair that had fallen across her face.

'My beautiful daughter,' he cried brokenly.

The nurse gave a discreet knock upon the door before entering this time.

'I just wanted to let you know that Dr Whittaker has just arrived. He'll be here in about ten minutes or so.'

'So soon?' asked the man in panic.

It was all happening so fast; there was so little time left.

Alone in the room once more he reached out for the

small bottle he kept in the drawer of her nightstand. His fingers shook as he tried to undo the stopper and several drops fell upon the pillow beside her. He dabbed some of the distinctive aftershave upon his hollow cheeks.

They'd told him a long time ago that she might still be able to hear and smell things, even from the depths of her coma. So he wore it always when he was here, hoping somehow the old and familiar fragrance could pierce through the veil and let her know that he was here with her. That she wasn't alone.

'You've been so brave, my love,' he whispered close to her face. 'I know you don't want to leave me alone. But I'll be all right.' He broke off then as the tears choked his words.

'I'm so proud of you,' he continued as the door handle turned and quietly the small room began to fill with people.

We paused by the lobby of the church. From behind the wooden doors we could hear that a hush had fallen from within. The guests were waiting, necks craned towards the doorway for our arrival. Sarah fell into place behind me as my father took my arm and linked it with his. He leaned over and kissed my cheek, his aftershave and the fragrance from my bouquet intermingling in an intoxicating aroma.

'I'm so very proud of you.'

'I love you, Dad,' I told him, bringing the gossamer veil down over my face.

From inside the church the organ began a familiar strain. It was our cue. The doors swung open and we began our procession up the aisle.

I knew every eye was on me as we walked, but I saw no one. Just him. He was standing at the altar, his body turned towards me, waiting, as he had been for so long, like a prince in a fairy tale. His eyes were so full of love that it took my breath away.

I wanted to fly to his side; felt almost propelled there by a swell of love from the small assembly of family and friends. Of course I was glad they were here to be part of this day with us, but the only people that really mattered were those standing beside and behind me, as I came to a halt next to the man I would share the rest of my days with.

Dr Whittaker entered the room with two other doctors he had never seen before. The nurse slipped into the room behind them.

'Good morning, Mr Wiltshire.'

The man had no voice to reply, just looked up at the doctor with red-rimmed eyes awash with misery.

The doctor approached the man and put his hand comfortingly upon his shoulder. From outside an ambulance siren sounded, a continual noise that the man scarcely noticed any more.

'You understand what we are doing today, Mr Wiltshire? Tony?'

The man looked up at the doctor in despair.

'And you're really sure? There are no signs at all? Nothing?'

The doctor shook his head sadly. He turned to one of his colleagues and spoke in a low voice.

'Is the paperwork all in order?'

The other doctor gave a single nod.

'It's just that sometimes I think she can hear what's going on,' the man burst out. 'And occasionally I feel sure she knows I'm here. I think she can smell my after-shave . . .'

Dr Whittaker shook his head sadly. He had heard this from so many other distraught families, who wanted so desperately to have hope when all hope was gone.

'She's given me a bottle of this every Christmas since she was thirteen years old,' the man explained to the nurse, whose professional composure was beginning to crumble at his words. 'It was like our private little joke . . .' His voice tailed off.

I don't remember the ceremony. I'm sure it was beautiful. I vaguely heard the hymns, and I guess I must have said my I do's in the right place, but really it was all lost to me in a wonderful dream-like haze. All I could really remember was the look in Jimmy's eyes as he slid the narrow golden band on my finger and gently lifted the veil from my face. A small cheer came from the pews behind us as he claimed my mouth in a tender kiss.

*

'Have you said your goodbyes?' asked the doctor kindly.

The man nodded, speech beyond him.

'Is there anyone here with you?' Dr Whittaker asked in concern, worried not for the patient, for whom he could do nothing, but for her father.

'No, there's no one,' the man said at last. 'It's just the two of us. She's all I have in the world.'

From behind the doctors, the nurse silently began to cry.

Dr Whittaker stepped over to the unit that was breathing for Rachel. Which had been doing so every day since she had been brought into hospital some two months earlier.

'See you soon, my darling girl,' the man whispered in his daughter's ear, as the doctor behind him flicked the switch.

'It will take a moment,' he said quietly.

The father took hold of his child's hand and squeezed hard to let her know he was with her.

We turned to walk back down the aisle. Joined together at last. Together for ever. As we passed the end of the pew where my father was sitting he reached out and grasped my hand, squeezing it hard. I looked at him and smiled. I held onto his hand even as we began to walk away, maintaining the contact until only our fingertips were left touching.

*

'She's gone,' the doctor said *quietly into the man's ear,
as the machine behind them confirmed his diagnosis with
a long, lamenting, continuous tone.*

A long and continuous note sounded from the church
organ behind us, before tumbling into the lilting strains
of one of my favourite love songs.

As we approached the entrance, the ushers flung open
the doors. Unusually bright February sunshine sliced
through the doorway, dazzling us with its intensity after
the cool darkness of the church.

Jimmy and I exchanged a deep and meaningful look
before walking together into the light.

Notes for your book club

✿   When we first meet Rachel, she has cut herself off from her family and friends. Do you think she is 'punishing' herself for Jimmy's death?

✿   Why do you think Rachel feels so responsible for the outcome of the restaurant accident? Do you think she would feel differently if Matt had died in Jimmy's place?

✿   When Rachel refuses to be her bridesmaid, Sarah asks her to reconsider. Rachel 'answers her' by showing her scar. Are there other places in the story where her scar plays a role? How do you think Rachel really feels about it?

❧ The novel begins with an accident. To what extent is Rachel's future shaped by events outside her control?

❧ Did you guess what would happen at the end of the novel? Did you finish the book feeling uplifted or sad?

❧ The story moves backwards and forwards in time. How does that affect what you feel about Rachel?

❧ Would you feel differently about Rachel if the book began as she woke up in hospital?

❧ By the end of the novel, do you feel any sympathy for Matt? What about Cathy?

❧ Which of Rachel's relationships do you think is most important to her – Jimmy, Matt, Sarah or her father?

❧ The characters encounter mirrors and reflections at several points during the story. Do you think the idea of mirror images relates to the way the author organises the story?

Acknowledgements

There are many people I would like to thank for making a dream I have had for a very long time, come true.

Firstly, I owe a huge debt of thanks to my incredible agent Kate Burke from Diane Banks Associates. Thank you Kate for loving *Fractured* the way you do; for finding me and taking me on the first steps of an exciting journey into a whole new world. Thanks also to Diane and Olivia for the very warm welcome and for all your help and support, I really appreciate it.

I would also like to thank my fantastic editor Laura Palmer at Head of Zeus, for her guidance, wisdom and patience, and for never making me feel that I was asking stupid questions (even when I know I was!). Thanks also to the amazing team at HoZ, whose warmth, friendliness and professionalism know no bounds.

When writing *Fractured*, I took the names of friends and colleagues and used them in a hybrid mash-up for my characters. Many of you didn't even know I was doing this, so apologies if finding a version of your name left you feeling a little surprised. Thank you for lending them to me, you are: Jimi Randall, Rachel Boyd, Matt Cooper, Cathy Johnson, Louise Boyd, Janet Boyd, John Kendall, Phil Wiltsher, Trev Chengabroyen, Jessica Sacco, Scott Tulloch, Dave Kelly, Sam Corcoran, Emily Frost, Laura Winter, Jamie Hunt, Max Isham, Joe Thorpe, Debbie Keyworth, Sheila Ellis, Kim Webb, Dee Whittock, Janet Brady, Ann MacRae, Megan Freeman and last, but not least, Kizzy the cat.

There are few things more important in life than really good friends, and for no other reason than that I would like to thank Hazel for always being there for me (even if, unfortunately, 'there' now happens to be in Australia).

Lastly I would like to thank my wonderful family for simply being the three best people in the entire universe. Ralph, Kimberley and Luke, I could not have done any of this without you.

And finally for my mum, Riv. I really wish you had been here to see all this happen for me, but I hope news of it has managed to reach you, wherever you are.